THE GARDEN PATH

Christina heard footsteps behind her on the gravel. She spun around. She had to arch her neck to look up at the man now so close to her, but she saw his face clearly. There would be a scandal if she were caught alone with him: the Marquess of Aldric.

"Good evening, my lord," she said hastily. "It is a pleasure to see you as always, but I must go back inside now. I promised Lord Arbuthnot that I would dance with him."

"You have developed an extensive court," Aldric observed.

"They only mimic you," Christina said. "They would pay court to a mountebank, if you did."

"Devil it!" Aldric said. "You are not a mountebank. You are a lovely young woman. I will show you how tempting you are."

Aldric took her mouth with his before Christina could comprehend what he meant to do. It was her first kiss. She had never allowed anyone else so close before. She had no idea what to do.

But the Marquess of Aldric most certainly did. . . .

A Heart in Peril

A Heart
in Peril

by

Emma Lange

A SIGNET BOOK

SIGNET
Published by the Penguin Group
Penguin Books USA Inc., 375 Hudson Street,
New York, New York 10014, U.S.A.
Penguin Books Ltd, 27 Wrights Lane,
London W8 5TZ, England
Penguin Books Australia Ltd, Ringwood,
Victoria, Australia
Penguin Books Canada Ltd, 10 Alcorn Avenue,
Toronto, Ontario, Canada M4V 3B2
Penguin Books (N.Z.) Ltd, 182–190 Wairau Road,
Auckland 10, New Zealand

Penguin Books Ltd, Registered Offices:
Harmondsworth, Middlesex, England

First published by Signet,
an imprint of Dutton Signet,
a division of Penguin Books USA Inc.

First Printing, June, 1994
10 9 8 7 6 5 4 3 2 1

Chapter 1

The Marquess of Aldric's appearance at Lady Ainsley's ball instantly excited a riot of speculation, for the marquess rarely appeared at such a tame, if exceedingly fashionable affair.

Some among the *ton* maintained he had long held himself aloof from his peers because he felt his virtual poverty too keenly, but another, equally large, faction held that even had the marquess not possessed the devil's own pride, he'd have had little time for purely social events.

Though his brother and sister were now fully grown and able to care for themselves, this group pointed out that Aldric had still the responsibility of maintaining his home, a castle of all the costly things, and his tenants, all on nothing. With such need driving him, not to mention pride, they thought it no wonder at all he spent his time at the card tables in London's gaming houses in preference to the ballrooms in London's fashionable homes.

Another contingent, comprised for the most part of men, argued yet another position on the matter of the Marquess of Aldric. They observed that while the other parties had made valid points, the truth was that Aldric had preferred the gaming tables to the dinner tables even before his father had made that shockingly disastrous wager. Indeed, they added, smiling knowingly, the only activity they knew of that Aldric preferred to gaming was bedding a beautiful woman, something he did quite as regularly as he gamed, and something he could scarcely do, if he were tamely making his bow upon the dance floor.

Emma Lange

As to why, specifically, Aldric should so unexpectedly make an appearance that night in March of 1816 in Lady Ainsley's ballroom, the opinion was no more unanimous. By far the largest party among the gossips believed that at long last the marquess had decided to humble himself, that is to sell his ancient name and august title to an heiress for her money. But a small group, again comprised primarily of men, disagreed. At thirty-one, they maintained, he had known too many women to wish to tie himself forever to any one of them. And it wasn't as if he needed an heir anyway, they observed. His younger brother serving with the army in France had a boy. No, if the marquess had not thought it necessary to leg shackle himself in the ten years since his father's tragic loss and subsequent death, he would not do so at this late date. They said he was scanning the dancers with those cool black eyes of his, for the simple reason that he wished to take one of the women, and here they disagreed among themselves, either for a mistress or a night's entertainment. They could not say which, but they were certain he did not look for a wife.

On one point, Lady Ainsley's guests did agree. For whatever purpose Aldric wanted the woman—wife, mistress, or temporary diversion—he would win her. There was something about him that drew women; something in his hard, uncompromisingly masculine face, in those fathomless black eyes, and even, it seemed, in his very indifference to them that attracted women like moths to a flame.

It would have been impossible to say whether the subject himself was aware of the interest he had stirred or even who it was interested him. The marquess appeared as aloof as ever as he flicked his black gaze over the dancers swirling before him.

Only the man by Aldric recognized the intensity in that veiled gaze, but the Viscount Molyneux was one of the few men the marquess called friend. They were oddly ill-matched, for all that they had been close since their school days. While Aldric was cool and possessed a dangerous tongue, the Viscount Molyneux was a fond mother's dream. Almost as tall, though not as broad-shouldered as the marquess, he possessed classical, blond good looks, an exceedingly amiable humor, and the most accommodating manners.

He nodded to several dancers he knew, smiling when he did, but, that evening, a really careful onlooker might have noted that there was about the viscount, as he sent his gaze roaming around the room, a certain intensity, as well.

After some time, Aldric finally spoke in an impatient undertone. "Is she here, Moly?"

A barely perceptible sigh issued from the viscount. "Yes, she is here. But damn it all, Johnny! I wish you would give up this scheme! It was not Miss Godfrey . . . "

"We have argued this since I learned the truth, Moly." The marquess cut off his friend with a flat, implacable look few would have cared to challenge. "You know my reasons. If my intent disturbs you still, then may I suggest that you take yourself off to Liza Rokesberry's willing arms? You should be able to forget my ignoble affairs easily enough languishing in them."

"Deuce take your temper, Johnny!" The viscount promptly relieved a passing waiter of two glasses of champagne and returned Aldric a look as mild as the marquess's was taut. "I'm not gainsaying you. I understand too well why you mean to do it, and yes, before you erupt, she is over there. Not dancing but speaking to the young pup who is lounging with such cheerful unconcern against the statue of Eros that Leda had Rupert haul back from Italy."

Aldric made no comment upon either the chubby statue of Eros or the taste of Molyneux's sister, his hostess, Lady Ainsley, as he looked in the direction Molyneux had indicated.

His eyes narrowed. "The one with the garish hair?" he asked.

"Garish?" Molyneux protested, looking across the floor to the girl in question. "Nay, but Titian would have celebrated her!"

"I wasn't aware Titian admired Amazons," came the cool reply.

"Well, I do grant she is tall for a girl," the viscount conceded. "But, really, Johnny, Amazons do not have fine bones. She is gracefully regal, I'd say. And elegant."

"No doubt you would say elegant." The look Aldric flicked his friend was dry, indeed. "'An elegant figure' is the euphemistic phrase people generally use when what they really mean to say is that the lady has no curves to speak of."

But Lord Molyneux could be, in addition to amiable, stubborn. "She may not be so well endowed in the bosom as your current mistress, Johnny, but I suspect those legs, if ever one could see them, would be magnificent."

Lord Aldric shrugged his broad shoulders. "You have never lacked for imagination, Moly. That I do grant."

Realizing that was all Aldric would grant, the viscount fell silent though he had thought to add something about how nicely supple he thought Miss Godfrey's slender figure to be.

Nor, though he had become something of the girl's advocate by default, was he tempted to mention that he admired her fashionable satin dress. Decorated with an exquisite embroidery embellished with seed pearls, it would have cost a small fortune, as would the pearls gleaming in her hair and about her throat, and he half tensed, waiting for Aldric to make caustic mention of the funds expended, but though the marquess did remark quite as caustically as expected, it was not about the girl's attire.

"She's willful as the devil, too."

Looking again, Molyneux saw what had prompted Aldric's observation. Miss Godfrey was arguing with the boy beside her, her arms crossed over her chest and her chin tipped to a haughty angle as she tossed her head in a gesture that summarily dismissed whatever the boy had said.

"Ah," Aldric exclaimed quietly, "here comes a rival. Let us see how the willful heiress likes competition."

"That is her stepsister, Miss Bexom," Molyneux remarked. "And surely not much in the way of competition. Faith, she is not even flawed enough in her looks to be interesting. But perhaps that is why it would seem she bears very little love indeed for Miss Godfrey. Lud, if her eyes were any sharper, they'd be stilettos."

But it was Miss Godfrey, Aldric watched. "I'd say there is not much love lost on either side, then. The heiress has not deigned even to acknowledge her stepsister."

It was quite true, in fact, that Christina made Cloris Bexom no greeting at all. She left the politeness to Will Palmer, standing by her, who inquired dutifully if Cloris were enjoying herself.

While Cloris put on the smiles that sweetened her face whenever a man was about, Christina waited, eyes narrowed fractionally, to hear the reason her stepsister had sought her company.

"But I have not come only to beg Christina to refrain from monopolizing you on very nearly your last evening in town, Will!" Cloris simpered then in the saccharine way that never failed to set Christina's teeth on edge. "I've also come to inform her that Mama wishes her company."

Christina felt a flare of satisfaction. Her guess had been correct. And judging from the smug look in Cloris's small, unprepossessing eyes, she thought she could make an equally accurate guess as to why her stepmother wished her company.

But first matters first. "How wonderfully limpid you can look, Cloris, when you beg," she declared, coolly observing the color that surged on the instant into her stepsister's sallow cheeks. "I vow your expression wrenches my heart, but I fear you've missed a vital point. Will is his own man and disposes of his company quite as he pleases. And as to my going to your mother, you may tell Louisa I shall not come to her until she detaches herself from that revolting creature she would push upon me for a husband."

"Oh!" Cloris fumed, unable, in her anger, to summon anything more trenchant. "You are . . . jealous!" she finally

spat, drawing herself up to her full height, which lamentably left her still looking up to Christina. "With your shocking hair and freakish size, you . . . oh, you are perverse!
Any other girl in the room would be in alt were Mr. Morley
to show an interest in them."

Christina appeared quite unmoved by her stepsister's remarks. As cool as Cloris was heated, she said dryly,
"Which only goes to show . . . "

" . . . that you are so high and mighty you think he is not
worthy of you!" Cloris snatched Christina's words and finished them with a hiss.

"I say," Will intervened, clearing his throat uncomfortably, "this quarrel is becoming a trifle heated for a ballroom, don't you think? I cannot believe either of you would
wish to earn a reputation as a shrew."

Christina only tossed her head as if she did not care a fig,
but Cloris turned a martyred look upon the young man.
"Oh, Will, you are right as ever! I do not know what we
will do when you leave!"

"Speak less frequently?" Christina queried with patently
false sweetness.

Cloris flushed angrily again, but she snapped her mouth
shut, and when she spoke, she turned to Will. "I can see
that I must go, as I have put Christina out of sorts by forcing her to share you, my dear. You will not forget the dance
you promised me though, will you?"

When her stepsister had departed, Christina glanced
wryly to Will. "You see what you do, you wretch, by taking
yourself off to Scotland? You leave me to battle Cloris and
Louisa alone."

"Fustian! You'll not persuade me to change my plans
with that particular argument, Ti," Will retorted with a
complete lack of concern. "You have held your own against
Lady Lely and her eldest daughter since the day they arrived at Fairfield five years ago, and you were no more than
twelve."

Christina did not thank him for his compliment, if compliment it was. She grimaced half wearily. "Perhaps I have,

but this new bee in their combined bonnet is wearisome. Since they discovered the intriguing notion that they may be rid of me by marrying me off, they have paraded me before so many prospective husbands, I feel like a fatted calf at the fair."

Will Palmer chuckled. "A fatted calf! What a thing to say, Ti! And saying it, you make my point. You've all the sharpness you need to keep any toad they wish to push at you at bay."

"Perhaps. No, certainly, I will not let them marry me off to Morley or anyone so unbearable," she said, then, because Will began to smile, she added, "However that may be, you've been in town less than a week! I want your company."

It was Will's turn to grimace. "At ball after ball? Dash it, Ti, Paxon's the best trout fishing Scotland has to offer! Carlisle will be there, and my cousin Duncan, too. I've not seen Duncan since ages before he married. Jove, I don't even known whom he married! You'd have me ignore my family just to dance attendance on you."

"You may see this long-lost Scottish cousin any time, Will Palmer." Christina elevated her slender nose so that she looked down it at the young man she had known since they had both been in leading strings. "I need you now."

"Need me? You've chaps aplenty hanging about you!"

"Fortune hunters! They circle round me, caring not a whit for anything but my purse."

"Now there you are fair and far out!" Will straightened so that he could look down his nose at her. "Any man would be proud to have you on his arm. You are a toast!"

"What I am, is an heiress," Christina returned quite as firmly. "It's my purse that's toasted not my looks. You know very well that while blond hair or brown hair or black hair may be extolled, red hair is most definitely not, and while pocket Venuses are the thing, I am a giantess."

"Lud, you're a goose, morelike."

"You may spare me that indulgent tone, Will. I know what I am, and I am not ill content to possess the ability to look down my nose at a goodly portion of the world. My eyes may be a plain gray, but they see clearly enough, and as to my bosom or lack thereof . . . well, I suppose even with you I ought not to discuss my less than ample endowments."

"Indeed you should not," Will agreed though mildly. "People will say you're fast, and that's not what you want."

"No, I don't suppose I do, but the point is that I can speak my mind with you, and you won't fly up into the boughs."

"Precisely the reason I should leave!" Will seized upon the thought. "Yes! As my father said, you've come to London to acquire a little town bronze, but with me about you'll continue to slip back into your less than polished ways, which won't do at all. You'll become a scandal."

Their eyes met and of a sudden they both burst out laughing. "Now that is why I want you to stay! I have not laughed with anyone else."

"Oh, ho! I saw you laughing with Sidley."

Mr. Sidley, Will's age and a friend of his, actually reminded Christina of her oldest friend. "I grant that Mr. Sidley is, if not as companionable as you, at least somewhat amusing."

"Well there you are!" Will exclaimed with the triumphant air of a man who has neatly tied up a worrisome problem. "You'll have Sidley to amuse you, and he'll help you to avoid Morley, too, if you wish. He can't abide the prig, either. So, there is nothing more you can say in objection to my going to Scotland." He expected Christina to laugh and finally relent, but when she did not, Will gave her a close look. "I know you are not afraid for me. There, you even look surprised by the suggestion! But, if it is not for me that you fear, can it be for yourself? Are you fretful because that cart crashed into your carriage yesterday? Surely, you're not so missish as to think such an accident will occur every time you leave the house?"

"No," Christina said. Will might have noticed that her

eyes darkened despite her denial, but he was off on his own train of thought.

"London is so dreadfully overcrowded! I am surprised people are not killed every day by runaway carts or carriages. Lud! Give me a few fellows in the country any day. I tell you there is no thrill like that you feel when you land a trout. The tug on the line . . . "

Christina failed to follow Will's rhapsody on trout fishing. She was thinking of the young footman who had saved her life. Had he not seen the cart rolling down that slight incline, gaining speed . . . she and her maid would have been killed.

"Everything will work out quite neatly, really," Will continued. "When I return, the Season will be over, and I shall escort you back to Hampshire. I think I shall invite Duncan to come to the Grange for a visit. He can bring his wife. . . . "

Will rattled on, confident of Christina's attention. Not much in the petticoat line, he had never taken notice of any other girl. He could not have imagined any reason he would. Ti was a dashed good gun, and he was exceedingly comfortable with her. Lud, they had grown up together, and she could outride him! He comfortably assumed they would marry eventually, after she had acquired her town bronze, and he got around to mentioning the matter to her.

Christina's thoughts were not running along so pleasant a path as marriage or even the coming summer. There had been two other accidents, neither remarkable in and of themselves, but together with the cart? A shot, presumably a poacher's, had missed her by a hair, while she had been out riding one morning in Hampshire, and before that, a cinch on her saddle had split. It was pure luck that she'd been walking her mare by then. Moments before she had been galloping as full out as was her wont.

Three accidents. That was not so many. Surely over a period of four months, anyone might meet with three accidents. Will knew of all the incidents. If the runaway cart had not prompted him to wonder whether some sinister force might be at work, ought she to be suspicious?

Perhaps not, but nonetheless Christina admitted with a restless movement that she was at least unnerved. Will, after all, had been away at school much of the time after her father's second wife and three children had arrived at Fairfield. He really did not know Louisa well, or Cloris even, and certainly not Robert. Christina did not count Millie. The youngest of Louisa's children, she was the only dear in the lot, but she'd had a different sire than Cloris and Robert, and it showed.

But was Robert or Cloris or Louisa vicious enough to commit murder? Great God, she was mad! The very question sounded absurdly melodramatic.

"Ti! Have you been listening? You look so grim."

Christina glanced into Will's frowning countenance and made herself smile. "Of course I look grim, wretch. My best friend is to leave for Scotland in three days. Had you not heard?"

"Oh bah, Ti! You're not on that again."

She was, but she felt a fool. What did she expect Will to do, run up an down every side street along every thoroughfare she traveled, checking for she knew not what? He would tire rather soon.

At the dry thought, Christina chuckled and threw off her grim, impossible thoughts once and for all. "Very well then, I'll not tax you about Scotland again, if you will do me the honor of escorting me to the refreshment table. I'd not dare go alone as Morley would instantly attach himself, and Lady Lattimer's lobster patties are reputed to be superb."

"Lobster patties?" Will groaned. "They are the merest nothings! I vow I will starve to death before I leave London."

"At home in Hampshire, you may have roast beef, Will," Christina chided but with a grin. "In London, however, you must suffer lobster patties. Come along now, or I shall think you are set upon being obstinate."

Will rolled his eyes, but he gave her his arm, and Christina grinned triumphantly.

From across the room, Aldric watched the pantomime with hard, unkind eyes. "It would seem the heiress has gotten what she wanted."

"Now!" Molyneux reproved at once. "How can you know that, Johnny? She is only smiling."

"Women do not smile like that unless they've gotten what they wanted," Aldric insisted sardonically. "Nor do young men look as sheepish as Fresh-face does, unless they've given in."

"Fresh-face?" Molyneux chuckled, diverted temporarily by the accurate description of Will Palmer. The boy even had freckles. And he did look like a man who was giving in, while Christina Godfrey looked quite like a girl who has gotten her way. Molyneux only differed from Aldric in that he did not think it so very bad that an attractive girl could talk a personable young man into some little something. It was the way of the world, but Aldric was determined to dislike Christina Godfrey, and Molyneux knew it was pointless for him to argue. The girl herself would have to persuade Aldric she deserved better than what he had planned for her. Molyneux rather thought she would, which was why he had not argued against those plans even more persistently than he had.

Unaware of his friend's somewhat traitorous thoughts, Aldric was marking how inattentive Christina Godfrey was to her enamored swain. While Fresh-face procured her a plate from the refreshment table, she gave no heed to his efforts but instead scanned the room. Aldric thought she scouted for fresh prey to add to her court, but had to concede he was wrong when he saw her gaze stop upon a sharp-featured, middle-aged woman with a tasteless excess of diamonds glittering around her thinnish neck.

Christina found her stepmother but failed to find the thoroughly unpleasant George Morley with her. Alarmed that he might be even at that moment approaching her, for he was insistent along with every other unpleasant trait, Christina swiftly searched the room.

She thought she caught a glimpse of Morley, but even as

she craned to be sure, her gaze collided with the gaze of a gentleman leaning against a column near the windows, and she forgot everyone else.

Christina had never seen the man before. Of that she was absolutely certain. He was not a man one would forget. If he was not classically handsome like the blond Adonis beside him, he was nonetheless the most striking man she had ever seen: tall with dark hair and contrastingly light skin, he'd strong, chiseled features and the blackest eyes . . . that were regarding her with . . . surely it was only a trick of the lighting . . . but it did seem to her bewilderment that his black eyes gleamed with a distinctly mocking amusement.

A plump matron and her lumpish partner wandered between them, releasing Christina from the hold of those mocking eyes. Immediately, she pulled on Will's arm.

"Who is the tall, dark-haired gentleman near the windows?" she whispered, adding impatiently when Will looked about vaguely, "The striking one."

"Jove!" William exclaimed, and Christina knew he had found her man, for the stranger was precisely the sort of man who would excite a strong reaction even in Will.

"Who is he?" she hissed.

"The Marquess of Aldric," Will replied. "He's a cool devil. Games a great deal but wins, unlike his father who frittered away the family's wealth. There's an old story, something about losing a fabulous amount, the bulk of the Beauchamp fortune or nearly, on a single wager, but I forget the particulars. Nor can I think why Aldric would be at a tame do like this. Lady Ainsley does not even have a card room. Perhaps he's after someone's wife for . . . well . . . "

Christina shot Will a dry look. "Surely you and I do not need to pretend that I know nothing of mistresses, Will."

He flushed and shrugged lamely, but Christina made no more of the issue. Whether Will could be frank with her interested her far less than the Marquess of Aldric. He exerted such a strong pull on her, she slanted a tentative, sidelong look in his direction, just to see . . . well, just to see.

He was not looking at her now. Will's surmise appeared to have been accurate. A well-endowed brunette with an elaborate array of plumes waving languidly in her hair had approached the marquess. As Christina watched, the woman trailed her gloved hand along his arm. Aldric's reaction was difficult to gauge. He did not disengage his arm from the woman's hand, but neither did he smile. The woman, however, was not deterred by the lazy, almost indifferent look he gave her. She all but poured her lush bosom over him as she leaned closer to pout coyly up at him.

"Ah, look! Here comes Sidley, Christina. He's cousin to the man by Aldric, the Viscount Molyneux. He may know more about the devil."

Christina dragged her eyes away from the intriguing little drama unfolding half a room away to make the pleasant Mr. Sidley a greeting. When asked, however, Sidley proved to know little more about the marquess than Will did, and it was a further disappointment to Christina that when she was able to look back, she found the marquess was gone. As was the lady. She wondered if they had left together, then abruptly laughed at herself. She was reacting with as much prurient curiosity as any old dowager. And to little point. From what Will had said she did not think it likely she would ever even see the Marquess of Aldric again.

Chapter 2

"There, he said it, Ti! Could you not make out 'Pretty girl'? Surely you did."

Christina looked with some amusement from the brilliantly green parrot sitting on its perch to her bright-eyed young stepsister. "I did hear three syllables of sound, Millie. And perhaps Alfonse did say, 'Pretty girl,' but I fear I could not swear to it."

"Did you hear, Alfonse?" Millie stroked the parrot's neck in a way she knew he particularly favored. "Ti could not quite understand you. You must try again and quickly. We haven't a great deal of time. Now, say, 'Pretty girl'!"

The parrot cocked its head to study Millie with an unblinking eye, then unexpectedly opened its beak and croaked out "Pretty girl" quite plainly. While Millie exclaimed with proud delight, Christina clapped.

"Well done, Millie and Alfonse! I heard 'Pretty girl' clearly."

"Isn't he brilliant?" Millie enthused, prompting Christina to allow with a wry smile that yes, indeed, one could certainly term the parrot brilliant. "You are the greatest dear to have given him to me, Ti!" the younger girl rattled on. "He is such a pet, and Sally is quite beside herself with envy over him."

Sally Warren was Millie's best friend, and not only a year older but, having been to London many times before, Millie's standard in all things.

"I am delighted Alfonse amuses you, puss," Christina returned. "And of course, I am equally delighted to know that you've turned Sally pea green for once. But why did you say you and Alfonse haven't much time? Are you going out?"

Millie's face fell. "No, it's nothing to do with me. It's Mama, Ti. She was very cross at breakfast, and, ah, she mentioned she would speak to you later. I think she was not pleased over something to do with Mr. Morley last night."

"And I think you have been listening at keyholes again."

Millie flushed a little, but her eyes reflected far more concern than embarrassment. "She sounded very angry."

"Your mother and I disagree about Mr. Morley, pet, but you need not look so anxious." Christina circled an arm about the younger girl's rounded shoulders. "I doubt we shall have a battle royal. Now give me a smile, before you take yourself off to give Alfonse his next lesson. Have you thought what it will be?"

Millie grinned, diverted. "I thought he might learn to say 'Bad boy' for Robert the next time Robert loses all his allowance at the tables in one night."

Christina burst into laughter, but their combined amusement did not deafen them to the sound of rapid footsteps in the hallway. Sobering immediately, Millie took up Alfonse's perch and whisked herself away from the library via the French windows that led to the gardens behind the enormous town house Lady Lely had thought an appropriate size for them to lease for the Season. No sooner had the girl disappeared from sight, if not, Christina knew, from sound, the door to the room was thrown open and Christina's stepmother swept into the room.

Even at that early hour she wore pearls around her neck, several bracelets upon each arm, and a ring on eight of her ten fingers. Christina had the diverting thought that Louisa looked like one of the dummies jewelers sometimes used in their shops to display their wares, but she forced both the thought and its attendant amusement from her mind as she faced her stepmother's narrowed eyes.

"Sit, Christina. I have a great deal to say to you."

There had been a time at the first of their acquaintance, when Louisa had made her stand during their confrontations, but that had changed the very moment Christina had surpassed Louisa in height. Now, Louisa had her sit.

Christina sat dutifully on the edge of the fine Adam couch behind her. With her spine gracefully erect and her hands in her lap, she watched Louisa choose a high-backed chair for her seat. It was a bit higher than the couch, and thus they sat eye to eye.

"I have often had occasion in the past to remark that you are a most unnatural child, Christina, but I had hoped that you had outgrown your customary obstinacy when you agreed to come to town for the Season. You have shown me how vain my hopes were though! I will not stand for it, Christina. I will not, I warn you, allow you to embarrass me again as you did last evening!"

Though Lady Lely had begun the interview seeming in cold control of herself, her anger got the better of her. By the end of the short tirade, her voice shook, and there was a riot of angry color on her high, bony cheeks.

By contrast, and in part because she had long since guessed how it annoyed her stepmother, Christina wrapped her composure around herself like a royal robe. "I regret your embarrassment, Louisa. Truly, I do, and I would not have you embarrassed again for anything in the world. We only differ on the cause of your displeasure. If you will but recall, I told you before we arrived at Lady Ainsley's that I would prefer not to dance with Mr. Morley at all."

"This is precisely what I mean when I say that you are unnatural, obstinate, and rebellious! Oh, you are all that is deference and understanding on the surface, but the only reason that you have taken Mr. Morley into dislike is because you wish to upset me!"

Christina bit back the sarcastic remark that Lady Lely figured not at all in her thinking about anyone or anything. "I am sorry you believe that, Louisa, for I can see how much the belief distresses you, but as we have discussed Mr. Morley before, I am at a loss as to what more I can say to convince you that it is on Mr. Morley's very own merits that I despise him."

"Despise him?" Lady Lely's lips thinned to naught. "You would set yourself up as a better judge of character than your own cousin Richard? As you know, Richard is the best of friends with Mr. Morley."

In fact, though Richard Brooks was the one who had introduced her to George Morley, Christina had seen very little evidence of real closeness between the two men. They were rarely to be seen together anywhere, and never referred to activities they had enjoyed with one another, but Christina forebore to mention her doubts principally because she was not certain of the truth, nor could she think why her cousin would lie on the subject.

Instead she said in a calm tone that did little to take the bite out of her remarks, "I can only say that Richard's friendship with Mr. Morley makes his taste suspect to me, Louisa. George Morley does not have an ounce of *ton* in his gross, overdressed body."

For a moment, Christina thought Louisa might not be able to find her voice at all she was so incensed. When she did, her voice quivered. "And what would you know about *ton*, you who have been buried in the Hampshire countryside all of your life?"

"A great deal more than Richard," Christina replied, ever so softly. "My mother was the granddaughter of an earl, Louisa, while dear Richard can claim no more . . . well, I am not certain what Richard can claim in the way of parentage. True, he was nephew to a baron, but my father's title was recently conferred. His line, I fear, is lamentably undistinguished, and, too, there is Richard's mother, who was, I believe, a tenant farmer's daughter. I beg your forgiveness, Louisa, if I sound unbearably high in the instep, but I think I have made the point that due to my birth alone, I've a better instinct for who does or who does not possess *ton* than Richard Brooks ever hoped to have."

Hearing her own words, Christina could have cringed. She'd have despised anyone who spoke so absurdly, but she knew Louisa well after five years. The first Lady Lely's bloodline was one thing the second Lady Lely respected.

"Mr. Morley is received everywhere," Louisa pointed out. The observation might have been a rebuttal, but Christina heard, with an infinitesimal lifting of her spirits, a new, ever so slightly considering note in her stepmother's voice. "And he is exceedingly wealthy!" Lady Lely's voice gained strength. "He could buy us—would buy you *anything* you desire," she amended, using emphasis to cover herself.

Christina did not fail to note the slip, but she had guessed long ago what Louisa's interest in the insufferable George Morley was. "Mr. Morley's wealth is indisputable, Louisa, and it is, I would maintain, the sole reason he is received as universally as he is. However, if you will but notice, the people of the highest *ton* may tolerate him but they are careful not to embrace him." For some reason Christina thought of the man with the black eyes at Lady Ainsley's ball whom Will had named the Marquess of Aldric. She could not imagine him even tolerating Morley, but she could scarcely hold up a complete stranger as a standard. There were others to name, however, "For example, tonight, when we attend her rout, you will not see Lady Lattimer encouraging Mr. Morley to pay his addresses to her niece. Only watch and see."

Christina considered her mention of Lady Lattimer a brilliant stroke, for Lady Lattimer was a leading light of the most fashionable set in society, just the position Louisa would have given her eye teeth to hold. Still, Louisa had an avid interest in money as well, and Christina thought it wise to add conciliatorily, "I do not mean to give Mr. Morley a disgust of me or my family. I understand that he is a friend to Richard, and I shall behave politely to him. If there is a place on my card, I will grant him a dance occasionally, and if he comes to call here at Morland House during visiting hours, I will receive him. What I will not do, however, is allow him or anyone else to believe that I've the least interest in his addresses."

Christina regarded her stepmother steadily. She had learned early that while Louisa pounced upon weakness, she could be brought to bow, if the opposing will was steely enough.

Louisa rarely conceded victory outright, however. "I shall think on what you have said, Christina," was all she would concede then, for example. "You have made an interesting point, but you are so young, and know so little of the world. There is a great deal . . . at stake here."

Even so equivocal a concession was a victory, and at any other time, Christina would have been smiling, with admittedly lamentable smugness, to herself. On that day, however, there was no smile at all in her thoughts. As she watched her stepmother depart the library, she was weighing the ugly possibility that their battle over Mr. Morley had been naught but a smoke screen anyway. Was Louisa vicious enough—and subtle enough—to pretend an interest in Morley's wealth while she plotted secretly to dispense with any need for a wealthy son-in-law? Did she thirst enough for the fortune her third husband had denied her? Did she hate her stepdaughter enough to arrange a fatal accident?

Christina shivered. She did not want to consider the possibility that anyone could hate her so much.

Damn Lely anyway, she swore in the next moment on a low, harsh breath. He had not only forced the Bexoms upon her, he'd made her a target for their resentment.

Of course he had not considered the effects of his actions upon her. She doubted he'd thought of her except as an instrument of his spite. Nor, of course, had he given her an explanation.

He had removed himself from Fairfield long before, finding it too modest for a man who had made the exceedingly lucrative investment he had on the 'Change that he had. His small, pleasant ancestral home would do for the wife who could not give him a son and her disappointing girl-child. And later, for his scheming second wife and her mob of annoying brats.

Lely had not even bothered to write himself to inform Christina of his second wedding. He'd left the detail to his secretary. But it had been Lely's solicitor who had come some five months later to inform Christina her father had changed his will to name her his sole heir, but for Fairfield, which Louisa was to have in the event of his death, along with a lump sum upon Christina's marriage. The solicitor had been able to make her no explanation for the astonishing change, nor had he been able to explain his second, equally shocking announcement that in no more than a day she could expect the second Lady Lely and her three children, who would henceforth be making their home at Fairfield.

It had been from her servants and Will that Christina had learned what she had. Louisa, it seemed, had made herself attractive to Lely and been his mistress for at least a year, and aspiring to more, had told him she was with child. Believing the male heir his first wife had failed to give him was finally within his grasp, Lely had married the woman, only to discover she had lied. Not only was she not with child, but she could not even have another, having had irreversible difficulties when Millie was born. Livid over the trick she had played upon him, Lely had exiled Louisa and her children to Fairfield, never to see them, or Christina for that matter, again. Within the year, his heart had failed him.

In the event Christina died underage, Louisa was to inherit, which left Christina squarely between her stepmother and a very great deal of money. To acquire the fortune Lely had come by so unexpectedly, Louisa had already proven herself willing to lie. But murder? Louisa was hard and rapacious, but was she that hard? Or sly, spiteful Cloris? There was Robert, too, who was not so openly hostile as his sister, but . . .

The sound of a tuneless whistle coming from the hallway outside the library interrupted Christina's exceedingly unpleasant thoughts, and hearing it, she grimaced with frustration. Had she summoned Robert merely by thinking of him?

Upon the thought, her stepbrother sauntered into the library. Four years older than Cloris and five years Christina's elder, he was a dandy of the first order, and in her view, at least, a scrounger of equally high degree.

She liked to avoid Robert on any day, as she could seldom tell what he was thinking except that when he looked at her he seemed to be mentally calculating what he could get from her. Damn Lely, she cursed again. He had allied himself to these people. He ought to have had to live with them, she thought angrily—and not for the first time—as she rose from her chair and made for the door that was opening even then.

"Hello, Robert. I am just on my way . . . "

She tried to pass him, but he stepped ever so casually into her path.

"I understand that Morley is out of favor with you now, Ti."

Only Millie and Will called her by the pet name Will had coined when as a little boy he'd not been able to get out Christina. She resented fiercely that Robert would presume and fixed him with a cold look. "Mr. Morley was never in my favor."

"Never in your favor! But Brooks said he was, and I put money upon him!" Robert regarded her as petulantly as if she had taken Morley in dislike merely to spite him.

"Then you have put your money in the wrong place as usual, Robert," Christina said crisply.

She sought to sweep by him again, but once more Robert backed into her path. "You cannot just leave the matter there!" he protested angrily. "I stand to lose a great deal. Who is in your favor? There must be someone in the crowd of gentlemen that swarms about you."

Christina's delicately arched eyebrows lifted markedly. "As the only male in my immediate family, Robert, I could have hoped that you would wish to protect me from the very sort of idle speculation and gossip you are, in fact, abetting. I am disappointed, though I know I have only myself to fault for that, as I have known you long enough to know that you are as close to being a gentleman as your wasp waists and absurd collars are close to being the dress of a nonpareil. Now, excuse me, Robert. I would go."

Her gray eyes frosty with disdain, Christina made certain to step by Robert then, but she did not pass him before she

saw his pale eyes narrow sharply. She could not be surprised after the dressing down she'd given him, and with a
stab of uncertainty wondered for once if she ought not to
curb her sharp tongue.

Robert did not share Cloris's passionate dislike of her,
but there was something unnaturally cold about him. The
only person he seemed to have any fondness for was himself. Even his mother he held at arms' length, and his sisters he disregarded entirely unless Cloris had some
interesting tidbit of gossip for him.

Surely, he was not so cold, however, as to try and kill
her, though it was true that through his mother he would
profit immensely, should she die. But, no! Surely Robert
was too squeamish. He shuddered at the mere mention of
disease or injury. Surely he would not have the stomach to
see her harmed.

But what was she thinking? Christina brought herself up
short of a sudden. Did she really believe someone had
arranged the three—only three!—accidents? And why
would the person have waited until now? If money was the
motive, and she could not think what else it would be, she
had inherited four years before at thirteen. She'd been more
vulnerable then, surely.

No! She had heard Millie describe the plots of her favorite penny dreadfuls too often. Her mind had begun to
run along those melodramatic, absurd lines. Will believed
there was so little need to worry that he was deserting in
favor of trout!

Christina managed a wan smile. She felt almost as if she
were losing her wits and decided she needed a little more of
Millie and her amusingly named parrot. Yes, they would
cheer her, and then for no reason at all the Marquess of
Aldric popped into her mind. Would he be at Lady Lattimer's? Christina had no more than formed the question
than she rolled her eyes. Here, indeed, was proof that she
was losing her mind. The man might attend Lady Lattimer's rout, but it was as likely that the sky would rain
gold as that the Marquess of Aldric would notice her again.

Chapter 3

"**Y**ou wish an introduction to Christina Godfrey, Aldric? I am . . . disappointed. I had hoped you deigned to grace my little entertainment because you'd pleasant memories of our so very short time together."

Aldric inclined his dark head, hiding the flash of regret in his eyes. He had devoutly hoped Lady Margaret Lattimer would either not recall the night they'd shared some years before or disdain to mention such an old tryst.

He schooled his expression soon enough, however, and even produced a smile of a gentleness that would have surprised all but the handful of people who knew him well.

"My interest in Miss Godfrey does not preclude pleasant memories, Meg. You are a superb woman, as you must know, but, ah, it is my future that concerns me now."

Lady Lattimer had her pride. She gave no sign how much she regretted Aldric's decline of her invitation, and Aldric breathed a sigh of relief for her exquisite manners. Truth to tell, he had never been particularly proud of that long-ago tryst with Meg. She had been the one to approach him, but he had encouraged her. Sometimes, as had been the case with her, he had only to meet a woman's eyes once, fleetingly even, to bring her to him. The prickly part for Aldric was that he knew he had used Meg to retaliate against her husband, a lisping fop with an unpleasant taste for blood, who once, in front a group of gentlemen at White's, had inquired of Aldric if the marquess "really and truly" wished to play at cards that night. He'd worn a most guileless expression, but everyone had understood. Lattimer had been insinuating Aldric could not afford the company. Aldric had replied by coolly whipping the man that night at cards and the next, flagrantly cuckolding him.

In those early years, the ones immediately after the loss as he called it, he had been raw with indignation. He, a Beauchamp and the Marquess of Aldric, could deposit less with his banker than any shopkeeper in the land, and he had almost looked for insults from his peers, he'd been so thin-skinned. Upon hearing some lately knighted bastard slur his father, he had challenged the man and promptly put a bullet through his arm.

With time, he'd cooled. And realized the truth about his peers. His troubles had been food for the gossips only so long as the news was fresh. Within a year they were pouring over someone else's troubles, but if they were fickle about their gossip, his peers unstintingly respected arrogance, and that he had in spades. He'd only had to disdain them to find to his cynical amusement that the gossips were lionizing him, and for years it had been the case that his peers kept their distance from him only because he held them there.

"Now look at you, Aldric!" Lady Lattimer lightly tapped the marquess's arm with her fan. "You've that closed, brooding look about you that proclaims how little you really care for my entertainment. That is not well done of you, when you have asked a favor of me!"

"Do you mean to deny me my introduction, Meg?"

His tone was lazy and even soft, but Lady Lattimer, a sophisticated woman, flushed. "No! Of course not! Indeed, I doubt I could deny you anything, Aldric."

She laughed as if to make light of the confession that had slipped out unintended and made a quick show of glancing about her ballroom for Christina Godfrey, but in truth, Lady Lattimer had meant that last. She remembered as clearly as if their tryst had happened the day before, how considerate he had been, how kind with his hands, how he had stirred her.

"She is very lucky," Lady Lattimer whispered suddenly, half to herself.

But Aldric heard, and it was not the charming, unexpectedly gentle man of whom she sometimes dreamed who glanced down at Lady Lattimer then. "Don't allow sentiment to cloud your judgment, Meg," Aldric advised, flint in his eyes. "I propose a business transaction to Miss Godfrey, no more. My name for her money."

Lady Lattimer had assumed the business side of the marriage. All marriages, proper ones, brought some material gain to at least one of the parties. Love was for affairs. Still . . . as she said rather wistfully, "But it is you she'll have on her wedding night, Aldric, not any other of ancient name and high title."

Aldric made no answer, but Lady Lattimer did not notice his grim silence. She had found Christina Godfrey standing with a small party on the far side of the floor.

Hearing the light, cultured voice of the hostess making a greeting to Louisa, Christina turned and suddenly, unexpectedly, her heart began to thud painfully against her ribs. Of all the people in the world, she had not expected to see him.

Dear heaven, nor had she expected that his effect would be so much more powerful at close quarters. It had been strong enough at a distance, but he was taller than she had realized, broader shouldered, though flawlessly elegant in black evening clothes, a white cravat at his throat. Christina saw Aldric speak to Louisa and noted the cool grace with which he bowed over her stepmother's hand, but she knew not what he said. She could not hear beyond the wild clamor of her heart. And that frightened her, for she realized she was excited, and she had never been excited by a man before.

He turned to her when she was still in tumult. Lady Lattimer made the presentation. Christina scarcely heard her hostess, as she looked up into the hard, handsome face of the Marquess of Aldric.

Meeting his eyes, she missed a breath. From the distance of much of Lady Ainsley's ballroom, she had understood they were black and even that they were compelling, but she had not understood his eyes were brilliantly black and that she would find it a struggle to look away.

She heard her name and remembered to drop into a curtsy. Head bent, she became aware again of the racing of her heart. Instantly it seemed a chorus of voices in her head cried alarm. "Watch out! He must be playing some joke. He can have no interest in you. He is so assured as to be indifferent to his effect! He could have any woman he wants. Why would he want a redheaded stick with colorless eyes and too much height?"

No voices came to Aldric's defense. It was her eyes made his case.

As she rose from her curtsy, Christina took in again the long, powerful, elegant length of him; the crisp blue-black of his hair; the refined, chiseled cut of his mouth even, then she was looking into his eyes again.

"I should be honored if you would dance this dance with me, Miss Godfrey."

Though it was a perfectly unexceptional invitation, Christina was aware of a faint, nearly undetectable hint of challenge gleaming in the eyes that held hers. Her chin lifted abruptly, yet after an infinitesimal hesitation, she heard herself say, "The honor is mine, my lord."

And Christina knew she did not allow Aldric to lead her onto the floor because Louisa would have killed her by slow degrees had she rebuffed a marquess. She had all but forgotten Louisa. She went, challenge or no in his eyes, because it simply would not have been possible for her to deny him.

It was to be a waltz. Her heart rioted in alarm, when Aldric took her in his arms. She had not expected such closeness so soon. She had not expected he would be tall enough she would be studying his cravat, if she did not force her eyes to his. For a half second, she thought she would be blinded by the whiteness of that cravat for the duration of the dance, but then she flung up her chin again.

It was angled haughtily to Aldric, and he had seen her hesitation before she would dance with him, too. It seemed she considered herself above a penniless marquess. A wave of bitterness threatened him, for God knew that he knew that with the father she had had, she ought to have dragged her chin in shame.

Coolly, his ostensible purpose in leading her out forgotten, he said, "I've the suspicion, Miss Godfrey, that you were not certain you wished to dance with me."

Watching her closely as he was, Aldric easily caught the flare of surprise in her eyes. But he had intended to throw her off her haughty, regal stride. What diverted him momentarily was the eyes themselves. He realized he had expected blue, the color he associated with red hair, not gray, and certainly not the misty gray hers were. Framed by long, curling lashes that were surprisingly dark, they were also very wide and unexpectedly direct.

"I mistrusted why you asked me to dance, my lord," Christina said after no more than half a second. "The only other time I ever saw you, you seemed to be laughing at me."

Aldric had had years of experience at controlling his expression. One did not play as successfully at cards as he did, if one could not, but she had taken him by surprise nonetheless. She was as direct as her eyes.

"If I was smiling when you saw me at Lady Ainsley's, you mistook why. I was not laughing at you, Miss Godfrey, but laughing with you, admiringly."

"And pigs are flying through the streets, my lord. You would not admire a too tall, too thin, carrot-topped, green miss were you blind."

It was not even her frankness that caught him so off guard this time, though he did not fail to mark it, of course. What caused Aldric an oddly unpleasant start was that she had all but repeated his own words to him.

He covered himself with ease, pretending to make a

close study of her hair. Moly, possessed of that chivalrous streak, had called it Titian, while he had termed it garish. Reluctantly, he took in that they had neither one been right.

"Carrots, I do believe, Miss Godfrey," he said, looking slowly back down at Christina, "are orange, while your hair, by contrast, is the color of old, well-polished copper."

She willed herself to dismiss the softness of his tone and even the glint just at the back of his black eyes. He was practiced!

"Coppery-topped young miss, then," Christina conceded, but with a challenging lift of her eyebrow. "Is it my purse you admire?"

She had gone too far. She had meant only to keep him at arm's length. But the question had revealed more about her than she cared for it to do.

If Christina did not want Aldric to be enlightened neither did Aldric want to be. He had taken for granted the benefits of being an heiress. Harboring no charity for her, he had not considered the disadvantages.

Quietly, with more sympathy than he wanted, he said, "If you sweetened that tongue a bit, Miss Godfrey, you might find you would not be obliged to ask such a question."

Christina's eyes flickered, as if she knew the truth in his remark, but would not acknowledge it. Soon enough, though, she met his eyes again and managed a careless shrug. "Alas, my lord, I was born with it already sharp."

"Perhaps if you were to put it to its proper use, you would find it softer and sweeter, too."

There was an unexpected light in Aldric's eyes. Christina found it oddly unnerving, but she did not understand it any more than she understood the significance of his remark. Another girl might have tried to pretend she did understand, but Christina could not. She flushed a little, but her wide, direct gray eyes on his, she said simply, "I am afraid I do not understand what exactly you mean, my lord."

"Devil it!" Aldric half shook his head. "I quite forgot your age. Forgive me."

Christina regarded her partner in some surprise then. She

had not expected rue or an instant apology. It touched her somehow; brought her to think of his mother. He was the most striking man she had ever seen, but of course he had not been hatched on high in an aerie. She'd even have wagered just then that he had at least one sister, younger than he, whom he had watched over with rather protective instincts.

"You are forgiven, my lord. I doubt I can be dreadfully affected by something I don't understand. But I think you are not much accustomed to younger ladies."

Aldric caught the flash of dry humor in her eyes as well as the emphasis on "younger," and he smiled, amused, without even remarking that he shared a moment of humor with Lord Lely's daughter. "And I, for my part, think I'll not touch that, my dear, Miss Godfrey. Instead, I'll ask, how old are you?"

She laughed. "Almost eighteen, actually."

"That would be seventeen, then," he said with mock exactness. "A delightful age."

"You remember it, then?"

"Devil take you. Certainly. Well, you may be obliged to jog my memory a bit."

"I doubt we've the same experience of seventeen, being of different genders," Christina told him, smiling still. "However, Will seemed to fish and hunt the year away."

"Will? Was he your swain at Lady Ainsley's?"

"My swain?"

It had been obvious to Aldric that night at Ainsley's that Christina had the boy wrapped around her finger, and so he supposed that she was playing coy. His tone dry as a desert, he clarified, "This particular one of your legions of swains was the fresh-faced fellow I saw making haste for the card room some minutes ago. You talked with him a long while at Lady Ainsley's."

"Oh, you do mean Will Palmer." Christina looked away again, remembering suddenly how alone she would be without him.

Aldric saw the darkening of her eyes, and misinterpreted

it. "Perhaps you have had a parting of the ways?" he suggested, his voice cool.

Christina heard the change in his tone, and if it mystified her, it also had the effect of pushing her annoyingly persistent fears to the back of her mind. "We will soon part ways, actually," she said, smiling faintly. "He is to go trout fishing in the Highlands with friends."

She spoke of the boy with obvious affection. "You have a *tendre*, then, for this Mr. Palmer?" Aldric pressed, wondering already how he would discredit such an ingenuous-looking fellow.

"Will is my closest friend," Christina told him frankly. "I've known him all my life. I doubt that means I've a *tendre* for him, but in truth, my lord, I do not know much about *tendres* or flirtations."

He wondered again if she was being coy, then decided almost grudgingly, after studying her clear, gray eyes, that she most likely was not.

Christina could not guess what Aldric made of her answer. He did not say, and his black eyes revealed nothing. At once she felt a spurt of frustration directed entirely at herself. Why in the name of heaven did she even try to read his enigmatic expression? What could it matter if he liked his ladies experienced or as inexperienced as she was? He was too desirable. He could have any woman in the room, and she did not like to think about the most probable reason that had brought him to expend his efforts upon her.

But then he spoke, in a low, lazy voice, something of that earlier gleam, the one that had unnerved her, in his eyes.

"It comes as a surprise that you know nothing of *tendres*, Miss Godfrey, but I find that I am very glad to learn your heart is not lost to anyone."

Christina could have laughed aloud. Her heart was most certainly not lost. She could feel its every beat. And it was not just the words he'd spoken, but the smile quirking the corner of his mouth as well.

Excitement raced through her veins, and he seemed to know, for the light intensified just there in the depths of his dark eyes. It made her breathless. And that alone made her wary all over again.

"You are playing with me, my lord."

"No," Aldric contradicted her with a sudden gravity that was entirely unexpected. "I am not playing with you at all, Miss Godfrey." Then, as quickly as it had come, the gravity disappeared and there was again amusement in his eyes. "You seem to think you are nothing but a bundle of faults, Miss Godfrey, but everyone is flawed, and I cannot see that you are unusually so. In fact, I do believe that if you would make a study of yourself in your pier glass, you would see the truth is you are not so flawed as simply out of the common way, a most uncommonly desirable thing to be."

Even more than she wanted to believe the flattery, she wanted to believe that Aldric believed it, but it was hard, so very hard to be that credulous.

"You may say 'thank you, my lord,'" Aldric prompted her, humor in his voice, for her war with herself was clearly reflected in her eyes. "I am not in the habit of doling out insincere flattery."

Christina flushed. He would think her ill-mannered, if not ill-looking. "Thank you, my lord."

"Very much?" He found himself teasing her.

And her eyes did light, most uncommonly nicely in fact. "Very much, then, my lord. It was an exceedingly handsome compliment."

If she was a trifle breathless, Christina could not much care. She knew Aldric had to have some understanding of the affect he had, and they had already established that she was infinitely less experienced than he.

"I've one more compliment," he said, still with that teasing light in his eyes."

"Too many and I shall doubt them all," she warned.

He laughed. "Not this one, I think. You dance very well."

"Perhaps it is my partner," she said, then dropped her eyes because she felt shy bandying flattery in that way. "And I do thank you, my lord."

"You are quite welcome. And I thank you, Miss Godfrey, for being of such a nice height that I was not obliged to bend in half to dance." That brought her eyes back to his, and she even gave a chuckle, grateful to him for finding some way to turn her worst attribute to seeming advantage.

The music came to an end then, and Aldric bowed as expected and said he had enjoyed the dance, a compliment Christina returned. She did not say he danced with the same natural grace and assurance with which he moved, but she imagined the sentiment, or near enough, was in her eyes, for she feared they must be shining, she felt so near to floating. Then Christina realized the direction in which Aldric was escorting her, and she came out of her distraction. "Oh, you are returning me to my stepmother, I see, my lord. I do not wish to go to her, however. I wish you to take me to Will instead. I can see that he has just returned from the card room."

"I cannot return you to Mr. Palmer, Miss Godfrey, however good a friend he is to you," Aldric replied flatly. "It isn't done."

That caused Christina's brow to lift. "And you would have me believe you are the kind of man who scrupulously minds all the niceties?"

Aldric returned her incredulous gaze with a suddenly narrowed one. "You will find, Miss Godfrey, that I do as I please, and in this instance I please to mind every nicety. And so," he went on, "you will go to your stepmother as is proper."

Chapter 4

"I simply do not understand why he danced with you, Ti! That is why I am continuing to belabor the issue, as you say. Good Lord, he's known for shunning eligible girls! Yet he danced with you."

Will eyed Christina stubbornly, but she returned him look for look. She did not want to discuss the Marquess of Aldric with Will. She wasn't certain why, she only knew that she felt shy about Aldric and did not want to think about him too closely with anyone, herself included.

"Will, for pity's sake! You are leaving in another moment. I cannot see why we must have this unpleasantness cloud our leave-taking. I have no idea why Lord Aldric asked me to dance."

"He cannot mean you well, Ti. You must see that! It is commonly accepted that he is not the marrying kind."

Abruptly, Christina's face cleared. "You are concerned he will give me a slip on the shoulder! Oh, Will! I do not know whether to laugh or hit you."

"Well, he's a rake!" Will defended himself against the suddenly amused look in Christina's gray eyes. "He's a practiced seducer who has women like other men have . . . brandy."

At that Christina could not contain herself. "Will! Oh, don't go! Please! I did not mean to offend you, and I will vow, if you like, not to become the marquess's next drink of brandy!"

Will did not laugh as she had hoped he would. With a gruff earnestness that forced Christina to bite the inside of her cheek to keep a smile from her lips, he admonished, "I hope you will be on your guard, Ti. Aldric's a reputation for being hard as the devil. Jove! I almost regret my trip now, but I'll not have an opportunity like it soon, and if I mean to go, I must do it now or Paxon and Carlisle will leave without me."

"Go with an easy mind, Will! I shall do quite well," Christina assured the young man one last time, and giving him a kiss on each cheek, wished him luck in landing the largest trout before she led him inside to the drawing room where Lady Lely and her daughters waited to bid him farewell, too.

When Will had finally exited, Millie spun around to ask, her eyes dancing with excitement, "Was Will cautioning you against Lord Aldric, Ti?"

"Now I wonder how you could make such an accurate guess, Millie?" Christina mused with mock thoughtfulness.

Millie giggled like a wicked sprite. "A lucky guess?" she tried.

Christina shook her head slowly, biting back a smile, but Cloris, watching, found little humor in their play. "You were eavesdropping again, Millie!" she accused. "That is how you know what Mr. Palmer said to Christina, and that is the lowest, most reprehensible . . . "

Millie wrinkled her nose with gross impertinence at her elder half sister. "You are only on your high horse, Cloris, because I told everyone that I heard Mr. Darnsworth say you are handsome for a woman of your age."

"Millie," her mother exclaimed rather perfunctorily, "you must not tease your sister so. It is unbecoming."

"Then you must ask her not to play mother to me, Mama. Cloris believes she rules me!"

"Because no one else tries to do so," Cloris retorted angrily, which, to Millie's delight, earned Cloris a cool frown from their mother.

With Cloris silenced for the moment, Millie returned her attention to Christina, who immediately shook her head. "If you know the details, you needn't ask me to repeat them, Miss Imp."

"I wasn't going to ask again what Will said." She shot her more formal sister an owlish look. I was going to tell you that Sarah says Lord Aldric is quite top of the trees."

The cant caused Lady Lely to make an exasperated noise, but Cloris cut a sly look at Christina and spoke before her mother could reprove Millie. "And did your chatterbox of a friend make any mention of Lord Aldric's pockets, Millie? I understand they are quite, quite to let."

Millie instantly understood the significance of the remark and shot an apologetic look at Christina. She had never meant to cause embarrassment to her stepsister, who was, in her humble opinion, the only reasonable person on earth except, perhaps, for Will Palmer, but then he forgot to notice her much.

To Millie's relief, Christina's head was bent, for she had, it seemed, discovered a piece of lint on her afternoon dress, and so Cloris was denied any visible proof she had drawn blood. Forthwith, Millie leapt into the breach and distracted Cloris entirely. "Sarah said nothing about Lord Aldric's pockets, Cloris, but she did say that Mr. Darnsworth's calves are known to be the spindliest in town, but I suppose, old spinst—"

"I am no spinster!" Cloris flared back, and despite, or perhaps because of Millie's smug look, went on to lecture her sister at length about manners, respect, and the foolishness of judging a suitor by something so trivial as his calves.

Christina made a mental note to present her younger stepsister with an entire box of her favorite chocolate bonbons. She needed the moment to recover from the swift stab of regret Cloris's news had cost her. So, it was her purse that interested him. In her heart she had known it. Her one outstanding attribute was her money.

Likely the suspicion was the reason for her reluctance to discuss Aldric even with Will. Understandable, perhaps, to wish unpleasantness away, but generally, as in this case, ineffective. Damn. She cursed to herself with swift, fierce violence, and then smoothed her face as she raised her head.

Millie and Cloris were still wrangling, but Christina found her stepmother's sharp, considering gaze upon her. "There are other heiresses out this Season, Christina," Lady Lely said abruptly. "Aldric did not choose to dance with any of them, though two, at least, are considered beauties. I do hope that you will keep that in mind, should he come to call, and that you will remember as well that he is not only the seventh marquess of his line, but that the Beauchamps are an ancient, ancient family."

The moment their mother mentioned Aldric, Cloris and Millie ceased bickering. In the ensuing silence, Christina wondered wryly if she should not call for stage lights.

"Thank you, Louisa. I shall certainly keep in mind Lord Aldric's admirable antecedents, should I chance to see him again. As to the other, I had not thought much as to why the marquess displayed an interest in me. I knew I need not worry myself as I had Cloris's sharp eyes and ears at my disposal."

"Not to mention her sharp tongue," Millie flung in, for good measure. "And she only said that anyway, because she is envious of you, Christina, and always has been. Ow! Mama, Cloris pinched me! Look, my arm is turning blue!"

Lady Lely paid her daughter's arm not the slightest heed. Looking over the offended limb at Christina, she said with an unusual trace of excitement in her voice, "I believe you will see Aldric again, Christina. He has never singled out a young lady before. No one at Lady Lattimer's could speak of anything else. Even Lady Alvanley remarked on his interest, and you know that little amazes Lady Alvanley."

Christina knew Lady Alvanley only by sight, but she understood nonetheless Louisa's principal point. Her wealth and Aldric's status made a perfect match, convenient for all concerned, and everyone knew it. Once again, if not so fiercely, she muttered an oath beneath her breath.

Louisa proved to be absolutely right. Aldric came to call during visiting hours that very afternoon. When Louisa's butler announced him, eyebrows all across the room lifted and it seemed a collective breath was taken as everyone present absorbed that, indeed, the tall, superbly self-assured gentleman in the doorway was John, Lord Aldric.

Only one person was unmoved. Christina raised her cup of tea to her lips and deliberately turned a shoulder to the door in order to address a question to young Mr. Sidley, lounging against the wall beside her window seat.

Aldric's eyes, dark eyes that had settled upon her the moment he entered the room, narrowed. Given their final exchange the night before, he had not known exactly what to expect from her this afternoon, but he had expected at least perfunctory politeness.

She was a spoiled thing. And had more coyness in her than he'd suspected. Evidently, she thought to test her powers over him, to bring him to her side with some abashed apology on his lips. A grim laugh nearly escaped him. It would be a cold day in hell before he apologized to Lely's daughter for anything.

And, he went on in the same nearly violent vein, the sun would shine at night before he reduced himself to vying with the three fellows clustered around her at that moment for her favor. Great God, but the boy she was laughing with even now, Moly's cousin, but Aldric couldn't recall the name, could not have been much over twenty. Morley, the newly moneyed monkey on her other side, was as repulsive as he was wealthy, and the third fellow, Hargreaves, or Hargrove, was an obsequious, sycophantic friend of Morley's.

A muscle worked in his jaw, but Aldric managed to remain in the room, though he made absolutely no move to go to Christina. Lady Lely, in decided contrast to her stepdaughter, came hurriedly to greet him, and Aldric allowed the woman to present him to her youngest daughter, an elflike thing who could not take her eyes off him, and then to Sir Adrian Trevor, whom Aldric had heard was paying court to Lady Lely. With Sir Adrian, Aldric spoke for a little of a mill that was to be held within the week at Tumbridge Wells, then Aldric observed casually to Lady Lely that though he did not wish to interrupt Miss Godfrey when she was so deep in conversation, he did wonder if Miss Godfrey would be free to ride in the Park with him in, say, an hour. He knew he had judged his woman correctly, when Lady Lely did not so much as blink at his arrogance. She did not intend to allow her stepdaughter to chase off a marquess, and hastened to assure Aldric that indeed her stepdaughter would be delighted to ride in the Park, without bothering to consult said stepdaughter.

From the corner of her eye, Christina watched Aldric do the polite with Louisa, Millie, and Sir Adrian, but when after a very few minutes, she saw him bow formally, as if he were taking his leave without even having so much as glanced her way, she ceased attending so closely to Mr. Sidley. She had gotten precisely what she wanted. She had managed to send another fortune hunter on his way, but she felt nothing of the relief she had felt with all the others, and she was powerless even to keep from rubbing salt in what she had the lowering feeling would be a wound by watching him take his departure from the room and likely her life.

But even as she lifted her chin in the direction of his lean, elegant figure, Aldric unexpectedly flung a swift, narrowed glance toward the window seat, catching her watching him. His expression was closed, as usual, giving no hint to his feelings, except when their eyes met. Then something almost violent crackled between them, and Christina felt as if he had lifted her from her seat then set her down with a thud before he flicked his gaze away and proceeded out the door.

Startled by the force of what had passed between them, too amazed even to realize that no one else could have done more than remark that Aldric had looked briefly at her, Christina scarcely heard her stepmother at first.

" . . . will return in an hour for you, my dear, with his phaeton."

"The devil!" Mr. Sidley exclaimed, and by so little did Christina realize Louisa had been speaking of Aldric.

Indignation blazed through her—he had not even nodded her way!—and she determined she would certainly not go with the arrogant . . . devil! Fuming, she only gradually took in what another of her visitors, a thin, obsequious fellow named Lord Hargrove, was saying. " . . . phaeton can't be his! He ain't got any cattle but that stallion."

"Molyneux's a new phaeton and a pair of matched chestnuts, however," Mr. Morley, sitting uninvited by her, upon the window seat, observed with a sly, unpleasant smirk. "I don't doubt Aldric wheedled the use of them from the viscount. Molyneux is very generous with him, all but supports him. . . . "

Toward Aldric, Christina felt a bright, flaming indignation that made her want to run after and berate him wildly for his arrogance and high-handedness. In relation to Mr. Morley, stuffed in of all things a wasp-waisted violet-colored coat, she felt a cold fury he'd have done well to notice. He did not, filled with the need to belittle a gentleman who hadn't a fraction of his wealth, yet possessed all the cachet he'd have given his eye teeth to have.

"Wheedled, Mr. Morley?" Christina interrupted ruthlessly, giving Morley a look that made him flush. "Did you say wheedled in reference to Lord Aldric? If you did, I commend you for being wise enough to wait until he left the room. I should think Lord Aldric might take offense, and he appears to be a gentleman who could"—she swept Morley's soft, fat figure with a contemptuous look—"successfully avenge any slight he thought done to him. As for myself, I cannot conceive of using the word 'wheedling' in connection with Lord Aldric, but then I cannot imagine him belittling another man behind his back. Now, if you will excuse me, gentlemen, I must go and make myself ready for my ride in the Park with Lord Aldric, as I do not care two bits whose cattle he is driving."

Christina stalked from the room with her chin high, but when Millie came tripping into the hallway after her, cry-

ing, "Bravo!" she flung the girl an exasperated look, and
did not listen as Millie, quite undaunted by that look, chat-
tered on about how "riveting" and "top of the trees" Aldric
was.

Christina did not want to see Aldric again. He'd cleverly
gotten around the point when they had discussed it at Lady
Lattimer's ball, but he was nothing more than a fortune
hunter. He had not been taken by her "coppery" rather than
red hair, or been pleased to find a woman with whom he
could dance without having to bend in two, or . . . or any
other thing to do with her personally. Likely he had thought
her Amazonian, forward, and bearable only because when
he looked at her he saw coins, lots of them.

And he had not even bothered himself to cross the room
to ask her if she wished to go to the Park! He had presumed
she would leap at the opportunity to be with him, no matter
how arrogantly he extended the invitation. Insufferable
man! No, she had had no intention of going to the Park
with him. He'd have come, and she'd have told him to his
face that he would have to consult her wishes before he
gave her lightning looks and stalked from the room, expecting her to do his will.

Admirable intentions, but all for naught now. She would
see Aldric, even go to the Park with him, because she had
become incensed by the sniping of two fatuous fools. As if
Aldric needed her defense! She suspected he'd not have
given a snap about their snide gossip. Both Hargrove and
Morley were negligible compared to him. Of a certainty,
when they had been announced by Louisa's butler, the entire drawing room had not gone silent. Cloris had not
looked up from Mr. Darnsworth's so-earnest countenance;
Millie and Sarah had continued giggling in their corner;
Lady Newell, Sarah's mother, had gone on gossiping with
Louisa, and so on. They had not made a ripple while Aldric
without the least effort, had brought the room to a halt.

With a half laugh, Christina tried to imagine what either
Hargrove or Morley would have done had the dozen or so
people in the room fallen silent upon the sight of either of

them. Hargrove would have gone beet red and fled, while Morley would have preened disgustingly. And Aldric? He'd been indifferent to the stir he caused, as if he encountered it so often he no longer even noticed it.

Yet—and she would receive no thanks from him—she had leapt to Aldric's defense and allowed herself to be goaded into dutifully appearing when he came to collect her. She'd not be pleasant, though. As Nancy scurried about, dressing her in a fashion the maid thought appropriate for a ride with a marquess, Christina determined not to be nice at all to Aldric.

Chapter 5

Aldric was half surprised to see Christina Godfrey descend the stairs of her stepmother's leased town house shortly after he arrived to collect her. He had thought her willful enough to balk at his high-handedness, but it seemed her stepmother had prevailed over her.

Lady Lely had turned her out smartly for him, too. She wore a well-cut carriage dress of a sky blue that turned her eyes a pearly, shining gray. Her bonnet was dyed the same shade of blue and was ornamented with an imported ostrich feather, a long, silky curved thing that set off the graceful curve of her neck. The cost of the feather alone . . . Aldric clenched his jaw. He would madden himself beyond the point of civility if he counted the cost of everything she wore.

And it would be difficult enough to be civil, he realized, taking in, as she approached, Christina's stubbornly averted gaze and tightly set mouth. It seemed she meant to make him pay for not dancing to her tune by inflicting the sulks upon him.

Aldric coolly ignored her, making his greeting a general one, and fixing his attention upon Lady Lely, though in truth he found the stepmother's fawning, presuming manners almost harder to bear.

Mercifully he had only to escort the stepdaughter out the door to be spared the woman's company. Going to the Park in an open phaeton with his tiger riding as good as on the seat between them, they would require no chaperon.

Fortune hunter; base, smooth fortune hunter. Christina

repeated the litany to herself as the marquess escorted her to the phaeton and assisted her to her seat. I go with you only to spite Morley.

The warning voices in her mind were pleased. Wise! they shouted. You are not in his style. Just look at him.

As Aldric swung up onto the phaeton, Christina flicked him an encompassing look from beneath her lashes, though the instant she sensed as much as saw the flashing black of his eyes, she looked pointedly away again. Still, she had seen enough to take her own point. Again.

He could not have looked more arrestingly attractive than he did in his biscuit-colored coat of superfine. Its color made his hair appear all the blacker by contrast and its close fit set off the powerful set of his shoulders. She thought of Morley, who had worn the latest fad in coats, several fobs, and half a dozen rings on his fingers besides. He had resembled a gaudy, corseted melon, while Aldric, in clothes that might as easily have been tailored last Season as this one, looked strong and lean and utterly out of her . . .

Without warning, a cart bowled out of an alley ahead of them and sent Christina's half grudging and entirely flattering ruminations on Aldric scattering. Going rigid, she took in the traffic all around them, the drays, the carts, the carriages, the riders, the pedestrians even. The dray before them pulled up to allow the cart room, but there was a carriage approaching from the other direction. Christina held her breath as Aldric whipped the phaeton's high-spirited chestnuts through the mess without hesitation.

From the corner of his eye, Aldric caught sight of Christina's slender hand gripping the phaeton seat. Her knuckles were white. He had thought her silent because she was stewing, and he had meant to leave her to sulk as long as she wished to make herself miserable, but when he flicked a glance from the busy traffic to her face, he saw she was pale and not staring off into some middle distance in a deliberate attempt to ignore him. She was staring rigidly at the congested street ahead.

"Are you anxious about riding in a high-phaeton, Miss Godfrey?" he asked, not without concern.

But she would not admit weakness to a man doubtless looking for weakness to exploit. "No, my lord, I am not at all afraid."

Christina forced herself to release her death clench upon the seat. Aldric watched her nestle her freed hand into the one lying in her lap, tightly he suspected. Her prickly show of bravery was absurd.

Yet, he found himself making an effort to distract her. "I had not the opportunity to say so before, Miss Godfrey, but you may be assured that you look very well this afternoon."

Christina shot him a brief glance that reminded Aldric the frightened-but-brave girl was only one side of Christina Godfrey. "Do I, my lord? I am relieved to know it, for I do try to turn myself out in direct relation to the graciousness of the invitation I am issued."

Christina refused to regret the remark she had rehearsed, but nonetheless, her cheeks warmed. He had a very cool way of looking, when he was not much pleased.

"I realize that is some sort of rebuke for my failure to apply directly to you, Miss Godfrey, about this outing, but I must admit I do not follow your reasoning exactly."

"I beg your forgiveness, my lord, for failing to make myself clear. The relation is in inverse proportions."

For a simmering moment, convinced he would make her a retort so devastating she would have to leap from the phaeton and run all the way home, Christina held her breath. And his black eyes did flash, but she realized finally the glint was lazily amused. "Very good, Miss Godfrey. Very good."

Even more than the spare compliment, that so very brief lightening of his eyes sent a thrill of pleasure streaking through her. Christina curled her hands into fists to fight it. By approving her setdown he had entirely negated its sting. And avoided making any apology for his insufferable arrogance.

"I wish you to return me to Morland House, my lord!"

Christina held herself stiff as a statue, while her eyes flashed indignantly at him. Aldric had not realized gray eyes could be so vivid.

"Do you?" He gave her an arrogant look that had the effect of causing her long-lashed eyes to go even wider. "Well, I'm afraid it is too late for that. The only place to turn this team about is in the Park. If you did not want to come out driving with me, then you should not have."

"Of all the high-handed things to say! And, it is a lie to boot." Christina heard the tiger riding behind them suck in his breath, but she was too incensed to care a whit if she'd shocked him or infuriated Aldric. Let the marquess call her out!

"A lie?"

Christina knew Aldric must be furious. Top of the trees Corinthians did not care to have their word questioned. She knew that much. "Yes," she snapped. "You've the skill to turn this team of chestnuts any time you want."

She could have bitten her tongue even before she saw the corner of his mouth quirk. "Thank you," Aldric said, and then looked at her to grin outright.

He looked a mischievous boy. And irresistible with that light dancing in his black eyes.

Christina blushed deeply. Before that, Aldric had not remarked her complexion. He had seen her only by candlelight with, presumably, a dusting of rice powder covering her. By daylight, he saw she'd skin the texture of cream and the color as well, but for the suggestion of rose that tinted her cheeks. Except, of course, that now the suggestion had become more a shout.

His smile deepened. "If I apologize for issuing my invitation so obliquely today, will you be persuaded to allow me to forgo displaying all my driving skills?"

She did not trust him—not his smile, not his words, not anything about him. He knew women too well, and he had good reason to use all he knew on her. But, if she was forewarned, what harm could there be in a drive around the

Park? Did she really want to return to Morland House and the company of the Bexoms?

Christina inclined her head. "It is, after all, a lovely day, my lord, and better spent outside than in a stuffy drawing room."

"My thoughts exactly," Aldric returned, his eyes gleaming, though he had the grace not to grin outright at her so guarded answer.

A post coach went rattling by, and they both returned their full attention to the busy street, though after a moment Aldric had the leisure to throw a faintly puzzled glance at Christina.

"If you recognized my skill as a whip, why is it you gripped the seat so . . . I'll not say fearfully, as you would protest . . . , but forcefully is not unfair, I think?"

His tone was dry, but it was not, she thought, disparaging, and Christina admitted, "I am not accustomed to London traffic." His response was a not unsympathetic nod, and suddenly Christina heard herself add, "In fact, I hate it! A runaway cart bowled into my carriage, and though the accident occurred some days ago, I can still hear the scream of the horses."

"Good Lord! Was it necessary to put any of them down?"

"No, no," she said quickly. "The horses were spared any harm, though the carriage was smashed to bits."

"Devil it! You must have been lucky to escape unhurt."

"I was, yes. My maid and I have a quick-thinking footman to thank. He noticed the cart and alertly got us out of the carriage just in time."

Aldric gave her a steady look. "I have never heard of such a thing happening, but I can assure you, Miss Godfrey, neither you nor these chestnuts will come near such harm while I am driving."

It was an impossible thing to assure, yet Christina felt unreasonably reassured. After all, he had threaded through the traffic with the ease of a sewing woman stitching a hem. Nor was it any detriment to her sense of security, she admitted, that Aldric was tall and broad-shouldered and arrogant enough that Fate would think twice before sending a runaway cart his way.

Christina smiled to herself at the improbable image of Fate quailing before the Marquess of Aldric, but after a little she began to consider the assurance that seemed innate, it was so offhand. Specifically, she began to wonder if it was real or only some fortune hunter's facade. He had not, she marked, admitted who owned the team he was so certain he could protect.

"I am grateful for your sympathy, my lord. Merely speaking of the incident has made me calmer, and I must say I can understand why you would wish to protect your team. Your chestnuts are exceedingly fine animals."

"The one on the left pulls a little," Aldric said absently. In much the same tone he continued, "And they are not mine, but the Viscount Molyneux's. As I've only a stallion, we should have been obliged to ride through the Park mounted double without his generosity."

Christina laughed to think of the brows they'd have lifted had they appeared in the Park mounted double on a horse, and Aldric chuckled, too, shooting her an amused glance. It was only the briefest meeting of their eyes, for they encountered more traffic, but Christina did not care how short the moment was. For the one glimmering moment, she and Aldric had been of one mind, sharing the same absurd vision without need of words.

And he had admitted who owned the chestnuts, had even confessed how little he himself possessed in the way of horseflesh. Perhaps he realized she would have been advised of the state of his finances, given the small world of London society. Perhaps he believed she did not care, given that she had gone riding with him.

And suddenly Christina was not certain she did care, at least so much as she had at first. The wish that he might have fallen in love with her at first sight was too idiotic, too impossibly romantic. She'd too many flaws for one thing, and for another, men of Aldric's experience and sophistication did not fall head over heels. And besides, what did his motives matter if she enjoyed his company, which she did? Christina decided impulsively that for once Louisa had given her good advice. She would take confidence from the thought that of all the wealthy young girls making their come-outs, he had singled out her. Surely there must be something he admired about her, something that had set her apart.

She could not guess what it was and did not bother herself to try. Merely believing that the man beside her found her interesting for herself in some way, however small, was quite enough, and she settled back in her seat, suddenly aware of the puffy white clouds overhead and the pleasant softness of the breeze.

And the man beside her, too. His shoulders nearly brushed her, reminding her of the impression of strength he gave. It was not the brute strength of a laborer, however, but the more subtle strength of a large cat. Yes, he was even sleek like a cat somehow, lean with flowing muscles. Noting Aldric's black hair from the corner of her eye, Christina thought suddenly of a panther, and then she all but lifted her eyes to the sky.

She was likening the Marquess of Aldric to a panther. Obviously, they could not reach the Park too soon. She clearly needed a diversion.

And she got it. From the moment they passed through the gates, heads turned. Christina had never experienced anything like it, though she had ridden in the Park several times. Men half stood in their seats to make them out. Women craned, then flicked open their fans and put their heads together to whisper excitedly. Though she kept her eyes fixed straight ahead, Christina turned pink with self-consciousness. Too easily, she could imagine what the gossips were saying. "Aldric with her?" the first would remark in astonishment, and the second would answer knowingly, "Ah, but she's an heiress, don't you know."

Casting a sidelong glance at Aldric, she felt a stab of resentment at how indifferent he seemed to the stir for which he, far, far more than she, was responsible. He lifted his whip to acknowledge the Viscount Molyneux riding by in a carriage with two women, but otherwise he paid no attention to the craning heads and the buzz of whispering Christina swore she could hear.

Just when Christina was adding herself to the list of things to which Aldric seemed indifferent, he asked conversationally, "Have you been in London long, Miss Godfrey?"

She glanced up at him, almost surprised by the sound of his voice, and wondered suddenly if he had not read her disgruntled thoughts, for his mouth was ever so slightly quirked.

He answered her question, proving he could, indeed, see a great deal with those black eyes. "Young whips who are foolishly eager to show off their driving abilities and invariably possess more team than they can handle often congregate at the gates, where there is, equally invariably, a ready audience for them. I have found in the past that it is wise to be alert there, but now that we are on a less-frequented byway, we may have all the conversation we like. With fewer people we will also be spared the distraction of scores of quizzing glasses gleaming in our direction, though I will say, by the by, that you appeared remarkably unaffected by the attention."

Christina ignored the pleasure of that "remarkably" in favor of answering frankly, "'Appeared' is the correct word. I was more than a little taken aback, in fact, but decided I could do no better than to attempt to mimic your imperviousness, my lord."

He inclined his head with mock seriousness. "I am glad I could set you such an admirable example, for I find such displays of curiosity about the affairs of others . . . "

" . . . common?" Christina finished for him, her eyes dancing.

"Just so," Aldric said, and once more, as their eyes met, there was a flash of understanding, of mutual humor, and even of pleasure in it that arced between them. In the next moment Christina thought she also detected a spark of something like surprise in Aldric's eyes, but she gave it little thought, for she was surprised herself.

The remainder of their outing was uneventful, if pleasant. Christina related to Aldric some of the more amusing antics of the Bexoms, which meant she dwelt on Millie a great deal, and she told him about Fairfield and Hampshire. She did not do all the talking, however, though she did do most, for he prompted her repeatedly. Before she returned to Morland House, Christina learned that Aldric's home was in Herefordshire on the border with Wales. He did not say so, but she gathered that his ancestors had been border lords, given the land in return for keeping the peace for whatever English king happened to be on the throne, and she found she was not the least surprised to discover that Aldric was the descendant of men who had been powers unto themselves.

But if there was that warrior strain in him, he was capable of gentle emotion, too. She also learned he loved his home, for when he told her its name, Pembridge Castle, she could hear in his voice how deeply he felt. She respected that caring. In London Christina had met too many gentlemen whose interests in their estates extended only as far as the income a steward sent them, and perhaps to a ball they might give in the summer to dazzle their country neighbors.

But in truth, the particulars of Aldric's history mattered less to Christina than did the moments when with a look they had communicated they were of one mind. It was a heady thing to have experienced that sort of understanding with a man like Aldric, and in contrast to her grim mood when she had left Morland House, when Christina returned, her blood was singing in her veins, and she had to fight against the desire to smile at the least nothing.

Chapter 6

"Johnny! You've returned."

Aldric tossed a wry look at Molyneux, who stood before his pier glass, inspecting his cravat. "As you see. I hope there is a touch of claret left in that bottle."

"My boy, you wound me! It is only nine o'clock."

Aldric laughed as he poured himself a glass of wine. "Having a quiet night, are you?"

Molyneux grinned wickedly. "Had a charming afternoon, rather. But the lady had other engagements this evening, and I'm left to do the family thing tonight. First it's dinner with my young cousin, Sidley, then we're off to Aunt Cecily's rout. She's rather commanded our appearance. Did Elise take your tardiness equably?"

The non sequitur did not give Aldric pause. Sprawling comfortably in a wing chair, he tossed off a healthy portion of the claret. "It would seem Elise can find nothing to do in her cottage without me. Pity she doesn't read. No," he corrected himself in the next moment with the glimmer of a smile, "I recant that. It is no pity that Elise's interests run in one direction only. She makes a delectable mistress."

"I cannot understand how it is her husband has never caught on to what she does when she hies off to their estate in Kent for a week at a time." Molyneux shrugged lightly as he gave his cravat a final pat. "I suppose it helps that the estate was hers, not his, and likewise the steward."

"The luck of the devil, one might say," Aldric observed with sardonic amusement.

Molyneux laughed, but when he turned from the pier

glass his expression was more curious than amused. "Did you tell her you plan to marry? Is that why you've returned a day early? Or did I get that wrong? Was it today you said you'd return?"

Aldric's smile faded. "I did not set a firm time of return, and no, I could see no reason to tell Elise anything of my affairs in town."

He lifted an eyebrow, waiting for Molyneux to protest again his plans in relation to Christina Godfrey, but the viscount could see from the belligerent set of that eyebrow that there was not much point. "You aren't afraid that Elise will come to town, learn of your interest in Miss Godfrey, and do something untoward out of spite?" he asked instead.

"She is tempestuous enough to do such a thing," Aldric allowed indifferently. He thought specifically of the wild tantrum his lush mistress had thrown because he had arrived two days late for their tryst. Still, she had managed to control herself when he had abruptly turned on his heel and called for his horse. "But in truth, I've little worry on that score," he went on. "She's a keen sense of what I will and will not abide, and anyway, she herself is married. But enough of Elise for the time. Tell me what has been happening in town. Anything interesting?"

"Well, there is a story concerning you that is making the rounds. I don't know it yet. Sidley does, however, and that is another reason, aside from our family ties, you understand, that I took it into my head to have dinner with him. So"— Molyneux tossed off the remainder of his glass of claret and fixed Aldric with a deceptively bland look—"rather than listening to news, you will be obliged to listen to me say that Christina Godfrey is not experienced enough to shrug off the unexplained disappearance of a gentleman who has paid her close attention for some three weeks or so."

Aldric did not care for the slight, unexpected pricking his conscience gave him. He had been his own master a long while and was unaccustomed to accounting to anyone, but particularly not to a young woman whom he had every reason to resent bitterly.

"Were there tears?" he inquired sarcastically enough that Molyneux's expression tightened. Seeing his good-humored friend's response, Aldric unbent a little. "Really, Moly, I was not away so long, only a few days. It did not occur to me to think she would mind. Has she made some scene?"

Aldric's difficulty imagining Christina Godfrey staging a scene for Molyneux's benefit told in his voice, and Molyneux managed a smile. "No, of course not. To everyone else, I am certain, she seemed to go on quite as usual, but then a veritable regiment of young men swarmed about her. Your interest in her has not gone unmarked, of course, and she seemed gay enough with her enlarged court, except that to the keen observer she spent rather more time than is customary looking expectantly to the door of whatever room she graced. And once, when I spoke with her, she seemed on the point of asking about you, but to her credit she managed to control her desire to even hint at what she wished to know."

It was on the tip of Aldric's tongue to say that he doubted Christina Godfrey knew how to hint. She was too direct, unusually so for a girl; no, for a woman of any age. She was astringency to honey. Honey was more common, therefore predictable; always sticky, generally murky, and even annoying, while astringency . . . ? Aldric scowled suddenly. So. The girl had a certain charm. He'd never maintained she would not, and his plans were not affected. His reasons for them were too compelling.

"At any rate," he heard Molyneux continue, "should you have some other prearrangement with Elise, you might think to give the girl a warning. It is what a true suitor would do." Even had Aldric had a response, Molyneux did not give him a chance to make it. Eyeing his friend perhaps a little warily, he made a mock bow. "And now, though I have made you suffer, of all things, a lecture from me, I shall have the further audacity to invite you to dine with Sidley and me. As I said, he's the one knows some story in which you figure, and after dinner, I am certain I can speak for the boy, he would welcome your company to his mother's. She'd be in alt to have you. You've always made Cecily's heart flutter absurdly, you know."

Not the least fooled by Molyneux's prattle, Aldric shot his friend a shrewd look. "Cut line, Moly. It's not your spritely Aunt Cecily you are thinking of. And I don't know if I'm in the mood to spare Christina Godfrey another evening of unrequited glances at doorways. We'll see. In the meantime, though, I am hungry as the devil and de-lighted to go with you to dinner."

"Excellent! We'll have a good meal and an amusing story for entertainment."

The viscount smiled his satisfaction, feeling no need at all to press his friend further about either Christina Godfrey or his Aunt Cecily's rout. After all, whatever Johnny's memory was, he distinctly remembered his friend saying he would return to town on Thursday; and yet, here Johnny was on Wednesday, a full day early. Either Elise was losing her touch or Johnny . . . Molyneux let the thought trail off, afraid even to think it for fear of putting a hex on it, but when he followed Aldric out the door, he was whistling merrily indeed.

Aldric suspected from the sly look in Molyneux's eyes that the story he'd been promised had not to do only with him but with Christina Godfrey as well. He was prepared for that, but not prepared for young Sidley to look so decid-edly undelighted at the prospect of relating the story in his presence.

"There you are, Sidley, m'boy!" Molyneux hailed the young man. "Come and sit down. Come on. Aldric doesn't bite, usually anyway. You do know each other, of course? Not formally! But Aldric, Sidley was hanging out after Miss Godfrey for a time. . . . "

Molyneux said it with the blandest of smiles, but the young man nearly choked on the claret his cousin had poured him.

Shooting a dismayed glance at Aldric's less-than-warm

expression, he cried quickly, "No, no, sir! I wasn't hanging out after Miss Godfrey at all. She made it clear early on that I could expect nothing more from her than friendship. And, too, she made quite clear the regard in which she holds you, sir."

"She holds Johnny in regard, eh?" Molyneux smiled. "Now why am I not overwhelmed to hear that? But what makes you say so, Sidley? Did she rhapsodize about his eyes, or perhaps, wax eloquent about that cool look of his. Has it on now, you'll mark."

Mr. Sidley made another strangled noise, perhaps meant to be a laugh, perhaps meant to be a warning to an elder cousin he feared had gone stark raving mad. But when he saw Aldric respond to the viscount with nothing more dangerous than a lazy glance, the young man managed to get out that Miss Godfrey, really, was not the sort to rhapsodize.

"No?" Molyneux's eyes twinkled, but otherwise he contained his humor. "Well, then, how do you know of Miss Godfrey's regard?"

"Well, sir, ah, well, she . . . "

"My boy!" exclaimed the ever-amiable Molyneux. "What could she have said that has you so undone? You are stammering as if your tongue's grown thick as a board. Here, soothe yourself with another glass of claret. It's quite excellent tonight."

Sidley drank gratefully. Aldric's dark, cool presence unnerved him enough without having Molyneux press him to tell a story he feared would offend the marquess as much as it might, hopefully, gratify him.

Finishing off the glass of claret, he began another, and Molyneux looked at him askance. "You need the fortification of three glasses of wine in order to relate what Miss Godfrey has said or done? Damn, Sidley, but I can scarcely wait to hear it!"

Regretting ever having accepted his elder cousin's invitation to dinner, much less having mentioned the certainty of Miss Godfrey's interest in Aldric, Mr. Sidley locked gazes with Molyneux, for he would be damned if he looked at Aldric while he told the story.

"Do you know Morley, sir? He's near my age and a pompous ass full of his own importance because he's a good deal of wealth. His grandfather made the fortune in trade, but he's conveniently forgotten that. Anyway, he, ah, made some remark about, ah, well, about who has and hasn't wealth."

Molyneux cocked a knowing eye at his young cousin. "You mean he mentioned that Aldric has successfully kept his family and estate afloat only because he has managed to win at the tables over the years?" The viscount's bald question was quite rhetorical. Before Mr. Sidley could summon an answer, Molyneux turned to Aldric to advise bluntly, "Call the fellow out, Johnny! He's an ass, and England would be far better off with fewer of his ill-bred ilk running about. They muck up the place awfully, forever posturing and strutting about. Makes a fellow want to quit town, even. Or perhaps we could enlist the services of a press gang. . . ."

Sidley could not be certain whether his cousin was only amusing himself, and his uncertainty made him more than a trifle nervous. He did not care for George Morley in the least, but neither did he care to be the cause of the fellow's death, which would surely be the result if Morley were obliged to face Aldric at twenty paces.

A little trickle of sweat rolled its way down his back. He shot a glance at Aldric, hoping inspiration would strike him and he would think of some clever, dismissive remark to defuse the tense moment. Unfortunately, Sidley found that Aldric was studying him, and when the young man looked into those hard, veiled black eyes, he could not bring any word at all to mind.

Yet, even as he was thinking to himself that the man would kill Morley without the least compunction, the ghost of a smile curved Aldric's mouth. "Disregard Moly, Mr. Sidley. He took Morley into some dislike the night the fellow lost a not inconsiderable sum to me and was less than gracious about his, ah, misadventure." Sidley had to bite his lip against a desire to babble that of course he would disregard his cousin, and even Morley, or particularly Morley, but already, Aldric was going on, "But now, if you will forgive me for pressing you, Mr. Sidley, I must admit I am curious as to how Miss Godfrey comes into your story."

"Bless him!" Molyneux laughed. "Johnny's remembered the point! What did the girl say, Sidley?"

Promptly, able even to smile now, Mr. Sidley declared, "She set Morley down so sharply she made his teeth rattle."

"Defended Aldric, did she?" Molyneux remarked, casting an exceedingly bland look at Aldric.

Mr. Sidley did not notice the look. He addressed Aldric, who did notice, but superbly ignored it. "Yes. It was a while ago, actually. You called at Morland House, sir, then returned after a little to take her for a drive in the Park. While you were away, Morley said something about the rig you were to drive being my cousin's and that you'd, ah, well, wheedled it from him. You ought to have seen Miss Godfrey. She was marvelous, rounded on Morley like a tigress! The fellow was red in the face by the time she had done telling him it was the man that signified with her, not his rig. Called him spineless, even, as I recall."

"Well, happily, she's some backbone," Molyneux murmured. "I admire that in a woman, you know."

Aldric did not take the bait, but he had long known the girl had backbone. What did surprise him was that she had defended him on a day when he had treated her less than amiably. As he recalled the scene, he had stalked out of her drawing room without a word to her. He'd thought she was being coy with him, and subsequently, that Lady Lely had somehow forced her to go driving with him. Obviously he'd gotten something wrong, but weeks later that did not matter so much to him as the remark about what signified to her. Interesting that, when after his father's cataclysmic loss had stripped his pockets so very bare, gentlemen he'd thought of as good friends had suddenly found reasons not to call upon him. Only a very few in fact, Moly foremost among them, had carried on as always. As he recalled, Moly had said something about not giving a damn what tailor Aldric patronized, as he certainly was not going to drink with his lordship's coat.

Over the rim of his glass, Aldric's eyes met Molyneux's. The viscount was looking . . . too bland by half. Damn him. Aldric's eyes narrowed. Neither of them could know why she had said it. She might only have wanted to trounce Morley and said the first that came to mind. And she might not have been telling the entire truth. A man's title might figure with her. . . .

"Well then, Johnny? What's it to be?" Molyneux rose from the table. Aldric thought he looked almost sympathetic. "Are you coming with us? Aunt Cecily's champagne's the best, you know."

Well there was that. He couldn't afford champagne himself. Yet.

Christina flicked her gaze to the entrance of the ballroom. No, her breath came in a rush of dissatisfaction. The man entering was not Aldric. He had not said he would attend Mrs. Sidley's rout tonight, nor Lord and Lady Rockingham's ball the night before, nor Mrs. Smythe-Carne's affair on Monday. She had only assumed he would, because he had made an appearance at almost every entertainment she had attended for a little over three weeks. Now, without a word, he was conspicuous in his absence.

She did not know why. He had not thought to advise her that he would be away, and the last time she had seen him, he had behaved no differently than usual. Actually he had seemed to enjoy himself at the Elgin exhibit. He had displayed a thorough knowledge of classical Greece, but his learning had not surprised her as much as that he had not been the least dismayed to find that she knew a bit herself. His eyes had lit, or she thought they had, when in the course of their conversation she had been prompted to observe how very improbable she found some Greek myths, most particularly the story of Leda and the swan. Had he somehow hidden that he'd actually been scandalized not only by her knowledge of the story, but her mention of it to a man?

No. Aldric wouldn't have bothered to hide his disapproval, if he had been disapproving, and certainly there would not have been that spark of amusement glinting in his eyes. Even now, she smiled to think of it, but perhaps his amusement had been fleeting, and he had decided he was bored by her. That did seem possible to Christina. How was she to know the signs that a man was bored? She hadn't known any man long enough, but for Will, and their footing was so entirely different.

"Christina! Here you are in the shadows, seeming to hide! I have been looking for you as Louisa did not know where you were, which I must say, is unforgivably remiss of her. I doubt your father would have named her your guardian, had he known . . . "

"Richard." Christina cut off the heavily jowled, thick-set gentleman who had been her father's nephew and was her only living blood relation. She wished she could like him, but his smiles never reached his eyes, and he'd a marked tendency toward complaining in one breath and criticizing in the next. Not one to pretend to feelings she did not harbor, Christina made no effort at all to inject enthusiasm into her greeting.

Richard did not appear to notice how tepid her greeting was. "I am pleased to find you alone for a moment, Christina. I have wanted to talk to you, and you are seldom free these days. I am glad to see that you have sent the Marquess of Aldric on his way. I know it could not have been easy for you to do. His title is an exalted one and his family the best, but he is a bad apple, Christina, a fortune hunter, no more. The best thing for you, as I am certain you have realized, is to marry a man equal to you in fortune. George Morley is . . . "

"An odious, pompous toad." There was a fiery light in the gray eyes Christina turned upon her cousin. He stiffened at the sight of it. "I detest Mr. Morley, Richard, and I will not under any circumstances consider him for a husband. I have told you as much before, and I do not expect to have to repeat myself every time that we meet."

"But he's rich as Croesus! And Aldric has barely a ha'penny to his name."

"Fortunately for me, I need not worry about the wealth a prospective suitor has to offer, Richard. I need worry only about his character, and there I find George Morley the pauper. But as to Lord Aldric, I do not believe he deserves to be termed a fortune hunter at all. He has not paid his addresses to legions of other heiresses, nor has he made the least secret of his finances to me."

"But"—Richard's fatuous smile had faded to an uneasy frown—"it is obvious that he has fallen out of your favor, Christina. Everyone has remarked how he's been least in sight these last several days."

Not by so much as a flick of her eyes did Christina indicate how that sent her spirits plunging. Lightly, if pointedly, she tapped her cousin's plump pigeon's chest with her fan. "You have been gossiping, Richard. It is not upstanding behavior, but I'll forgive you this once, as I know how marvelously interesting Aldric is. Excuse me now, will you? I've a profound need to slip out onto the terrace for a momentary respite from the suffocating hothouse in which I find myself."

Chapter 7

Christina did not refer to the warmth of the ballroom. It was London that was the hothouse to her, with everyone gossiping about everyone else's affairs. Aldric's interest in her had stirred up a furious amount of attention, but his disinterest was likely to stir even more as the gossips seemed particularly to delight in blood. Her shoulders sagging momentarily, Christina acknowledged that gossip about his interest had been easier to bear than gossip about his rejection would be.

"Moping, Christina?" Robert Bexom strolled up, uninvited and unwanted. "That's not like you at all. Is it true that Aldric's deserted you, then? I hadn't thought he would. You seemed to amuse him, somehow."

Her fingers tracing a pattern on the rough stone of the balustrade, Christina turned a singularly cool look upon her stepbrother. But for his sister, perhaps, he was the last person she wanted to see at that moment. "What do you want, Robert?"

"Oh, nothing," he protested too smoothly. "I only came to keep you company when I saw you slip out here alone."

"How filial of you, Robert, but I slipped out alone, because I wished a moment to myself. Now I think I'll just continue out into the gardens."

Robert ignored the hint. Like a gnat he continued to buzz in Christina's ear, even as she moved to the steps, but unlike a gnat, he had something of a sting.

"Actually, I did have a little request to make of you, Christina."

"Oh?"

Her ironic tone failed to affect Robert. Falling into step beside her as she descended to the gardens, he nodded quite as if she had begged him to tell her what she could do for him.

"Yes, it is not much, but you see I have fallen head over heels for Miss Bellingham."

That did bring Christina up short. "What?"

"I cannot understand why you are surprised, Ti! Miss Bellingham is delicate as a piece of china, she is so small and pretty. And she's sweet-tempered besides! I vow she is never without a smile."

"Well, Robert, this is interesting news. I am, ah, happy for you, but I don't see quite what I can do for you. I do not know Miss Bellingham well at all. Cloris might, though."

"No, she doesn't." Robert dismissed his sister with an idle flick of his hand. "But you, Christina, know Lady Lattimer, who is Miss Bellingham's aunt."

Since Lady Lattimer had presented Aldric to her, the fashionable hostess had taken to acknowledging Christina every time they met, and as her public recognition had done a good deal to ease Christina's way in society, Christina was duly grateful. However as she'd the suspicion that Lady Lattimer's attention had more to do with something between the dashing woman and Aldric than any feeling Lady Lattimer might have for her. Christina's response, while all that was courteous, had also been reserved.

"I know Lady lattimer only a little, Robert."

"You know her well enough to invite her to tea, I daresay, and Miss Bellingham with her. Then, when they are at Morland House and you have Lady Lattimer happily occupied, I shall find some way to whisk Miss Bellingham aside for a private coze. I know she yearns to have me to herself. She has all but begged me to find a way."

Tired of the rout that seemed sadly flat for reasons she could too easily guess, Christina began to drift toward the closest path into the garden. Over her shoulder, she advised, thinking that would be the last of it, "Take her for a ride in the Park. You would be alone then but for your tiger."

Robert kicked out at the gravel lining the walk. "Do you think I am a boy, with no notion at all of how to go on? I have extended Miss Bellingham more than one invitation to ride in the Park, but her mother has forbidden her to accept. Confound the woman and her objections to me! They are hideously unfair. She says I haven't enough substance."

Christina's mouth twitched, but she did not think it quite the appropriate time to observe that Lady Lattimer's sister was wiser than she had realized.

"Well, it does not seem your suit with Miss Bellingham has much hope, then, if her mother does not approve of you, whether she comes to tea or not."

"Her mother and father dote upon her," Robert returned flatly. "They'll not deny her what she wants. I merely have to convince her she wants me. She'll come around, I know it, and if she does not . . . but of course she will come around. She's as deep a *tendre* for me as I have for her."

Had he not made the one slip, Christina might almost have believed Robert's assertion. She had not seen him with Lucy Bellingham, but neither party had interested her enough to watch. Entertainments in London were generally enormous affairs, often packed with hundreds of people. It was entirely possible that Robert could have spoken repeatedly with the girl, and Christina not know it, particularly as gossip held little interest for her.

But he had slipped, and Christina recalled that Lucy Bellingham was heiress to an estate almost as large as hers. She shivered slightly and not because the air that night was cool for May.

"If you ceased gaming for such high stakes and gave up that rather nasty crowd of spoiled young pups you've fallen in with, Robert, I imagine Mrs. Bellingham might change her view of you . . . "

Before Christina could add that he would not then be obliged to sneak around like a thief in the night, Robert snapped curtly, "That would take too long! My debts are pressing now, seriously. Soon my vowels will not be accepted. It is intolerable! But I'd have all the credit I want the moment my engagement to Miss Bellingham was announced. You must help me, Christina! By Jove, you've never done anything else for me."

"I've put up with you, Robert, which is a great deal more than I wished to do. If you want Lucy Bellingham, then you'll have to reform your character to get her. Who knows? It might be the making of you, but whether it is or not, I'll not assist you in whatever nefarious scheme you really have in mind. And now I should like to continue my walk alone."

"Oh, would you?" Robert asked, a sneering note in his voice. "Well, I don't care to go just yet." When Christina turned to leave him anyway, he grabbed her arm. "You'll not turn your back on me!" he hissed, bringing his face unpleasantly close to hers.

"Robert!" Christina attempted to jerk her arm from his grip. "Release me this instant! You are hurting me!"

"I will not! Who are you to give me orders? To turn your back on me? You are . . . "

"She is a lady who desires your absence, as I heard it."

"Aldric!"

Robert let go of her arm as if it had transformed itself in an instant into a live coal.

Christina scarcely noticed as she stared at Aldric. She had thought it entirely possible she might never see him again.

"Did he hurt you?"

She had to think to remember whom he meant. Robert? No, it was not Robert had hurt her by absenting himself for days without a hint of warning. She had not realized how anxious she had been. She'd held the uncertainty, and the pain that would surely follow it, at bay, numbing herself, going through the motions of life like an automaton. But now, as when blood rushes into a foot that's fallen asleep and the very return hurts more than the absence had, Christina felt such an ache it frightened her. She had no claim on Aldric at all. Damn him and damn him and damn him.

"No," she said in a voice that did not sound quite her own. "He did not hurt me. He was just leaving, I believe. Good night, Robert."

Christina turned from the two men even before Robert could command his feet to move in a careful arc around Aldric. He mumbled good night, but Christina certainly did not hear him. The gravel beneath her feet crunched in a distracting staccato as she walked rapidly away into the shadows of the garden. There were lanterns along the path, but their light was dim and infrequent. Christina was glad of the dark and the sharp air that had kept most of the guests inside. She did not want anyone to see either how glad she was or how wretched that very joy and relief made her.

Most of all she did not want Aldric to see, but she was powerless to turn and demand that he not follow her. She feared what might burst out of her mouth, or what, even if she managed to control her tongue, he might read in her eyes. And he did follow her. She did not need to look to know he was there, a little behind her, his stride long enough that he could stroll and still easily keep pace with her. She could hear his footsteps, feel his presence, even his eyes upon her, though she kept her chin down and her eyes fixed on the shadows of the walk.

Christina had not chosen a path so much as she had had one appear before her, but the one she walked not only failed to loop back to the house, it ended in a remote, private cul de sac in the center of which stood an ornate, iron bench. She stopped dead when she realized there was no exit behind the bench, somehow uncertain what to do, and stared blankly at the bench, the white gravel beneath it, and the dark line of evergreens that made a solid wall around the cul de sac.

It was the most isolated place in which she could have found herself, and as abruptly as she had started out, Christina whirled, prepared to return the way she had come at the same determined pace.

But Aldric had not followed her all the way to the middle of the clearing. He had paused at the entrance to the small enclosure. Christina faltered, unwilling to come so close to him as she would be obliged to do, if she attempted to brush by him.

She stared stubbornly at his trousers, waiting. He did not move. She could see his hands were thrust into his pockets, his feet a little apart, and from the very casualness of his stance, she thought he looked prepared to stand there all night. Finally, impatiently, she flicked a glance upward. There was only one lantern lighting the cul de sac. By it, Christina could see the set of Aldric's mouth was unsmiling, but there was not enough light to read the expression in his eyes. She could feel them upon her, however.

Aldric watched her fling up her stubborn chin. It was likely a belligerent gesture, a prelude to a demand that he remove himself from her way. But with an uncomfortable tug he also recognized it as the move an inexperienced pugilist is likely to make in order to ward off an expected blow.

"What did he want?"

He meant Robert, she realized, after she recovered from the unexpectedness of hearing his low voice shatter the silence of the garden.

"Nothing unusual."

"Money?"

She couldn't understand why he was belaboring an issue that interested her not at all. "The same as money, I suppose."

"Is it Bexom's custom to lay his hand on you like that?"

"I cannot see . . . " She caught herself before she could betray bitterness. "No, Robert generally keeps his hands to himself."

"He'll not do it again."

There was such certainty in his tone, Christina realized that he meant he would speak to Robert. Well, she would be damned before she would thank him. "You will do as you like, I imagine," she said, her gaze steady on him, though her heart was beating uncomfortably hard. "But I can manage Robert. I am not at all above giving him a kick in the shins."

But was she really able to manage Robert? In her desire to keep Aldric at arm's length, she'd forgotten the "accidents." Should she reverse herself, tell Aldric of those?

No! He must think her mad already. She had made him no greeting after his absence. Quite the opposite, she'd stalked off into the garden without a word. And she had no right to this simmering sense of ill usage. No right at all. He was not her betrothed. He had made her no vows, not even promises.

More acutely aware than ever of how vulnerable she was as far as Aldric was concerned, Christina turned her back on him again and began to walk restlessly toward the back of the enclosure.

"Why do you tolerate him at all?"

Aldric fired the question at her from closer than she had expected. She hadn't heard him approach, and suddenly, she felt crowded by him and by his incessant questions. "I don't know!" she flared, addressing the evergreens. "I suppose the fact that I live in his mother's house has something to do with my forbearance. I've some constraints, you see, being a girl of seventeen and having a guardian. I am not as free as the inimitable Lord Aldric to do as I please."

Damn! She bit her lip too late. Her tongue had gotten away from her, after all. Crossing her arms at her waist, Christina stared blindly at the dark greenery before her, wishing mightily she lived in a fairy-tale world where hedges could suddenly grow around her, cutting her off from his sight.

The silence dragged out between them. Then she heard his footsteps upon the gravel, and as suddenly as she had turned her back, Christina spun around again. She had not listened as closely as she thought. Aldric was just behind her. She had to arch her neck to look up at him, but she could see his face clearly now, for all the good it did her. His eyes betrayed nothing of his thoughts.

"Let us forget, Robert, shall we?" She burst into speech, unable to hold her tongue before Aldric's steady enigmatic regard. "He did in fact upset me, and I have acted, I am certain it must seem, peculiarly as a result. I apologize, not least for omitting to bid you good evening even. Good evening, my lord. It is a pleasure to see you, as always, but I must go now. I promised Lord Arbuthnot that I would dance with him."

Aldric remained where he was, close enough so that she'd have had to scramble sideways like a crab to get by him. "I saw Arbuthnot circling Lady Lely inside. There were at least half a dozen other fellows swarming her as well. You've developed an extensive court, Miss Godfrey."

She did not trust the tender note in his voice, but it undid her nonetheless. Studying the gravel to the side of them, Christina shrugged.

Aldric had already been aware of her shoulders. She wore a dress cut lower than usual, and the intermittent light of the lanterns had caught on their smooth, graceful roundness. Now, when she shrugged, he found himself studying her décolletage. Her breasts were not heavy, it was true, but they were high and firm, and swelled sweetly above the low neckline. His eyes swept up from their rise to the smooth, satiny skin just at the hollow of her neck, where her pulse throbbed visibly.

" . . . only mimic you," he suddenly heard Christina say. "They would pay court to a mountebank, if you did."

It took him a moment to comprehend what she had said, or perhaps it was the note submerged so deep in her voice that he could not readily identify it that held him still for a half second. But when he did identify it, he found he was not at all proof against that hint of anguish, and swearing beneath his breath, he caught Christina's chin and forced her to look into eyes that were not particularly gentle on her, "Devil it! You are no mountebank! You are a lovely young woman, as you would know, if you would look at yourself dispassionately, but as you likely will not—and as you say I may do as I please—I shall show you how tempting you are."

Aldric took her mouth with his before Christina could comprehend what he meant to do. And it was not, at first, a gentle kiss. There was a roughness to it, an urgency even, that ought to have frightened her. It was her first kiss. She had never allowed anyone else so close before, but Aldric did not ask for permission. Nor was Christina frightened, only stunned for a moment that he should desire to kiss her. Then all at once she became aware of the feel of his mouth on hers, of his lips trailing fire across hers as he pulled her up to him.

Her pulses leapt wildly and even as she thought helplessly that she did not know what to do, her lips acted with an understanding of their own. They softened for Aldric, yielding to him.

Instantly his arms tightened about her, bringing her almost sharply against his hard body. She went weak with the thrill of it, sagging, and caught at Aldric's shoulders. They were so wide. She skimmed her hands across them, up to his neck, and then she was standing on tiptoe, pressing her lips harder against his.

It seemed to Christina that her blood was on fire and that her heart was pounding so hard he must feel it, and then her lips, again as if they knew what to do, parted fully for him. He groaned. Christina felt the groan as much as heard it, and, though she had never heard such a sound before, she understood it, understood Aldric was as molten hot and lost to all reason as she. She whimpered, overwhelmed, if not afraid.

Aldric had more experience by far than Christina. Presumably, given his experience, he had more control as well. Belatedly, very belatedly he would admit later, he remembered to exercise that control.

It was her whimper that finally penetrated, bringing him to his senses. Unless he wanted to ruin the girl it was time to stop. Abruptly, before he could do more than register how little he wanted to relinquish her mouth, Aldric lifted his head. He could not, though, quite yet find it in him to let her go. Nor had he the strength to resist laying his forehead on hers. They were both breathing hard.

"I didn't mean to do that," he whispered so softly he might have been speaking to himself, but Christina heard.

She pulled back just enough to look up into his dark eyes. "I am not sorry," she whispered back.

She was watching him, breathless with what had happened, looking for confirmation of what the kiss might imply, and so she saw the flash of some emotion in his eyes. For a split second, she thought it was regret she saw, a searing regret out of all proportion to the size of the offense, but then he smiled a lopsided sort of smile, and she could have laughed at the trick the light had played on her. A man of Aldric's experience would not regret something so small as a kiss!

"It seems I may not always do precisely as I please"—he laughed wryly—"for I've precious little desire to escort you back to your stepmother just now, but it is time and more."

Aldric straightened away from her, and though Christina regretted the loss of him, she made no protest. It was enough that he had wanted to stay with her in the dark seclusion of the gardens. Not once as they walked back in silence did she think of that flash of regret. He had kissed her! She could still feel the touch of his lips on hers.

When they approached the lights of the house, Aldric subjected Christina to a brief inspection. Almost to her surprise, she stood quietly for him as he tucked a stray, fiery curl behind her ear, feeling none of the self-consciousness she ought to have felt. She had allowed him to take an enormous liberty, and she'd returned his kiss with an abandon she'd never even imagined she could feel, yet she felt no shame or embarrassment at all. Aldric had wanted her. He had wanted to kiss her and not merely lightly. For Christina, that was enough to make everything right between them.

Aldric tilted his head to judge his efforts, and his mouth lifted in again in that wry, faintly lopsided smile. "You look like . . . you've been thoroughly kissed, I'm afraid. But go inside, anyway." He put her away from him, turned her, and even gave her a little push, when she did not move on her own. "You'll sober soon enough in the lights. No," he went on, answering the question Christina only spoke with her eyes, "if you returned with me, everyone would know instantly why it is your lips look as rosy and soft and utterly appealing as they do just now."

Chapter 8

"Oh, Ti!" Millie spun into Christina's room, interrupting her as she inspected the fit of a dove gray riding habit. "Sally says Lord Aldric must be head over heels for you!"

Christina turned from her pier glass. The habit nearly matched her eyes, and Nancy said, with her height, she looked elegant in it, but she was not sorry to be diverted. Her hair gleamed more brightly against the light gray than she'd expected.

"Head over heels?" she echoed Millie, a dry note in her voice.

"Yes, head over heels!" Millie affirmed, spinning once more for the pleasure of watching the skirt of her new walking dress flare. "He must be!" she went on when she wobbled to a stop. "Sally says nonpareils never suffer younger children, and yet Lord Aldric suffered me yesterday when he met us at Hookham's and invited us to Gunther's for ices. He could have waited to see you at Lady Hampton's soiree, but he was so eager, he accepted me."

"I thought he rather enjoyed himself," Christina observed softly, remembering how surprisingly good Aldric had been with Millie, and remembering as well how she had not been able to look at him without remembering the kiss he'd given her the night before in Mrs. Sidley's gardens. "And," Christina went on in a firmer tone that indicated she wished to rein in her thoughts, "though I applaud Sally's keen eye for nuance, in this case I fear she began with the wrong premise. The rules that apply to other people, even to non-pareils, do not necessarily apply to Lord Aldric."

"Oh, I do agree that he is quite different somehow!" Millie exclaimed, collapsing dramatically upon Christina's bed as if the mere thought of Aldric could strike her down. "I can scarce take my eyes off of him when he comes to call, Ti. He is so . . . thrilling! I should die, if I were you and he meant to ask for me today!"

There was a half moment's silence and then Christina asked with deliberate casualness, "Wherever did you get the idea that he means to ask for me today, Millie?"

The young girl sat up promptly. "Mama said she thought so! She thinks it is very significant that Lord Aldric has asked to take you riding. He said you had told him how much you like to ride, but she said she thought he wished to have you alone, as there will be no one in the Park so early in the day."

Christina's heart raced. She had battled against the same line of reasoning, wary of getting her hopes up. "Louisa told you that?" she asked, and got the diversion she needed. Millie turned a guilty pink, and Christina grinned. "You were eavesdropping, Miss Millicent."

"I could not keep from hearing!" Millie protested. "Mama and Cloris were in the drawing room with the windows flung wide, and I was in the garden. I should have had to clap my hands over my ears to deafen myself."

Christina chuckled. "While in truth, your natural inclination is to cup your hands behind your ears, minx."

"But what do you think?" Millie returned to her far more interesting original point. "Will Lord Aldric ask you to marry him today, Ti?"

"I do not know Lord Aldric's mind," Christina pointed out with perfect truth. "I have no notion what he will do today. Were he anyone else, he'd have asked Louisa for permission to speak to me, but he's not anyone else."

"No. And he will ask you!" Millie insisted. "I know it. Oh, you are so lucky, Ti! To marry such an exciting man!"

"I must say, Millie, that you are not only certain of Aldric, but me as well."

"And should she not be?" Christina turned sharply to find Cloris standing in the door Millie had left open, her eyes narrowed slightly with interest. "Would you really refuse the so-thrilling marquess?"

Christina did not care for her tone, nor even for her interest. Cloris would be seeking an advantage to herself somehow or other. "Should I accept him, Cloris?" she inquired, deliberately baiting the older girl. "You were the one pointed out Aldric's interest in me was scarcely romantic. Why would I marry a man who only desires a marriage of convenience?"

Rather to her surprise, Christina watched Cloris flush. "Well, I thought your relations with him had changed. I mean that at first it seemed to me he was drawn to you for your money only, but now he seems to have changed toward you. He has been most attentive. Everyone has remarked it."

Christina smiled thinly. "When Aldric was away for a few days, everyone remarked that. How quickly everyone's opinion changes." She waved her hand before Cloris could make any further protestations on Aldric's behalf. "I thank you, Cloris, for your, ah, remarks. I am certain you do wish me to marry Aldric and be gone as soon as possible, but we shall have to see whether or not I shall accommodate you. Just now, I think I would like a little air. Perhaps a turn in the gardens will help me decide."

Christina gave Millie a farewell look before she took herself from the room and Cloris's gimlet-eyed company. The girl had a positive genius for putting her back up, and Christina observed half wryly to herself that merely having Cloris support Aldric's suit could conceivably turn her against him.

It wasn't true, of course, and it was Millie who had really unsettled her with the prophesy that matters were coming to a head. She felt a rush of uncertainty, and the need for a quiet place in which to bring her thoughts into some control, but Christina did not make her escape to the peace of the gardens without event. As she approached a rarely used small formal sitting room next to the library, she heard Richard Brooks speaking behind the closed doors and immediately slowed her step, for she had not known he had come to call.

"I am her only living male relation, Louisa, and whatever the terms of Lely's will, I should have some say in what is best for Christina!"

"I am afraid that I see the matter quite differently." Louisa sounded as if she were speaking with her jaw clenched, but Christina was too weary of Richard Brooks to have an ounce of sympathy for him.

"The marquess is totally unsuitable for her!" Richard burst into heated speech before Louisa could say more. "Morley is a far superior match! I cannot understand why you have not encouraged his suit as you have this . . . rake's."

"Your candidate failed, Richard," Louisa retorted sharply. "He failed. Do you understand? She does not care for him in the least, and I can scarcely drag her to the altar. I will hear no more on the subject!" Louisa snapped, evidently to forestall Richard from further speech. "Out of consideration for you, I tried to further Morley's cause, but she prefers Aldric, as, I might add, any girl or woman would."

"But he's not a crown to his name!"

"It matters not a whit to me whether Christina's husband has a farthing to his name or not! I will not see any of his money, or hers, after she marries. But it is not quite the same with you, is it?"

"That is quite enough! My concern is for . . . "

"Yourself," Louisa cut in coldly. "Let us cut to the heart of the matter, Richard, and have done with it. You have all but admitted Morley paid you a tidy sum to promote his cause with Christina. Nay, don't waste your breath on a protest! You gave me that gold bracelet when I invited Morley to dinner, and I know full well you've not the blunt to buy such a thing. As to the future, I've the suspicion that you stood to earn another tidy sum did he succeed in marrying her, so you may cease playing the fine, upstanding male relation with me. You are out for your own gain, no more, no less."

"And what if I am?" Richard retorted in a low, rigid voice Christina scarcely recognized. "I didn't get a farthing from Lely. Oh, I know he denied you the bulk of the estate, preferring to toss it to her just to spite you, but at least you got something. I only stand to inherit a piddling amount if she dies without issue, and she is very young, Louisa, and about to marry a man who will certainly get her with child. But you will prosper even does she marry him! Not monetarily. His needs are too great. I'm told that estate of his is enormous and after ten years of neglect . . . well, he'll not be giving you gold bracelets, but he has something else you want, doesn't he? A woman of your background—or is it no respectable background—cannot hope to climb to the very highest reaches of society unless she's the cachet of a marquess, can she now?"

Christina left then. Though she had not heard anything about Louisa she did not know, and she found she wasn't rocked with astonishment about the reason for her cousin's championship of Morley, they both sickened her. She'd have liked to charge into the room and shout how contemptible she thought them, but she did not want to be in the midst of a flaming argument when Aldric arrived. Likely he had some guess on the matter, but he needn't know for certain her family was so despicable that even her one blood relation would actively try to sell her.

In the garden, she turned her face up to the sky and tried to clear her mind entirely. It was the future that mattered, not the present, or even the past. She bent to sniff the sweet scent of a purple hyacinth, then walked slowly to a seat on a bench near the house, where she watched a wren, tail saucily alert, hop by, cocking its head curiously at her from time to time.

She would see Aldric soon.

Was he head over heels in love with her? At the thought

of Millie's pronouncement a wistful smile accompanied a definite, negative shake of her head. No. Green boys might fall head over heels, but not wild, untamed hawks like Aldric.

But if he was not anything so childish, was it possible nonetheless that he loved her? A bed of tall, elegant lilies stood by her seat. Christina picked one, and began to play a variation of the age-old game, "He loves me, he loves me not."

She tapped the first petal, but registered little of its velvety smoothness. She was thinking of that kiss, a secret smile suddenly lurking at the corners of her mouth. She remembered Nancy making an ill-advised remark once about knowing a man was interested if he was breathing hard. Christina hadn't understood it then, but she did now. Aldric had been breathing hard at the end of the kiss, as had she.

He liked something about her. He must, or he'd not have kissed her like that. Not that he sang her praises. She went on to the next, arched petal. A lover was expected to sing his love's praises extravagantly, but in fact, she counted it in Aldric's favor that he did not. She'd not have trusted him had he told her that her hair drove him mad with delight or that he could drown in the depths of her plain gray eyes. True, he had told her before he kissed her that she was lovely, but she did not believe him. With that fulsome compliment she thought he had been seeking to make amends for his absence, yet unexplained.

No, much as she'd have liked to believe he thought her lovely, what she did believe were the more circumspect remarks he made. After a swift, raking look, he would say something like, "That color of blue suits you, Miss Godfrey," or "You do exceedingly nice things for that high-waisted style." That little pleased her, and to an inordinate degree.

It was true that he had teasingly called her "Gray Eyes" more than once, and that she had felt a frisson of pleasure each time, but it was the familiarity she liked. Christina could not imagine that he found anything about her gray eyes remarkable.

He teased her, too, she told the next petal of the graceful flower. Sometimes elaborately. Her rather tentative smile grew bolder. He'd invited her to a production of *The Taming of the Shrew*, the outrageous man. When Cloris had learned of it, she had nearly choked on her spiteful amazement, but Christina had laughed. Living as closely as she did with people for whom she'd strong likes on the one hand and strong dislikes on the other, she knew which group she teased, and which she did not.

It had been a wonderful night, too. Louisa had declined the invitation extended to her, saying she had never cared for "all that language" of Mr. Shakespeare's. For a chaperon, Aldric had produced his great aunt. Half deaf, Lady Marston spoke at a shout, and at the end of the evening had trumpeted to Christina, "You'll do, girl! Yes, you will. A pity about your hair. You might be considered a real beauty if it were not so red, but I like you very well anyway. You've a thing or two to say for yourself, and that's refreshing. Yes, you're out of the common way, indeed."

How could she not have relished the old woman, Christina thought with a wry laugh. To have her second greatest fault dismissed as ultimately unimportant, and her first, her height, not mentioned at all? And then to be told she'd do, because she had a thing or two to say for herself. Her eyes had met Aldric's over the top of his great-aunt Marston's head, and she had thought her heart would race away when she saw the amused, perhaps even approving, gleam in his eye. Of course two days later he'd disappeared from sight without a farewell or explanation, without even a word, in fact, but still, the night had been a delight.

At the end, he'd asked her what she thought of the play, and when she had replied that she thought Kate's spirit delightful, he had looked exceedingly bland and murmured something about wonders never ceasing. "And don't you find it interesting," he had continued in the same exceedingly idle tone, "that while you admire Kate, Miss Godfrey,

I have always found myself quite taken with Petruchio's brilliantly firm handling of her?"

Their eyes had met and suddenly that lopsided smile had broken out on Aldric's face, quite ruining his attempt to appear ever so innocent. She'd laughed outright, and had been about to say that perhaps the most instructive point was how well the match, that had begun so poorly, had finally ended, but Lady Marston had come awake when the carriage hit a rut and she started to shout about the deplorable state of the roads.

So. He enjoyed her at least at times. But did he love her?

Christina twirled her flower swiftly around and around. She didn't know much about love. Her parents surely had not been in love. She had no memory of ever seeing them together. Even when her father had still lived with them in Hampshire, he'd had his cronies and sporting events and card games, and her mother had her friends and teas and shopping excursions to town. After her father had decided to set himself up in London, her parents may have seen each other there, though she doubted it, but her mother certainly had not pined for him. She'd gone on precisely as she had before.

The only question, then, that Christina could hope to answer was, did Aldric have the same feelings for her that she had for him?

He could be critical of her. Instantly she thought of a time when they had met by chance on Bond Street. Aldric had greeted her sparely, and there had been a less than warm gleam in his eyes as he glanced to the several footmen trailing her, laden with bandboxes. He'd mockingly called them her retinue, and then casting a sardonic eye toward a discharged soldier begging on the corner, had inquired bitingly whether she had thought to spread some of her wealth among the needy, or whether she confined her largesse to merchants.

Nor did he comply with her every wish. For instance, he had not even deigned to answer her when she remarked, not so obliquely, that she would dearly love to try her hand at driving Lord Molyneux's phaeton. She had, in that case, taken the matter a step further, appealing to Lord Molyneux, who had readily given his approval, just as she had expected he would. When she told Aldric, though, the arrogant man had only lifted one of those black eyebrows and remarked coolly that as she and Molyneux had agreed on the matter, she could take the reins when the viscount escorted her to the Park.

And there were whole days, not to mention the one stretch of several in a row, when he had not exerted himself to see her at all. Louisa, not surprisingly, had pleaded his case, saying it was only natural that a man like Aldric would not dance attendance on a young girl every evening. Waving vaguely, she'd said something of clubs and alehouses and gaming and finished with an even vaguer, "and so on."

Christina had not pressed for particulars, but she had understood Louisa's point to be that none of those pursuits, gaming or drinking or "and so on" had to do with Christina. They were simply what a man did.

But she had answered her question. He did feel differently than she. While he could forgo her company in favor of a game of cards, she counted the minutes until she saw him. She wanted him to call every afternoon at Morland House, no matter that he had come the day before, or even the two before that. If he did not make an appearance, the afternoon seemed wasted. And every evening, at each entertainment, she attended with only half her mind to what was said to her, to how people looked, to the refreshments, to her host and hostess, to anything but the door, as she waited to see whether Aldric would be announced.

Would she marry him nonetheless? He would ask. She had not been entirely honest with Millie. She might not know when he would ask, but she realized that he would not have gone to the bother of courting her, making appearances at all those entertainments he tolerated so poorly, had he not decided for reasons of his own that it was time he married.

What would she say?

Was there any possibility that one day he might wait impatiently for her to come to him? Might he ever ride home at a gallop, eager to take her in his arms? Surely there was some possibility, given that kiss.

For a moment, Christina lost herself in the memory of that powerful embrace, and then from nowhere came the thought that Aldric was an experienced man. He had kissed other women like that.

It gave her a wretched pang even to think that, but her mind raced on to worse: what if they married? She did not think she could bear it if he took a mistress. Nancy had often said she felt things too keenly. Perhaps it was the truth, but it did not matter. She could not do as her mother had done, turning a bland eye to her philandering husband and eventually establishing a separate life.

Christina bit her lip, thinking of the scenes she would likely make. Kisses in the moonlight were one thing, but marriage quite another. What would she say to Aldric if he did ask her?

She rose suddenly and began walking with her face buried in the fragrant lily. Of course she could not hide in a flower forever. She wouldn't want to. She had never been a coward, after all. Perhaps she might best ask herself another question. Did she wish to see Aldric married to another heiress?

The answer was clear. She . . .

From just behind her, Christina heard a great rushing of air. It was the only warning she had. Even as she whirled around a piece of the cornice from the roof crashed into the bed of lilies, smashing them to pulp.

Chapter 9

Christina froze. She had been sitting so close . . . just inches from the lilies . . . the piece of stone would have killed her. She came alive on the thought and sent her gaze flying up to the roof, but no one was standing there, and she was not given the time to search the shadows and peer around the opening in the cornice.

The crash had been loud as a gunshot. In seconds, half a dozen servants swarmed out into the gardens, followed by Louisa, who exclaimed irately when she saw the lily bed and looked up to the broken cornice. Under the terms of the lease, she was responsible for repairs. If she realized how close Christina had come to harm, she gave no sign as she began issuing orders to the servants to clean up and to Millie to keep out of the way, when the young girl came flying out from the music room where she had been practicing.

Millie took one look at the shattered piece of decorative stone and clapped her hands to her mouth in horror as she whirled to ask Christina if she had been anywhere near at the time it fell. The young girl's response was all that Louisa's had not been, for when she learned how close Christina had been, she ran to put a comforting arm around her stepsister's waist.

Looking over the child's head, Christina saw Robert lounging in the door of the library, watching with no emotion at all on his face. Movement at the window of a sitting room on the second floor caught her attention, and she saw Cloris, but her elder stepsister did not believe the commotion in the gardens of sufficient interest to bring her down for a firsthand look. As to Richard, it seemed he had left the house earlier, for he made no appearance at all.

"Miss Godfrey? Your butler said there had been an accident." It was Aldric striding into the gardens. Just the sound of his voice made her feel safer, and Christina betrayed herself with a small cry as she turned. He frowned sharply down at her. "What has happened. You're pale. Are you all right?"

She wanted to fling herself into his arms, but that would never have done, and she had to content herself with holding his steady gaze.

"That piece of stone from the cornice came loose and fell."

"And Ti was sitting on the bench only seconds before!" Millie blurted.

"Devil it!" Aldric took her hand, holding it tightly so that for a moment she could not have spoken if she had wanted. "You will think London is a hazardous place if this sort of thing keeps up," he said.

Something or someone was hazardous to her. Christina feared there could not be doubt now. The fourth accident had tipped the balance in her mind, but she could not yet speak of her startling fears to him and so said in a voice that was only a trifle low, "I am fine, really, my lord. The, ah, accident shook me, nothing more serious."

"I should think it would have been horrid!" Millie shuddered. "I don't think I will ever sit on that bench again."

"Good day, Lord Aldric." Louisa came hurrying forward with the exceedingly pleasant smile she always had for Aldric. "I am dismayed you had to come upon such a scene! When one leases a house, one never knows quite what one will get, but I had thought Lord Bascom had kept his home in better repair. Why, now we shall be put to the bother of seeing to the results of his neglect."

"Quite a nuisance I am sure, Lady Lely, but I am certain you are as relieved as I that Miss Godfrey escaped her close brush with disaster." Dismissing Louisa with that pointed remark, Aldric swung his dark gaze back to Christina, and she did not think she imagined that his expression softened. "Do you still wish to go riding?"

"Yes, very much! I shall just go . . . "

But she did not have to go to get her hat. Nancy, her maid, had learned of the near accident just after she had learned of Lord Aldric's arrival, and at that moment came trotting out into the garden, her round, country face creased with concern, the small jaunty hat clearly forgotten in her hand. Gesturing with it, she wailed about the close call her "lamb" had had. Louisa made a sharp, displeased sound, but Christina patiently endured the fuss. Nancy had been half servant, half mother to her since well before her own mother had died of sudden lung inflammation, and patiently she reassured the older woman she was fine, before she slipped the hat from Nancy's grasp and said she was to have just the remedy she needed, a good ride.

Nancy only then appeared to realize the audience she had. To Aldric's amusement, she didn't much seem to care that she had kept a marquess, not to mention her charge's not so indulgent stepmother, waiting. Nancy would not hear of Christina putting the hat on herself, either, and herded Christina back into the house to put the final touches on her "lamb's" toilette.

Nancy took pride in her work and went about it with such care, Christina was soon fretting impatiently. "Please, Nance! I'm sure that angle will do!"

" 'Twon't hurt him none to wait on you a bit, lamb," Nancy muttered around a handful of pins she held between her teeth. "You don't want him to start out takin' you for granted, and besides, you want to look yer best when he asks you to be his lady."

"Don't say such a thing! You have no idea if he means to ask me today, or any day for that matter. Oh, Nancy, what if he never does?"

"Then he's blind and you don't want a blind man," Nancy answered stoutly, but when she had finished with her pins, she looked into the pier glass and smiled broadly.

"He'll want you, you'll see. You're out o' the common way, and he knows it."

"How can you know what he knows?" Christina demanded. Her tone may have sounded dismissive, but she was watching Nancy closely.

The older woman shrugged. "He's a bonny man, love, and could have any lady he wanted. As it's you he's come after, it stands to reason he thinks you're above the rest of 'em. Be glad, lamb. He's strong and fit. He'll take care of you, you'll see."

Their eyes met in the pier glass, and neither was thinking of Aldric. "That stone was so close, Nance. I must get away."

The country woman nodded sharply. "Aye, lass, and you must get away to a strong man who can protect you. His lordship's a godsend."

Thinking what Aldric might say if he heard himself called a godsend eased Christina's expression. "Well, then, as we've settled upon my champion, how do I look? Will he have me? You are certain the habit suits me well enough?"

Nancy stepped back to survey her mistress critically. "Aye," she said after a minute. "that cut suits you well. Shows off your narrow waist and those long legs of yours."

"What of the color?" Christina wanted to know.

"'Tis a good one. Makes your eyes lighter, like a sparkling mist."

"Oh, Nance! A sparkling mist, indeed. It's my hair that concerns me. Does it look too red?"

"Too red? The man knows you've red hair, lamb. He's not blind. But no," Nancy added, when Christina made an impatient face, "Yer hair looks fine."

In truth the light gray did bring out the red in Christina's hair. At that moment, the long, shining mass pinned atop her head and more shown off than covered by the narrow hat, gleamed like polished copper, and Nancy thought there could not have been hair any more beautiful in all of England, but she knew it was pointless to try and convince

Christina so. In the maid's mind, the girl's sensitivity to her hair was not the least sin for which her father, Lord Lely, would be obliged to answer on the Day of Judgment.

"Wager you his lordship tells you first thing how fine you look," she said on impulse.

Christina regarded her shrewdly. "I would only believe he spoke from politeness if he did, Nance. Leave it, though I do thank you for trying to make me feel the ugly duckling become a swan."

Aldric had elected to await Christina in the entry hall, and as she descended to meet him, he surveyed her in the slow, deliberate way he had, taking in, it seemed to her, every inch of her from the little peaked hat she wore, to the crisp white stock at her neck, to the close fit of her severely cut habit. As usual his inspection made her stomach flutter.

When he lifted his black eyes to meet hers, there was a gleam in his made her stomach flutter again. "May I say, Miss Godfrey, how exceptional I find you to be? Any other woman would by lying prone on a couch, having a fit of vapors after what nearly happened to you."

Christina stifled a pang of disappointment. She ought to be delighted he found her character uncommon. That was certainly more important than her looks.

"You may say so, my lord, and I shall even thank you for doing it."

His smiled deepened. "I was going to ask if you are certain you do wish to ride out, but I see now the question is unnecessary."

"It is, indeed. A good ride is just the remedy I need." That and escaping this house.

Aldric did not miss the flash of darkness in her eyes. "You really are certain?" he asked, taking her hand in his.

"Oh, yes." She knew she clung to him a little, but could not help herself. "I would like to ride very much."

"Then we are in harmony. And may I add"—Aldric lifted her hand to his lips—"that I find you more elegant than you've a right to be after such a fright?"

Christina became lost in his eyes for a moment. They

were so soft on her. "You may say that, my lord, though I run the risk, with so many compliments, of having a dreadfully swollen head all day."

He chuckled, unexpectedly sounding wry. "I think the risk exceedingly small with you, Miss Godfrey. You've precious little vanity, but that is a subject for another time. Just now the morning is waiting, as is the mare I have brought for you. I hope you like her."

What did he mean that she had "precious little vanity"? Should she have had more? And why had he sounded like that? Christina would have liked to shake him for uttering such an intriguing remark only to dismiss it. Then she entertained the secret, delightful thought that she would have a lifetime to learn what he meant.

The morning had, indeed, become dazzlingly bright, she found when she stepped out into it on Aldric's arm, and the mare he had brought for her was a beauty as well.

Aldric lifted her onto the horse with such ease, she felt light for once in her life. "You are up to her, Miss Godfrey?" he demanded, when the mare pranced sideways as Christina took a moment to adjust the skirt of her habit.

"I am," she affirmed. Then, when she met his eyes and saw the frown in them, she smiled. "My riding is the one accomplishment upon which my father ever complimented me. I rode almost before I could walk, and I am delighted to have a mare of such spirit. You needn't worry for me."

To Christina's gratification, Aldric took her at her word. Without another word, he swung up on his stallion, and led the way, while Christina followed half a length behind him, and her groom several lengths behind her.

"Beau is accustomed to running now," Aldric said when they reached the Park. "Are you and the mare up to a gallop?"

"We are up to a race, in fact," Christina returned, her eyes dancing. "To the elm there in the distance."

Aldric's sudden grin was the only signal Christina needed. She kicked her mare to a gallop, but even with the tiny head start, Aldric passed her before they were halfway to the elm.

The mare didn't fade, however. The gallant animal dug deep, and Christina arrived at the elm hard on Aldric's heels.

She was smiling brilliantly despite the defeat, but Aldric, the winner, did not look so lighthearted as he walked his stallion back to her. "You tried to cheat," he said, his gaze dark and seeming rather hard.

Unable to believe he could truly be angry about such a playful attempt to best him, Christina nodded outright. "I did, indeed, my lord. The little mare deserved some chance to best your Beau, after all. He is a magnificent stallion. I do not think I have ever seen a finer animal."

She was relieved to see his expression lighten, as he leaned forward to pat his stallion's gleaming neck. "Thank you. I am lucky to have him. And you, Miss Godfrey, are as fine a rider as you claimed." He lifted black eyes that were warm again. "On any other mount I might have lost the race."

She was pleased by the compliment, but it was the warmth in his eyes that made her so lighthearted. "I doubt you'd have lost, my lord, but if you had, I vow I'd not have told anyone."

At that bit of impertinence, Aldric's smile broke through to give Christina an almost giddy sense of pleasure. "I am vastly reassured to know how secure my reputation is in your hands, Miss Godfrey. It makes the prospect of racing you in the future far less alarming."

He expected them to have some future together. Christina seized upon the thought, then felt her heart leap uncontrollably, when Aldric asked, "Shall we walk awhile, Miss Godfrey? We can leave our mounts with your groom. He's caught up with us."

She sensed that it was the moment she had awaited, and yet, now it had come, Christina was seized with such nervousness she could do no more than nod. As Aldric did not seem interested in chatter either, the only sound to be heard was the sound of their feet upon stones of the walk as they climbed a small hill and came to an opening in the trees that commanded a view of the grassy stretch across which they had raced.

From the corner of her eye, Christina saw Aldric turn to look at her, but though she had spent more minutes than she cared to acknowledge imagining the very scene about to take place, she could not, for the very life of her, meet his gaze.

"Miss Godfrey?"

She could not breathe, much less command her head to turn, but then he took her hand, and her eyes lifted to his of their own accord.

She almost wished they hadn't. Aldric's looks struck Christina with such force it was almost as if she had never seen him before. He was so unconscionably well made with that imposing height and those strong, broad shoulders. Too vividly she remembered the feel of them beneath her fingers. And his mouth on hers. Her throat went dry, and she wished for a cowardly second that he were not so striking; that his features were not so well cut; that his hair did not gleam blue-black in the sun; and most of all that his eyes were not so brilliantly black and did not give the impression of seeing so much.

"You must have some inkling why I have invited you here."

Christina did not have it in her to be coy and simper that she had no idea what he intended, but neither did she seem to have it in her to nod, and say, of course, she understood he meant to ask her to marry him. Nor was Aldric much help as she gazed up at him mortifyingly tongue-tied. His eyes had never seemed more veiled and unreadable, but scarcely seeming to mark her lack of response, he went on. "I believe you know something of my circumstances. I am, as they say, land poor, and I've little to offer in return for your hand. Nevertheless, I am presuming to ask, Miss Godfrey, if you will do me the honor of marrying me?"

He did not speak of love, but she would have distrusted

him if he had. Yet, Aldric had rarely seemed more distant to Christina than he did at that moment, the one when he ought to have seemed closest. For a distracted moment, she wondered if he would always address her so formally, if after years of marriage she would remain Miss Godfrey to him.

She searched his eyes and found no answer. They were as impenetrable as night. It was his pride, she told herself. He did not like having to say that he, Aldric, was poor, even if it was only land poor, and that he brought so little to a bride. Still, she looked away to scuff at a rock with the toe of her boot.

"You are right, my lord," Christina found her voice at last, and was relieved to hear it sounded steady, if a trifle low. "Your circumstances are not unknown to me. London is a talkative city, but your finances are of little consequence. Mark my heedlessness as the one luxury of being an heiress." A laugh of sorts escaped her. Hearing the dry, not so very amused sound of it, Christina shot a swift glance at Aldric from beneath her lashes. He understood. She saw a flash of something, sympathy she thought, disturb the darkness of his eyes, and in a rush she heard herself say, "It is you I fear will get the poor end of the bargain."

"I?" Aldric asked.

Christina took heart. Surprised, he did look quite so remote. "Yes." She nodded, finding she could look at him fully again. "You will get a redheaded marchioness of absurd height and thinness not to mention ready temper and tart tongue."

"Ah, well I will grant that you're no simpering nodcock, Miss Godfrey." Aldric had not called her Christina, but she scarcely noticed, for he was smiling faintly, lopsidely down at her. "But I must disagree about your hair, I fear." As Christina's ears filled with the unsteady beat of her heart, Aldric took a strand of her hair between his finger and thumb. "How can I do otherwise, when you even misname it? Your hair is nothing so simple as red. It is flame and sunlight all at once, a heady combination, indeed." The eyes Aldric lifted lazily to hers gleamed with a new light, one that made Christina go meltingly warm. She stared at him as he continued. "You have no idea, do you, Gray Eyes? It is the greatest mystery that you do not, but the truth is that any man who looks at you finds himself wondering whether your hair would burn him, if he took it down from all those pins and let it swirl around him in all its glory."

Her breath lodged in her throat as her mind caught on an image of her hair swirling around Aldric. Without really being aware what she waited for, Christina dropped her eyes to his mouth. Then he let go of her hair and feeling almost bereft at the separation, she spoke without thinking.

"Will you kiss me, my lord?" Christina went furiously hot the moment she uttered the words, and feeling as awkward and foolish and uncertain as a young chick in the presence of a cock, whispered idiotically, "Millie says the gentleman always kisses the lady when he asks her to marry him."

"What a minx that child is," he murmured, but something volatile flashed in his eyes, and Christina's heart was racing wildly even before Aldric cupped her cheek and bent his face to hers. His kiss was not hard and demanding this time. Quite the opposite, it was so soft and tender, she could not have said why it released such a flood of warmth in her that she felt dizzy. But even as she went up on tiptoe in her eagerness to give to him, Aldric pulled back.

"Someone is coming," he murmured gently.

Christina had not heard the voices, and even now that she did, she did not know if she cared. His black eyes were soft as a summer's night.

"Will you marry me?" he asked.

"Yes." She cleared her throat, and said it again."Yes, I will."

Chapter 10

Aldric straightened just as two nannies, three children in tow, appeared in the clearing. Christina wondered if she looked as bemused as she felt. She was to be Aldric's wife. He had asked her. And she had said yes.

Without a word, he took her hand, and they began to return down the hill, but about halfway Aldric stopped abruptly. When Christina saw that his expression had closed again, something tightened in her stomach.

"Though I very much fear my wishes may disappoint you, my dear, I would like to marry as soon as possible, within a fortnight, no more. I . . ."

"Oh, I do, too!" Christina cut him off, too relieved that his remote look came from a fear of disappointing her to hear him list the reasons he was impatient to marry. She suspected they would have to do with getting her money to his needy estate, but she had her own distinctly unromantic reasons for wanting to leave her stepmother's guardianship as soon as possible and did not fault Aldric. She did not intend to tell him about the series of suspicious accidents though, still too uncertain of him to trust he would not think her mad or perhaps worse, a melodramatic fool. "Yes." She nodded smiling, because he looked nonplussed. "I would marry within the week even, if we could, but another thing I would like is to marry in Hampshire. My friends are there, you see. Would you object, my lord?"

It suited Aldric's purposes perfectly to have a small, quiet wedding ceremony in Hampshire. "Not at all. I should prefer Hampshire to London, actually, and I shall speak to the archbishop today about a special license. Do you think Lady Lely will make a fuss about putting on the affair in a week's time?"

Christina chuckled aloud. "I think if you said you wished to wed me tomorrow, she would not lift so much as an eyebrow in argument against you, my lord."

Christina had it right. When Aldric spoke to her, Louisa betrayed a flash of disappointment that she would not be able to put on the kind of grand wedding of which she had evidently dreamed, but she mastered herself quickly, and ever eager to please the Marquess of Aldric even agreed to go over the settlements that afternoon that they might be done with business matters before she and the household left in haste for Hampshire the next day.

Millie reacted with rapture, while Cloris said something sly about why a couple might wish to wed so hastily. Christina scarcely heard her. She was in a kind of dazed blur of amazement. Occasional bursts of energy overtook her during the week, enabling her to select a dress, write the few invitations she would send, and decide whether to serve roasted duck or pheasant at her wedding dinner, but more often she felt such a panic at the thought that she would be Aldric's marchioness, and so soon, that she could not think about anything at all.

Somewhere near midweek, when she was at Fairfield without him, it occurred to Christina that she really knew very little about her husband-to-be. Trying to imagine herself in charge of his home, she realized that all she knew was the name, Pembridge Castle. She did not know how large it was, if it was really a castle, nor even precisely where it was located. Nor did she know much more about his family. His father's passing, Will had mentioned, along with something about the previous marquess losing his family's fortune on a wager, but Aldric himself had never said anything of the event. He had never mentioned his mother, either; had never spoken of brothers or sisters or any other relatives. Why she had never thought to ask, she could not imagine, but she had not, and he had not thought to tell her. Nor was he inviting anyone to their wedding except for Lord Molyneux, who would stand up for him.

Aldric's silence on all that was close and personal to him was unsettling. Christina fretted about why he had been so reserved on the subject, imagining half a dozen plausible and implausible reasons, until finally she decided that the most likely reason was simply that he did not have much family, and was too proud to wish to discuss his father's tragic story. And anyway, she assured herself, she could ask him about all the things she wanted to know when he came before the wedding, but on Thursday, the day on which he was to have arrived at Fairfield, she received a note from Aldric in which he asked her forgiveness for a change in plans. It seemed an urgent matter had arisen in town, and he would not be able to come to Hampshire until Saturday, the very day of the wedding.

When Cloris made a barbed remark about reluctant grooms, Christina found she was not so immune to her stepsister's barbs as she had been, but she bit back the retort that at least she had a groom. She was not absolutely certain she did. More than anything she'd have liked to have Will, with all his practical steadiness, on hand, but though she had sent off a letter to Scotland before she left London, she knew he would not receive it in time to arrive before she married.

Aldric did come, though, just as he had said he would, around noon on Saturday. Christina was eating luncheon with the dozen or so people Louisa had invited to stay at Fairfield for the affair, and when Aldric was announced all of them leapt up to block his entry, crying that it was bad luck for the groom to see the bride before the wedding. Christina protested, but as she could not admit that the particular reason she wished to flout tradition was that she knew too little about her husband-to-be, she failed to carry the day.

When she encountered Lord Molyneux as she was leaving the dining room that he and Aldric might enter and have their turn at the table, Christina considered speaking to him, but she once more found herself at a loss for words. Nor did the viscount's expression encourage her to admit to her anxieties. His usual smile was quite absent, and indeed Christina thought with a spurt of alarm that he seemed strained.

But then there was no time for anxieties. She was being dressed by what seemed an army of maids operating under the stern direction of Nancy. Millie ran about her room, chirruping excitedly about nothing in particular and even Louisa came to fuss and twitch this side of the dress then that. Christina forgot to worry about what she would find at Pembridge Castle as she worried about more pressing matters, to whit how she looked and whether she could get herself down the aisle without fainting from nervousness.

It was Richard Brooks who escorted her. She'd have preferred Squire Palmer, Will's father, but Richard was her cousin and to have denied him would have caused more controversy than she cared to face. Aldric stood waiting before the altar of the small, stone church, and at the sight of his tall, dark figure elegantly turned out in gray, she felt a thrill of such excitement it routed all her doubts. He was the most striking man she'd ever seen, and she was to wed him.

He regarded her gravely, more gravely even than Lord Molyneux had, but she had expected Aldric to look so. He was taking an enormous step, allying himself to her, and besides, Christina imagined she looked rather grave herself.

She could not have described the actual service afterward. She was too conscious of stray details, of the deep black of Aldric's eyes when Richard gave her away to him, of his body so near hers, of the steadiness of his hand when he slipped a wide gold wedding band on her finger, of the quiet authority in his voice as he repeated his vows. She thought her own voice sounded unnaturally small, but she did not really know if it was, for then the vicar, Mr. Johnston, advised Aldric that he could kiss his bride, and Aldric lifted her veil. His dark eyes met hers only an instant before he bent to place a kiss upon her lips. It was the merest, lightest brush across her mouth.

Louisa gave a small wedding dinner for them. The guests were the members of her family staying at Fairfield, Richard Brooks, and the vicar and his wife, for the Palmers had excused themselves, saying Mrs. Palmer did not feel well. Their absence disappointed Christina, for they were like a favorite aunt and uncle to her, but by then she had more to concern her than the Palmers.

Aldric seemed to grow more reserved with every passing moment. He was not rude. He responded to the toasts that the company proposed, for example, but with a spareness that did not encourage further rounds of jovial hoisting of glasses. Christina might have found that natural enough in Aldric, if she had not also thought that the few smiles he did unbend enough to give all seemed forced, nor did she think she imagined that his eyes never quite met hers, or if they did, met hers only glancingly. Increasingly unsettled, she glanced to Lord Molyneux and was not reassured to see the viscount actually avoid her glance. His expression as he looked away to no one in particular was grimly set, and that despite the fact that he had had more than one glass of champagne.

Finally the meal was done. Louisa rose to announce that tea and brandy would be served in the drawing room in order that Aldric and Christina might make their final farewells before they went up to their room. Their plan was to spend their wedding night at Fairfield before they set out for Herefordshire the next morning.

There was quite naturally some good-natured teasing on the subject of the wedding night. Christina ignored it. She was not afraid of what would happen in the master suite that had been prepared for them. Nancy had given her some notion of what to expect, and besides it was one area in which she did trust Aldric implicitly. However, it was impossible to contemplate the kind of intimacy that even to think of could make her cheeks go hot and take her breath away in a room full of people. And particularly it was impossible when Aldric seemed so remote, her stomach was wound in a tight knot and she was suddenly uncertain of everything.

Christina had just drifted away from Louisa's mother, who had had too much champagne and was winking and saying she had some excellent advice for a bride, when someone behind her said, "My lady?"

It took a proud prodding from Mrs. Johnston, the vicar's wife, before Christina realized it was she Whitley, Fairfield's butler, had addressed. Afterward she would always remember how Mrs. Johnston laughed at her unfamiliarity with her title and said how she would soon become so accustomed to being Lady Aldric that she would scarcely notice it.

"Yes, Whitley?"

"Mr. Palmer is here, my lady."

"Will?" Christina stared, the niceties of address forgotten. All week, she had been longing for Will's level head and now miraculously he had come. "But where is he, Whitley? Why does he not come to join us?"

"He wished me to advise you, my lady, that in order to arrive before the end of the evening, he was obliged to come in his traveling clothes and would prefer to see you privately. I have shown him into the library."

Christina glanced in Aldric's direction. Richard and Mr. Johnston were standing near him, speaking, but Aldric was looking out the window into the night, seeming as removed from their conversation as he was from his own wedding celebration.

Christina shivered imperceptibly. He was infinitely compelling. Even then, abstracted as he was, he dominated the room with his looks and his self-assurance.

She ought to have been the happiest woman alive, yet her stomach was in a knot, and she had to remind herself to smile. It would all come right. Surely it would. They were married, but she was not sorry to have a reason to escape the room and that remote, even grim look on her so very new husband's face. She would enjoy Will for just a moment alone, then she would return with him to the wedding party.

"Will!" Christina smiled her delight. "Whyever did you not come into the drawing room? We'd not have minded your traveling . . . "

Her voice trailed off as Will stepped abruptly into the light. His eyes were red-rimmed, as if he had not slept in days, and his mouth was a taut, humorless line. He caught her by the arms, startling her. "What have you done, Ti? Why?"

"Why?" she repeated, taken aback by his manner rather than his question. She knew there was only one thing of moment she had done of late.

"You married him!" Will actually shook her a little. "Why? Did he compromise you? Is that it? You needn't remain married to him. We'll ask for an annulment. I'll call him out."

"Will! What are you talking about?"

"How could you have married him?" Christina stared, trying to grasp what was happening. Now Will, too, seemed as good as a stranger to her and, bewildered, she shook her head.

"I don't understand, Will."

"Ti! Why did you marry him? I thought . . . didn't you realize . . . surely you did . . . we . . . us, I thought we would marry!"

"We would marry?" Christina stared, the bottom of her stomach seeming to drop. "But! Oh, Will, you cannot mean it! You never said anything!"

"I thought you knew!" He was all but shouting now, but neither of them noticed. "Our mothers planned for us to marry from the earliest times."

"I knew nothing!"

"No? Perhaps your mother did not speak because you were young yet when she died. I should have realized, but it never occurred to me! We get along so well together!" He was hurting her, he squeezed her arms so tightly, but the pain seemed minor compared to his distress. "Great God,

Ti! I could not believe it when I read your letter. You cannot imagine! I thought you understood that I would ask you one day, that I had wished a few years . . . a young man doesn't marry right out of school, damn it! But it needn't matter!" He went on, his tone changing to urgency. "You can get an annulment. There may be a scandal, but I shan't mind. We neither one care for the opinion of the *ton*. And I don't care a whit that he compromised you. I know you'd not do anything really wrong."

"Will! Oh, Will. Aldric did not compromise me. I am so sorry to have to say this, but, Will, I wanted to marry him."

There were tears glistening in her eyes. She had played with Will all her childhood, had ridden over half of Hampshire with him, escaped to his home, the Grange, whenever hers became unbearable. And now she had made him go pale with shock.

"He seduced you!"

"No, Will! He did nothing of the kind. I . . . I fell in love with him."

"No! It was the bitterest cry she'd ever heard, and she squeezed her eyes shut against the sound of it.

"Please, Will. I . . . "

"He did seduce you!" Will shouted. "With words! With all that bronze of his and those looks. Dear God, but those cool looks of his can heat women! They all pant after him . . . "

"Stop it, Will!" Christina shook off his hold, but Will seized her hands, tightly grasping them between both of hers.

"I'll not stop it, Ti. I cannot! He despises you. I thought I might spare you, but now you must know. You must! I had it from Duncan, my cousin. You remember that Duncan married a girl I didn't know? He married Aldric's sister! Aldric's deceived you from the first. He's married you for the worst of reasons."

"Will, please! I know of Aldric's financial state!"

"It is not only that. He . . . "

The clicking of the library door sounded loud as a trumpet. Will jerked, pulling Christina with him. They had not heard the door open, only close. Aldric stood there, looking with those piercing black eyes from Will to Christina and then down at their clasped hands.

Time seemed to stop. The room went as quiet as a tomb, and then Aldric looked back at Christina, and she thought that his eyes were not so impenetrable after all. Something that looked deadly to her flashed in them.

"Aldric!" she cried, trying to free herself from Will's stubborn hold in order to make some calm, reasonable explanation.

But neither man cooperated with Christina's desire to defuse the scene. Will tightened his grip upon her hands, keeping her with him.

Aldric gave her a slight, sardonic bow. "Yes, it is I. De trop, it would seem in this cozy scene taking place on my wedding day between my wife and her good, good friend. I will hear an explanation for it. Mr. Palmer?"

"Oh, you'll have your explanation, Aldric," Will promised, suddenly dropping Christina's hands and taking a step forward as if he meant to attack the marquess. Angry color had surged into his face, and when he clenched his hands into fists, Christina grabbed at his arm, but he shook her off. "Leave off, Ti! I'm not afraid of this, this devil, who's married you to do you harm."

"Will!" Christina caught his arm this time and shook it hard as she could. "Stop this! Please, it is done. I wish. . . ."

"Ti, he detests you!" Will roared, so beside himself he turned on her again and began speaking rapidly, his words blurring. "He wrote it all to his sister, who told Duncan, who, drunk as a lord on his Scots whiskey, spilled all to us. Your father cheated Aldric's, Ti! He fixed that race. Aldric's father lost everything and died within six months of shock. He never knew he'd been cheated. No one knew until early this year when the rider repented on his deathbed and confessed. Aldric formed the plan then to strip you as he was stripped. Not to marry you! He means to leave you tonight, declare you wanting, and apply for an annulment.

He would see you humiliated, Ti. He despises the name Godfrey, and . . ."

Will broke off as Christina dropped her hold on him and took a step back. Her face was white and set as marble. Until then Aldric had seemed frozen by the words spilling from Will, but when she moved, he did as well. Christina caught his step forward and came to life, whirling to face him, her gray eyes flashing wildly in her blanched face.

"Don't come near me!"

Aldric stilled abruptly. "Do I receive no hearing?"

"Is Will's story true?"

He seemed to hesitate, but she knew what he would say. Too much made sense now. His reply when it came served only to sear her. "Yes. Your . . ."

He got no further. Christina said simply, in a low, raw voice, "I hate you."

Aldric stood between her and the door, but she brushed by him as if he did not exist. As to Will, Christina had forgotten him the moment she turned to look at Aldric and read the truth in his eyes even before she heard it on his lips.

Chapter 11

Aldric stood facing Will in the sudden silence. The young man's eyes were fastened on the door, as if he could not quite believe Christina had left without so much as a look to him. Aldric was half surprised himself, but he'd little room in him for satisfaction at that point, if it was satisfaction he'd have felt. He was consumed with a white-hot anger, that was all the more intense for being completely unexpected.

Not all of his anger was directed at Will, but the young man served as a most convenient target, and when Aldric spoke at last, his voice was taut, as if he had himself under the thinnest control. "I will meet you in the copse of trees behind the gardens after I make her excuses to the guests."

It was all he said, but Will, jerking to awareness, understood completely. His own anger charging back in full force, he nodded once curtly and wheeling about, let himself out the French windows of the library.

Aldric went directly to the bellpull to ring for brandy and Molyneux in that order. As a decanter of brandy was kept in the library at Robert Bexom's order, Aldric had some fortification before the viscount arrived. Succinctly, he explained what had happened.

"But how the devil did the boy get the story?" Molyneux demanded, irrelevantly at least to Aldric.

"Does it matter?" he snapped. "Oh, he learned from Duncan, who loves his Scots whiskey as much as he cannot keep a still tongue when he tosses it off. The point is that she learned the truth from Palmer and she did not . . . " His voice trailed off as he recalled the chalky white of Christina's face, unrelieved entirely but for that sizzling flash of hatred in her gray eyes. Grimly, he continued, "She did not receive his revelations well. There will definitely be an annulment. I must go now and make some sort of excuse to the cozy group Lady Lely gathered to wish us well. That I can do alone. I believe Miss . . . ah, blast it!" He glared so hard at his glass, Molyneux feared the fragile thing would shatter in his hands, but then Aldric bit out, "Christina. She is Christina now to me. She'll have have had an attack of nerves, I believe. Tomorrow, she can give out that she discovered whatever dark secret about me that she cares to invent. What I need from you, Moly, is company when I go to the copse behind the gardens. Will Palmer is waiting for me there, and I would have someone neutral present."

"You've challenged him, Johnny? But you intended to tell her the truth, even to achieve the end he has achieved for you. She's Lely's get, as you said often enough."

A dangerous light glittered suddenly in Aldric's eyes. "Aye, she is that, but I like to do my own truth telling, Moly. The fellow will pay for interfering in my affairs."

In the drawing room, everyone appeared to accept Aldric's announcement that Christina wished him to make her farewells as she was felling a trifle indisposed. They nodded knowingly, smiled at one another, and made various remarks about a new bride's nerves. If Louisa sensed something more might be amiss, Aldric's expression discouraged her from pressing him for a fuller accounting, and he soon excused himself from the small gathering with the excuse the he wished to go to his wife.

Then he went to the copse of trees, where he did, indeed, make Will pay for his interference. To stop Aldric, Molyneux was obliged to throw a bucket of water on him.

"What the hell?" Aldric jerked around, brushing his arm across his face to clear his eyes of water.

Molyneux did not flinch before the fierceness of Aldric's look. "Do you mean to kill him, Johnny?" the viscount asked, gesturing to the young man who had sagged to his knees. Blood streamed from his nose and lip, and he clutched his sides as he gasped for breath. "You will, if you keep on like that."

Will had never had much of a chance, really, Aldric trained regularly at Gentlemen Jim's when he was in town. He was also infinitely cooler than Will, not to mention larger and more powerful. Aldric shook his head as if to clear it of anger. "I was afraid what I might do to him, Moly," he said between deep breaths. "It's why I asked you to come. Help me with him, will you? I cannot just leave him here to fall onto the grass. If we enter through the library, we should manage to go undetected."

Aldric's reasoning was excellent. The library was seldom used at night, but Cloris Bexom was there. He ought not to have been surprised. It was Cloris who had come to him earlier and whispered that she thought it would be in his best interests if he went to the library. She had not said that Will was there, but she must have known and now it seemed she had come to see what her contrivings had achieved.

She clapped her hand over her mouth when she saw Molyneux and Aldric half dragging, half carrying Will between them. The young man had lost awareness and his bloodied head lolled limply to the side; one of his eyes was swollen completely shut, and there was a great deal of blood on his clothes.

Cloris turned a wild look upon Aldric.

"What have you done to him?" she shrieked.

"What did you imagine I would do when you sent me to find him with my wife in the library, Miss Bexom?" Aldric demanded coldly. "Applaud him? On the contrary, I have beaten him insensible. Now you know, you may leave us." When Cloris hesitated, looking uncertainly to Will, Aldric cracked out, "This instant!" forcefully enough that she fled the room with a cry.

When Molyneux insisted they ring for towels and water for Will, Aldric made no protest, and Whitley earned himself the unending respect of both gentlemen by not so much as blinking an eye when he caught sight of Mr. Palmer lying prone and obviously well beaten upon the couch. When he returned with a basin of water, towels, and a fresh supply of brandy, Aldric took his leave of Molyneux.

"I don't think it would aid the cub's recovery if he were to arouse and see me bending over him. And I'd not have him faint dead away. He's brave and loyal, if stupidly brash."

Molyneux nodded, understanding how it was Aldric could beat the boy to a bloody mess and yet admire him afterward. "He's loyal enough to take her now, you think?"

Aldric regarded Will. When he had let himself into the library and found Will clasping Christina's hands, the two of them close as lovers, he had been stunned to feel anger. She was Lely's get, daughter to the man who had killed his father, or as good as, and paupered the Beauchamps. He didn't know how to account for the outrage he'd felt, except that he had been on edge all that week, wanting to get the affair over at last, yet dreading it, too, for he had made his plans before he had known her. Somehow the sight of them had caused his unpleasantly and even unexpectedly mixed feelings to coalesce into rage. Perhaps he'd a stronger streak of possessiveness than he'd ever realized. Or, as he'd told Moly, it might simply have been that he liked to do his own truth telling.

But Molyneux had not asked about his feelings regarding the girl, who, temporarily at least, could not be called Miss Godfrey. Aldric flicked his glance to the viscount. "Aye. He'll take her."

"Well then, she'll be fine," Molyneux said, his voice betraying relief. "There will be gossip, of course, but the scandal should not affect her much here in Hampshire with her neighbors. They seemed fond of her, and with the squire's son to support her, she should come through well enough."

An ironic smile flickered in Aldric's eyes. "Are you trying to reassure me, Moly? If you'll recall, it was my intent to do her harm."

"At the first, perhaps. But I think you lost the desire to her outright hurt some time ago."

"As you yourself said, she is Lely's get."

Molyneux disregarded the provocative note in Aldric's voice. "Aye, she's that. And you may not care to ally yourself to Lely's only offspring for longer than is necessary to recover what he cheated you of, Johnny, but I do not believe you feel hatred for his daughter anymore."

Aldric shrugged, feeling suddenly weary, and he turned away for the door. "It doesn't matter, really, for now she hates me quite as fiercely as I ever hated her."

Aldric was halfway up the stairs before it occurred to him that he'd nowhere to go. Christina's room had been given to Lady Lely's sister. She could not have gone to it, and must, therefore, have gone to the room allotted to the two of them. He did not imagine she would care to share it with him.

Still, he continued up the stairs. He did not think he had ever felt so tired. The master suite would have a dressing room. If there was no cot there, he would make a pallet on the floor. He'd slept on the ground in Spain, when he'd served there with Wellington. He could contrive to rest upon an English floor.

And in that willingness, there was rich irony, indeed, as he admitted with a grim, unamused smile. When he had first learned of Lely's insidious, despicable perfidy, he'd have killed the man by slow, agonizing degrees had he been able to get his hands on him. But Lely had gone beyond his reach. Lely's daughter had had to suffice as the focus of his rage. And his need for vengeance. His plan at the first had been all Will had said: he would marry her, gain possession of the wealth to which she had no right, then publicly proclaim that he found her wanting and leave her. He had wanted to scar her, as every member of his family had been scarred by her father.

Even before his father's death, his mother had been so shocked at the loss of the only way of life she knew that she'd suffered an attack that had left her paralyzed. It had been a blessing, really, when she had died within a year of his father. His sister and brother had fared better. They had not died from shock, as his parents had done, but both had been denied the place in society they'd have had, had Lely not stolen the privilege from them. And him? Aldric shrugged. It was impossible for him to say how his life would have been different. He was a bitterer, harder man, perhaps. Nay, he was. He'd learned how shallow most men were; how few so-called friends he could trust.

Yet now that he'd brought his bitter plans to fruition: now he'd Lely's daughter in his control, what would he do? Sleep on the floor because he was unwilling to disturb her rest? Or embarrass her by calling for a cot? His ancestors would have thrown her in the dungeons at Pembridge and been done with her. Was he growing soft, he wondered tiredly? Perhaps. He didn't know, couldn't think about the matter carefully enough just then, only knew . . . what? That he had come to know her? That beneath that willful, sharp-tongued exterior there was wit and pride and intelligence and an unexpected vulnerability?

And passion, too. He'd not expected that, not planned for it. And his own response? Aldric scowled. He was a man, after all! And not made of ice.

Damn. He did not want to think about the girl. Christina . . . Beauchamp, temporarily. And he needn't. She would, as Moly had said, do well enough. Sometime ago he'd given up the thought of shaming her. He would allow her to apply for annulment and say whatever she wanted about the reason for it. He'd even somewhere along the way decided he would not strip her of all her fortune, though he had the right through a clause he had had inserted in the marriage contract that Lady Lely had, in her eagerness to ally herself with a marquess, quite overlooked. Despite the annulment, all Christina's estate would remain his, but he meant to return to her a portion roughly the equivalent of what he'd been able to win at the tables for his sister's dowry. That seemed just to him and would be enough to allow her to go to young Palmer with pride.

Abruptly Aldric flung open the door to the dressing room. His aged valet, Gadston, had awaited him fully clothed, and came awake with a start that became alarm when he saw the blood spattering his master's coat. Aldric suffered Gadston's mutterings as well as his ministrations to a bruise he sported on his jaw.

Once or twice his eyes strayed to the door that let to the master bedroom. He wondered if she slept. He could not hear any signs of life, but he had not expected to hear sobs. Most women he knew cried easily. His sister had used to cry over every hurt, physical or otherwise, and Elise produced tears whenever she wished to get her way, but . . . as clearly as if she stood before him then, Aldric could see how straight Christina had stood, how high she had held her chin, and the hatred that had blazed from her eyes. No, she would not be crying.

Suddenly he cocked his head, interrupting Gadston.

"Stop, man," he ordered, but quietly when Gadston protested. "I heard something."

It came again. A dull thud. Had she thrown something at the wall in anger? He could envision her doing that, but surely the sound would have been harder, sharper? Listening intently, he heard a muffled sound. Perhaps she was speaking to someone? There it was again. It sounded as if . . . but surely it was not a cry being stifled.

Aldric rose from his chair so abruptly he left Gadston with his hand hanging in midair. He did not knock at the bedroom door, though he did not really believe caution was necessary. He simply did not wish to disturb Christina if the sounds had an innocent cause, and so he was in no way prepared for the scene he encountered when he silently cracked open the door to the master bedroom. Luckily there was a full moon. It had allowed him to make out Will Palmer's jaw plainly enough and now it came to his aid again. With a sense of disbelief Aldric realized he was staring at a hooded figure bent low over Christina. She was struggling with the person, man or woman he could not tell which, wrestling against hands that encircled her throat.

With a fierce cry, Aldric flung open the door and leapt into the room. Christina's assailant jerked about, froze for a half second, then scooped Christina up from the bed and flung her headlong into Aldric's path.

Aldric reacted instinctively. He caught Christina before she fell to the floor, and her assailant fled through the open window onto a balcony.

"Are you hurt?" Aldric demanded, steadying Christina.

He thought she might need a doctor, but she shook her head and managed to croak out a low, "No." Immediately Aldric shouted for Gadston and ran on for the balcony.

There, he bit out a vicious oath. He had not realized the balcony ran the length of the second floor of the house. There was no sign of the devil in the hood and there were innumerable windows opening onto the long balcony. Nonetheless he plunged forward, running to look in every window, heedless of who might be within.

He awakened Robert Bexom from what seemed a sound sleep. Further down, Cloris, too, started up in surprise; Lady Lely screamed when he threw open her wardrobe, and finally in the last room, Christina's cousin Richard Brooks slept so soundly he did not awaken at all. Quite naturally the ones Aldric had disturbed demanded to know the meaning of the disturbance. Aldric noted that all three Bexoms were in their nightclothes and seemed to have been sleeping. But sleep is easily feigned and anyone of them would have had time to run to his or her room, shove the hooded cloak into a recess, and leap into bed. Grimly, he informed them what had occurred, then had Lady Lely arouse the servants for a search of the house. Her face a study in consternation, Lady Lely did so at once, but as Aldric had feared, the search was unsuccessful except that it brought Molyneux pelting upstairs. He had been tending Will Palmer in the library still, administering several medicinal doses of brandy when a servant came rushing in with a garbled account of what had occurred.

With Molyneux, Aldric took a contingent of servants

outside to search the grounds for some trace of the attacker, but again nothing was discovered and Aldric was swearing fluently when he and the viscount entered the house by way of the library.

More than a trifle befuddled by the amount of brandy Lord Molyneux had thought he required and somewhat dazed by pain besides, Will had not taken in why Molyneux had raced from the library. Nor had he cared. His only desire had been to lie down on the couch again and go to sleep, hopefully forever.

His rest lasted a considerably shorter time. He was roused by the sound of Aldric's harsh curses, and though he understandably flinched from the anger evident in the marquess's tone, when he heard Christina's name, he pulled himself to a semisitting position and fixing his one working eye on Aldric, demanded to know what had happened.

Aldric told him. Almost absently propping a pillow behind the boy, he related the story, and as he did, he bethought himself of the piece of cornice that had fallen at Morland House. "Devil it! And there was that runaway cart!"

Aldric did not realize he had spoken aloud until Will said, lisping a little on account of his split lip, "Good Lowd! Fowgot it! Lud! And there was a shot in the woods before that!"

Instantly Aldric dropped down to sit eye to eye with the boy and demanded the story of the shot. Wincing as he struggled to sit upright, Will told him that the incident had occurred just after Christmas. He could be certain because Lady Lely and Christina had been arguing at that time as to whether Christina should have her comeout that year or the next. Christina had wanted to wait, but after the shot, though everyone had thought it had come from a poacher warning her away from his traps, she had lost the will to argue.

Aldric fixed Will with an odd look and took both the young man and Molyneux by surprise. "A shot, man?

Given that and the incident with the cart, how could you think of going to Scotland and leaving her alone?"

Will colored fiercely. "Well, I did not dream that . . . "

Seeing the young man wince with pain, Molyneux interrupted. "Of course you did not dream such a thing! Good Lord, who would dream that someone wished to hurt, nay, dear heaven, to murder her?"

The enormity of what they discussed caused all three men to fall silent a moment, then Aldric abruptly announced that he was going above to stay with Christina for the night. When Will tried to heave himself from the couch to go, too, Aldric snapped flatly, "Sit. She is my wife and Beauchamps protect their own. If you must do something, keep guard downstairs with Moly on the off chance the villain has hidden somewhere and hopes to escape when the house quiets."

Chapter 12

Aldric expected Christina's stepmother would be sitting with her, but it was the maid who cracked the door when he knocked. She did not welcome him. "Miss Christina does not wish to be disturbed, yer lordship," she said and would have slammed the door in his face, but Aldric put his booted foot in the way.

"For the sake of your mistress's safety, I will speak with her, now."

The issue did not hang in the balance, Aldric was accustomed to being obeyed, and was already moving by Nancy before he finished speaking. He found Christina sitting on her bed, her back against the headboard and her knees drawn up to her chest. Something tightened uncomfortably inside him. She looked close to the end of her rope. Even the bright flame of her hair seemed somehow subdued, but her eyes, wide, dark pools against the pale background of her face, asked for nothing from him. On the contrary, they regarded him stonily, and if fear flickered like a shadow in their depths, she did not betray any fear when she spoke.

"I do not want you here."

Aldric had not imagined she would welcome him. "I do not doubt that," he replied, walking across to her anyway. Her hair lay in a thick braid across her shoulder, hanging he noted irrelevantly, nearly to her waist. Before she could divine his intent, he lifted the braid and examined her neck.

Unable to escape, Christina did the opposite. She straightened, affording Aldric a better look. "Fitting bruises for Lord Lely's daughter, my lord?" she taunted bitterly.

Aldric's eyes flicked to hers and held. She jerked her braid from his loosened hold, as if she could not bear even so little of his touch.

Aldric looked over his shoulder to Nancy. "Leave us," he commanded quietly. "I would speak privately with your mistress."

"No! Don't move, Nance." Through clenched teeth, Christina emphasized, "I do not wish you to go."

"Christina," Aldric said levelly. "We must discuss the gravest of matters, and to do that fully, we must have privacy."

He had thought her subdued, but she came to furious life then. She crashed her fist down upon the night table by her bed. "Get out!" she cried, all the fury and pain of that disastrous day in her voice. "Get out! I despise the lot of you and your false sympathy. We have nothing, nothing to discuss! Get out!"

She had lumped him in with Robert Bexom, the cold fish, with the sly, conniving Cloris; and with their grasping mother. It was the intensity of his desire to argue that surprised Aldric. He came close to laying hands on the distraught girl before him and shaking her. Abruptly he wheeled about. He was tired beyond reason, that was all. He did not care what Lely's daughter thought of him. Of that he was certain. He only wanted to get to a bed, but to do that, he must understand the nature of the threat to her.

"All right," he said when he had summoned a degree of calm. "Your maid may stay, but I stay as well. Christina!" he growled when she cried out in argument again. "You told me of the incident with the cart yourself; I was present only minutes after the piece of cornice fell at Morland House; and now I have heard of a stray shot from the woods here. I must understand what is happening."

"You must understand?" Christina's eyes blazed. "What the devil do you care? Had the cart and the other incidents not occurred before that sham marriage ceremony, I'd have considered you the chief suspect!"

She had landed a hit. A muscle leapt in Aldric's jaw, and

it was a long moment before he could allow himself to speak. First, he had to remind himself how deeply her pride had been wounded; how afraid she must be; and, surely, how tired. He took a breath and expelling it, released the urge to throttle her into retracting the charge that he was capable of cold-blooded murder.

"However," he said in a determinedly reasonable tone, "the incidents did occur before I could have had anything to gain, and I would know more of them."

But Christina was quite beyond being appealed to by a reasonable-sounding tone. "Why?" she all but screamed at him. "I am your worst enemy's daughter! Lely's daughter! You will never see me again. Get out!"

"In the name of God!" Aldric thundered, provoked beyond his limit. "I do not intend to leave you dead on the floor! Whatever else you are, you are also my wife and a Beauchamp. Now, madam, would you care for some tea before you tell me about any other so-called accidents that have befallen you, or would you like to begin forthwith? The sooner you do, the sooner I will be gone."

Absolutely the last thing Christina intended to do was to turn to him. She flung up her chin defiantly as her wide, gray eyes clashed stubbornly with his commanding black ones. How the battle of wills might have been resolved, it is impossible to say, for Nancy took it upon herself to intervene.

"Now, then lamb!" the maid cried, bustling over so that she stood between her mistress and her mistress's husband of only a few hours, "O'course, you do not want to relive all that's happened. I'll tell the tale. You listen and correct me as y'wish. Nay, donna argue," Nancy went on in a pleading tone when Christina's eyes flashed angrily. "You need him, lamb, more than you need yer pride. He can help you. He saved yer life, after all."

She had almost lost her life. Christina shivered. Unable to sleep, she had been sitting on her bed in the dark when she had heard something and turned to the window in time to see that mysterious, doomsday figure slipping stealthily into her room. It was odd how terrifying the detail of the hood had been. Had the man been plainly dressed, she knew she would have screamed at once. But though she had opened her mouth, it had been as if her throat had closed from fright. She remembered how her hand had gripped the sheet as if to summon sound, and then she had tried to scramble off the bed, but the intruder had reached her before she could escape. He had flung her down, trapping her with his body, and then those gloved hands had encircled her neck despite her every effort . . . Christina buried her head against her knees. Withdrawn from Aldric and Nancy, both, she made no effort thank Aldric for his rescue, but neither did she forbid Nancy to speak.

When Aldric waved Nancy to a seat, she settled herself near Christina upon the edge of the bed. He pulled a chair nearer and listened intently as the maid described each threatening incident that had occurred, including the cinch that had snapped.

"Did you get a look at it?" Aldric asked Christina, who sat still with her face against her knees and her arms wrapped around her head. She did not look up, but she had heard him, and she shook her head. Nancy spoke up to explain that as the split cinch was the first of the threatening incidents, Christina had had no reason to be suspicious. "Even the shot from the woods was not so worrisome," Nancy went on. "There are poachers hereabouts, and we thought one o' them was trying to warn Miss Christina away. But after the cart . . . "

"Who stands to gain from Christina's death?" Aldric asked the maid, though he glanced to the slender girl who was his wife.

Succinctly, Nancy replied, "All o 'em, until she wed. Lord Lely left it so her portion of the estate, most of it, would fall to Lady Lely, if Miss Christina died, except for a bit that would go to Mr. Brooks."

A movement from Christina brought Aldric's sharp gaze to her. She had lifted her head, and he knew he had never seen such bleakness as he saw then in her wide, gray eyes.

"Richard stands to inherit his dab until I have a child, actually."

"Oh!" Nancy cried meaningfully. "Then he's the only one with reason to attack you tonight."

"Perhaps." Christina shrugged almost listlessly. "However, I cannot imagine Richard doing anything so forceful. And there is no way to say what arrangements he might have with Louisa. He gave her a bracelet to throw me in Morley's way, after Morley paid him and"—Aldric growled an oath, but Christina went on as if she had not heard—"he has been friendly at times with Robert, and no one is friendly with Robert without reason." She shrugged again. "Robert did leave me alone in a room with Morley once. Perhaps that is all Richard and Robert plotted together, but it would be impossible to say. And there is Cloris, of course. She would have little love for me whether I had stood through a marriage ceremony or not."

Aldric noted the subtle way Christina avoided saying she was married, but he was remembering with more interest that Cloris had been below only a little before he found her seemingly asleep in her bed. "Is it possible the person who attacked you was a woman?" he asked.

Christina remembered the strength of the hands squeezing her throat and shook her head. "No." Her voice turning hoarse, she repeated, "No. He was so strong . . . "

Though both Nancy and Aldric started forward when Christina's shoulders began to shake, her maid was closest to her.

Irresolute for one of the few times in his life, Aldric watched as the maid encircled Christina's slender shoulders with broad, thick arms and leant her a stout shoulder upon which to bury her head. Next to the sturdy countrywoman she looked as fragile as an elegant piece of porcelain would look beside an earthenware mug.

But she'd the strength to fight the sobs that wracked her. Though her slender body shook, she made no sound at all, and he'd the urge, strong enough he had to fight it, to catch her to him, to make her cry aloud like anyone else would do and find some release.

She would not thank him, he knew. She would fight him as hard as she fought herself. And it was absurd anyway, this desire to comfort her. He'd not threatened her life, but he had done as much as he could, and deliberately, to hurt her. She was Lely's daughter. Tainted.

And for the moment at least, she was his wife. Not knowing if she would hear or even care, he murmured aloud before he left, "I shall make arrangements to be certain you are safe tonight, Christina."

Christina slept little at all, though Aldric's arrangements included a cot for Nancy in her room and a cot for himself in the dressing room next door. A hooded, faceless man lurked at the edge of her awareness, waiting to pounce violently upon her each time she came close to drifting into sleep.

Starting awake, she lay wide-eyed, her breathing quickened from fear, and listened intently to the sounds of the night. She heard nothing untoward, but awake, it was impossible not to relive the attack; impossible not to wrack her brains trying to think who hated her enough to have her killed. She knew the people who had obvious motives. She knew they were none of them nice and had little love for her. But to wish her strangled? Great God! And yet someone had tried.

What could she do? In the dark, with Nancy's soft snores for accompaniment, Christina tried to imagine living at Fairfield. Every smile would be suspect. Every corner, every dark nook, every open window would threaten. She would end by cowering in her room afraid of everyone. It was insupportable! Yet . . . she had nowhere else to go.

Nowhere else to go. She squeezed her eyes tightly closed, but the pain welled up anyway from somewhere deep inside her, filling her until she thought she could not bear it.

Dear God! She gave a bitter, silent wail in the night. To

think she had taken heart from the thought that he had chosen her from among all the heiresses coming out that Season. She tossed, trying to elude the pain of it, but it came again and again. He had hated her! Because he despised her, he had paid court to her rather than petite, pretty Lucy Bellingham.

And she had thought the most compelling man in London had singled her out, because he had found something about her to admire. A wild, hysterical laugh threatened to escape her, and Christina clasped her fist so tightly to her mouth that she ground her lips against her teeth.

How could she have forgotten the mocking smile she had caught gleaming in his eyes that very first time she had seen him? How could she have been so eager to accept the way he'd brushed it off? Or the biting remarks he'd made about her wealth that day on Bond Street? He'd counted his own pennies in those bandboxes!

He had hated her. All along. That kiss . . . how he must have laughed when she returned it with such eagerness. Oh dear God! All the acting he had done, and she had fallen . . . no! She would not say it. It was not true. She had only been infatuated with him. She would forget him soon enough after he had gone. She would, by heaven, and just now she would think of herself, and what she was to do.

But when morning finally came, Christina had no answer. She could not even go to the Grange. She had lost it as a refuge along with Will yesterday, her wedding day.

Nancy, coming in to rouse her, took one look at her bleak, shadowed face and clucked sorrowfully.

"Ach, lamb, I see you didna sleep well. 'Tis little wonder, but sit up now and have some of this tea. You'll feel better after it and some breakfast."

Christina let her cluck and took the tea, though she avoided the food, and then she allowed Nancy to dress her in a simple pale blue muslin, tied beneath the bosom with a darker blue sash. But when Nancy voiced the opinion that

Christina might find a walk just the thing for her spirits, Christina shook her head.

"Not just now, Nance. Go on. I know you've things to do. I'll just finish the tea."

Nancy collected the tray under protest, muttering something about the perils of being all alone, and when there was a knock at the door only a few minutes after she left, Christina assumed Nancy had found some excuse to return and keep her company.

But it was not Nancy. It was the very person Christina had meant to avoid by staying sequestered in her room. Aldric strode in, reducing the spacious, airy room into something as cramped and uncomfortable as a closet. Her eyes met his for the time it takes a heart to beat, then Christina swung sharply about and crossed to the window.

She'd have been pleased to know he interpreted her action as a snub. Anything but that he guess the truth. It seemed she could not summon at will the flinty anger that had allowed her to face him squarely the night before. Perhaps it was too early in the day for anger. Perhaps her nerves were raw from lack of sleep.

The sight of him gave her a physical hurt. It was as if she had expected him to look as ugly as what he had done to her, but the gods were not so kind. His shoulders were as broad, his hair as black, his features as chiseled and even beautiful in their way, and his eyes . . . She couldn't look at him.

For a long moment, Aldric studied the slender back Christina presented him. Nancy had neatly coiled her hair atop her head, leaving a few tendrils to wave softly along the graceful column of her neck. At another time, he'd have admired the contrast between the fire of her hair and the creamy white of her skin. But he had seen the hollows dark as purple bruises beneath her eyes, and his mouth tightened rather than softened.

"Squire Palmer is below," he said into the silence of the room. Though Christina gave no sign that she listened, Aldric went on levelly, "He has come in his capacity as magistrate. I have spoken with him as have your step-mother and the servants. In due course, the squire has arrived at the opinion that your attacker was merely a thief who chose to enter the house by the wrong room."

"What?" Christina spun around, astonishment at a theory that fit few if any of the facts, shoving into the background the pain Aldric had dealt her. But there was more surprise to come, and even as she met his black eyes and remembered how stunningly they had deceived her, Aldric was saying something so unlikely that she actually ended by staring hard at him.

"I understand how astonishing his conclusion must sound, but I think it might serve our purposes. . . . Hear me out!" Aldric ordered, when her eyes flashed furiously at that "our." "Your life is at stake, here, Christina. Whatever else may lie between us, you must agree that it is paramount that we discover the source of the danger to you before one of these attacks actually succeeds. And if you consider a moment, I think you will agree that the person threatening you is far more likely to betray himself, if he does not know he is hunted."

Christina shivered at the choice of words. She was the one who felt like prey.

Aldric saw the shiver, and the unconscious gesture of revulsion and fear confirmed the decision he had come to in the night. He would exert himself to protect Lely's daughter, though had anyone told him he would do so only a month ago, he'd have laughed aloud.

More abruptly than he had intended he said, "You cannot stay here." When Christina's eyes widened at his tone as much as at a sentiment that reflected her own, Aldric gestured impatiently. "Surely, you see that. You know as well as I that the person behind these attacks must be at least one of these wretches around you. You are not safe here until you know who it is threatens you. Your only choice until we have contacted Bow Street and have discovered the villain's identity, is to come away with me."

It took Christina a moment to accept that she had not

heard him amiss. Then she shook her head with complete conviction. "Oh, no," she said. "No. That is not possible."

"I did not expect you would agree easily, Christina, but if you will think calmly for a moment, you will see that you must do it. Or else, you will as good as offer yourself up to be slaughtered."

"Stop it! You are trying to frighten me senseless. I am not going anywhere with you. I cannot bear the sight of you!"

"You will have to bear it!" Aldric snapped. "I am not leaving you here to be killed."

"I intend to go to the Palmers!" She did not, but he did not have to know that. "They will protect me."

"The Palmers are too close to Fairfield." Aldric dismissed her suggestion with a powerful slash of his hand. "You could not ride at all, could not even go for a walk with any assurance of safety. And though the pup may mean well, he's not proven the most reliable protector in the past. What happens if he receives another invitation to fish with his sporting cronies? He'll reject the first, perhaps, but time will drag on. He'll receive a second. And he will end by telling himself his servants will provide you adequate protection. And as to his father, the squire is too simple a man to comprehend the danger you are in. No. The Palmers will not do. I am taking you to Pembridge where no man has the power to cause you harm."

Was he not a man? To date he had done her more irreparable harm than the hooded man. Bruises fade, but not the kind of pain Aldric had given her. Christina shook her head from side to side, stepping back slowly, thinking of the balcony window and flight. But Aldric guessed her intent and came at her. Christina flung up her hand. "Stop! Stop, right there. You will not bully me into doing this! I vow it!"

Aldric stopped moving, but it was the only way in which he relented. "I am taking you with me, Christina," he said, enunciating each word. "If I have to fling you over my shoulder to do it, I will."

"You wouldn't dare."

For answer, his black gaze never wavered.

"I'll not let you!" Christina cried, a note of desperation in her voice. "I won't. I'll scream. The servants will come. They are loyal to me."

Still Aldric said nothing, nor, really, was he obliged to. By law she was his. He could flog her, if he wanted. As to the servants, there was no court in the land would acquit them, if they laid so much as a finger on a peer of the realm.

"What is it to be, Christina? Do you walk to the carriage or do I tote you like a sack?"

In that moment, she hated him almost as much as she had when she had learned the truth, and her hatred flashed in her eyes. "I will make your life hellish."

She got a smile for that, a hard one, hard enough to cut. "You've your father's example, after all."

Christina went as pale as if he had struck her, but Aldric did not see. He had turned on his heel and was walking to the dressing room door. "You've one hour to pack," he warned coldly over his shoulder. "The rest of your things can be sent on later. And, be advised, I will return, if you do not present yourself in the hall below."

Chapter 13

"It is time to awaken, Christina. We are nearly there."

Christina did not stir, though she was not asleep. she had feigned sleep since Aldric had joined her in the carriage Lord Molyneux had presented them for their wedding trip, as the viscount had imaginatively termed the journey upon which Aldric had all but dragged her.

She had not needed to go to such lengths to avoid her temporary husband the day before. Aldric had left her to herself, preferring to ride his stallion, Beau, than travel in the carriage with her, and when they stopped for the night, he had taken his meals separately.

But after luncheon on the second day Aldric had caught Christina by surprise, overcoming his reluctance of her company and swinging up into the carriage behind her and Nancy, unannounced. Christina scooted hastily, and admittedly inelegantly, along the seat, but it had been impossible to put enough space between them. Aldric's size rendered the previously spacious carriage wretchedly small.

She made him no greeting at all, even averted her face as if she would pretend he was not there, but Aldric had other plans. He had not spoken solicitously; had not inquired if their dashing pace exhausted her or if the entirely new countryside she saw interested her. His expression cool, shuttered even in that way it could be, he said in even, careful tones that suggested he meant to behave politely even if the effort killed him, "It may interest you to know whom you will meet today at Pembridge, Christina.

Perhaps he'd have touched a sore nerve no matter what

he said, but her ignorance of what awaited her at his home
was a particularly raw one. Now Christina understood, of
course, why he had said next to nothing of his family and
home. He had intended that she would never need the information.

"Nothing about you or your home interests me, Lord
Aldric," Christina returned with a cool lift of her gracefully
arched eyebrows. "I intend to take to my room for the duration of my stay and so will need no information. Now, if
you will excuse me, the motion of a carriage inevitably puts
me to sleep."

Forthwith, Christina had turned her head away and
closed her eyes. She had succeeded in silencing Aldric. He
did not attempt speech with her for the remainder of the afternoon, but she failed miserably at shutting him out of her
awareness.

He sat not two feet from her. She heard him shift his position; listened as he stretched out his legs comfortably
upon the seat across from them. The carriage hit a rut and
bounced, causing her eyes to fly open momentarily. She
closed them with an image of gleaming black boots into
which tight buckskins disappeared etched in her mind.
He'd long, firmly muscled legs. She saw every inch of
them against her eyelids. Indeed, she saw every inch of him
from the tips of his black riding boots to the top of his
black head. With almost unbearable keenness she was
aware even of his hand lying casually upon the seat between them. Were he to move it only a little, he would
touch her. That would never happen, of course. Those long,
tapered fingers might long to throttle her, or better still,
drop her like a used handkerchief, but they would not reach
out to touch her.

"Are these your woods, then, my lord?"

Nancy's voice startled Christina from her less than pleasant thoughts. The maid sat across from her and had not spoken to Aldric even once except from necessity. Christina
resented that she did now and particularly that there was a

note of wonder in her tone. How spectacular could woods be?

She slitted an eyelid and saw a dense green forest of old oaks and hawthorns. For counterpoint there were dabs of white here and there, wild Narcissus, she thought.

"We've been traveling through Pembridge woods for an hour or more," Aldric was saying to Nancy. "Soon we'll come to a bend of the road, and you will be able to see the house."

Christina felt more than saw Aldric turn his gaze on her and promptly snapped her eyelid shut, but she was again lured out of the deceptive pose by Nancy.

A little later, as the coach swung to the left taking a bend in the road, Nancy gave such an inarticulate, marveling cry, Christina would have had to be made of stone not to peek. She saw only forest, however, when she peered out from beneath her lashes. It was out Aldric's window she had to look, and so she let her head sag the other way as if she were moving in her sleep and lifting her eyelid a fraction, looked beyond him.

The site of the house struck her first, for it was splendid. Pembridge sat on a knoll, commanding a view of the thousands of acres of valley that had belonged to the Beauchamps since their ancestor, one Roderick, had fought victoriously for King Edward against the Welsh. Behind the knoll, protecting its back and flanks, rose high, steep foothills covered by a dense forest that was interrupted here and there by outcroppings of huge, sharp, jutting boulders. Halfway to the top, behind the house, a waterfall plunged recklessly over a cliff.

Christina followed the spume of white spray down to the house. Castle, she corrected herself, then changed her mind again. It was both a, castle and house. The oldest part, a massive tower, was obviously left over from the days when the Beauchamps had required fortification to hold their land. She could almost see soldiers keeping watch in the guard tower, or a Beauchamp wife, mayhap, waiting for her husband.

Peace had come eventually, though, and the Beauchamps had not been content to live in the gloom and chill of a castle. Over the generations they had gradually transformed most of the bulky, massive castle into a stately, elegant home. The new part, the greater part of Pembridge Castle, was built of the same gray rock that had bean used for the original building. It was the rock Christina had seen above, jutting out of the hills, but now the blocks were smaller, and put together in graceful lines, and there were windows, too, banks and banks of them to bring light into the seat of the Marquesses of Aldric.

Despite, or perhaps because of, the love Aldric had betrayed for his home the one time he had made mention of it to Christina in London, she had hoped Pembridge would be a sinister and forbidding pile of rock. She'd gotten the rock right, but even the low, threatening clouds that darkened the day failed to make Pembridge forbidding. Its gray rock gleamed softly in the low light, its windows winked a welcome, and the mist the clouds trailed across the tops of the foothills seemed to set the knoll apart in some enchanted kingdom of its own.

Then the road turned sharply, taking the house and its setting from her view. Woods rose around them again, but Christina scarcely noticed. She had flicked her gaze to the owner of Pembridge, curious to see what emotion, if any, he betrayed about his home that day. But he'd not been studying the view he must have seen hundreds of times before. Dismayingly, she discovered her attempt to mimic sleep had not fooled him in the least. While she had been lost in admiration for Pembridge Castle and its setting, Aldric had been watching her, and there was a gleam in his eyes that to her defensive eye looked like satisfaction.

Gall shot through her, and Christina immediately threw off her sleepy pose. "You've a magnificent home, my lord," she said, conceding the opinion he must have read in her eyes. "But I own I am surprised," she continued coolly. "Given the price you've exacted from me, I expected my father had left you with little more than a crofter's hut."

Christina got what she wanted. She wiped that light from his eyes, but her satisfaction was exceedingly short-lived.

"Had I exacted a fair retribution for the effects of your father's crime," he said in a taut voice that made her straighten in her seat, "I'd have left you to the mercies of your hooded friend. On account of your father, madam, my father shrank before my eyes, turning into a wasted, dazed, pitiful man before he died within six months of that iniquitous race. Due to your father's craven dishonesty, my mother suffered an attack that left her paralyzed and without speech for the year it took her to follow my father to his premature grave. And Pembridge!" He was all but snarling now. "Shall I warn you how uncomfortable you will find yourself? But no. I forget. You do not wish to hear about anything that pertains to me."

As if he could no longer bear the sight of her, Aldric jerked away to glare broodingly out his window. He left Christina sitting as rigidly as if he'd lashed her with a whip.

She had known her father devastated his family, but to know the particulars of the devastation he had wrought! It made her sick to think of his father wasting away, dazed and in shock, because her father had cheated him. And his mother, paralyzed! Dear God, Aldric could not have been much older than she was now, when he had been left to carry on all alone and with so little.

She bit her lip to keep herself from trembling. He had much reason for the anger that had spilled nearly undiluted onto her. He certainly did, but she was not the just focus for it! Her sense of ill usage surged up sharply, tightening her lips. Aldric had deliberately hurt her, seared her, on her father's account. Her father's! A man she had scarcely known and who had cared little for what he knew of her.

And what of the money that had been the cause of all the sorrow and anger? What had it brought her, who had ended with it? Louisa and Robert and Cloris, for three. Heaven knew she could have done without them, if not Millie. And she mustn't forget her London Season. How delightful it had been to have so many of the select flutter about her with such determined pleasantness while their eyes had skimmed beyond her to that plump purse. Someone had tried to kill her. And her husband . . . With a grimace, Christina straightened her spine. She would break if she dwelled upon all the good reasons she had for self-pity, and she had no intention whatsoever of breaking. She would outface Aldric just as she had Louisa.

Feeling militant, she decided it was absurd not to speak to Aldric if there was something she wanted to know. He was not the one who lost if she kept silent. On the thought, Christina turned to him. "There is one thing I ought to know before we arrive at your home, my lord. How do you intend to present me?"

Aldric was slow to rouse from whatever dark thoughts he brooded upon, but when he finally did, he shot her a sardonically questioning look. "My wife. How else should I explain your presence? As my mistress?" He paused only long enough to eye the color that surged into Christina's cheeks. "No? Well, I cannot see that you will have any difficulty playing the less than enamored wife that you are. As you say, you will stay in your room. . . . "

Aldric's voice trailed off as if he had remembered something. Whatever it was seemed to bring him grim amusement, but he did not enlighten Christina. Looking back to her, he said with deliberate mysteriousness, "Well, you'll see for yourself soon enough. But there is another matter I wish to address now that the motion of the carriage would seem rather miraculously to have ceased affecting you." This time Christina met his dry look without flinching. She did not care if he knew she'd gone to such a length to avoid conversation with him. She wanted him to know. He returned her the ghost of a smile, mocking her defiance, she knew, but he did not refer to it when he spoke.

"I mentioned in passing before that Moly and I had formed the plan to engage a Bow Street runner to discover who it is means you so ill. He is a man we know, named Samuel Thompkins. Moly will see him as soon as possible and dispatch him to the Palmer cub, who has agreed to hire him on at the Grange as a groom." Christina's eyes betrayed her surprise at Will's involvement. Aldric's own eyes narrowed fractionally, but he bit back a comment about it being the least Will could do, given his interest in Christina. If she was pleased, so be it. "Thompkins is good. In the seemingly inconsequential position of groom he'll be able to ferret out more information than anyone in an official capacity could. In time, he will discover your enemy, and you needn't thank me. It behooves us both to get to the bottom of the matter."

"That was a gratuitous barb, my lord." Christina lifted her chin, though she was not, in fact, pleased to have to be grateful to him. "We may each be eager to be quit of the other, but I've rather more at stake in the matter, I think, and I am grateful to you, as well as Lord Molyneux, for your efforts."

Contrition may have flashed in his eyes. Something did, but Aldric was inclining his head in the next moment, and Christina was telling herself she did not mean to concern herself over an emotion that came and went so quickly it left no trace.

"You are welcome," he said, but distractedly, for the carriage hit a rut then, and he looked outside to see where they were. "Ah. We have arrived."

A panic, that was none the less for the fact that she could have prevented it by allowing Aldric to advise her what she could expect, seized Christina. She did not know whether she would see a dauntingly long line of servants formally turned out to welcome the woman they supposed to be their new mistress or a half dozen family members swarming down the steps intent on vengeance, or both.

As the one constant thread in her unpleasant fancies was people, Christina was considerably surprised when she peered out the window and saw no one at all upon the great stone steps leading to the house.

Nor did anyone appear when their carriage rolled to a stop. It was the Viscount Molyneux's footman who came to open the door and let down the steps. Aldric descended first, and turned to hold out a hand to Christina. Ordinarily, she'd not have taken it, but a drop of rain splashed upon her nose and startled her into acting without thinking.

As Aldric hurried her up the steps that had been worn smooth in the middle over time, she thought that perhaps it was the threat of rain that had kept their servants indoors, but if so, no one was on the lookout for them. Aldric had to pull the great brass studded door open himself, and then they stepped into a great hall.

At least Christina supposed it was a great hall. The narrow windows at the top let in precious little of the gloomy day's light, and there were no candles lit. Had Aldric not stopped beside him, Christina would never have seen the white-haired man fast asleep in a chair by the door.

"Morton."

Aldric spoke quietly, but the old thing jerked awake with a start. "Eh? What's this? What . . . ah, m'lord!" He beamed with almost childlike pleasure, though Christina was surprised that with such milky eyes he had been able to recognize his lord. Shuffling about on his chair, he pulled on a bellpull behind him. "I'll just call for Mrs. Gryn. Ah, what's this now?" He creaked slowly back around as Nancy blew in out of the rain. "A lady?"

"This is Nancy, my lady's maid, Morton, but here is Lady Aldric." To direct Morton's gaze to her, Aldric placed his hand on the small of Christina's back. She instantly moved forward out of his reach, but he continued as smoothly as if nothing had occurred, "My dear, I should like to present Morton to you. He has been at Pembridge all of his life, and knows more about the place than I ever shall."

"Lady Aldric!" His thin voice quavering with emotion, Morton came to his feet. "Oh my! How we have waited for this day! Lord Aldric is the kindest of masters, indeed he is, but he is most remiss in this instance! He did not send word ahead of your arrival, and we have prepared no welcome for you!"

The old man wrung his hands with such distress Christina could not have played the cold, removed part she had envisioned for herself, had she even thought of it in the midst of an arrival that was so entirely different from anything she had imagined.

"I need nothing but your words to welcome me to Pembridge, Morton," she hastened to assure him, even managing a smile warm enough to cause the old man to turn pink with pleasure. "You have made me feel quite at home."

"I am glad! Mrs. Gryn will be here shortly. I called for her, and then . . ." Seeming to run out of words, he looked pleadingly again to Aldric, who said in the softest voice Christina had ever heard him use, "It is all right, Morton. Lady Aldric understands our situation."

She understood nothing, as the devil well knew, but Christina was obliged to forgo shooting a daggerish look at Aldric in favor of smiling comfortingly again at the old, befuddled butler. The tremulous smile he gave her back nearly broke her heart. She could not imagine what he was doing at the door. He ought to have been in his bed with a hot brick at this toes.

"Ah, here is Mrs. Gryn," Aldric announced, and Christina looked up to see a broad-hipped woman with hair nearly as white as Morton's emerge from a side door. The branch of candles she held aloft illuminated little of the cavernous hall but did at least allow Christina to see, when the woman came closer, that she was younger than Morton, and judging by her shrewd brown eyes, nowhere near her dotage.

Summoning again the right husbandly note of familiarity, Aldric said, "This is Mrs. Grynydd, my dear, though we call her Mrs. Gryn. She has the distinction of being the world's most faithful housekeeper. Mrs. Gryn, I have brought a new Lady Aldric home to you, without, and I do apologize, any warning."

Had a cannon exploded beside her, Aldric's housekeeper could not have reacted with more astonishment. "Lady Aldric!" she cried in a voice softened by a Welsh accent.

"Merciful heaven! Oh, 'tis glad we are, m'lady, to welcome you to Pembridge! Bless me, but I feared at times I'd never live to see this day!" To Christina's excruciating discomfort, tears plainly glistened in the woman's delighted eyes. "Oh, but what you'll be thinkin' of us, I cannot imagine, what with this havey-cavey way m'lord's brought you home. You ought to have sent us a warnin', Master Johnny!"

Master Johnny? Christina glanced sidelong to see his Lord Aldric would react to being addressed by his childhood name, and to being chided to boot. She did not know what she had expected, but it certainly was not the affectionate smile she found him bending upon his housekeeper. She had never seen that smile.

"Now, Mrs Gryn, don't cut up so. Lady Aldric did not want you to work yourself to death merely to welcome her. We'll have work enough to do in the coming days. We are going to have changes. Good ones, finally."

"Oh, Master Johnny! Never say you've come about at last! Oh, thank God! Thank God, you've come about as you deserved."

Tears were streaming from her eyes, but even so, it astonished Christina that Aldric would put his arm around his housekeeper's stout shoulders. He was a marquess, but it was not even that so much as that he was Aldric, aloof, half indifferent, untamed Aldric! The *ton* would have collectively gaped.

"The time for tears is past, Mrs. Gryn," he was saying with a kind of gentle humor that gave Christina an unpleasant ache. "Come now, it is time to smile. We are welcoming Lady Aldric to the castle, dilapidated though it is."

"Ye'll be thinkin' I'm daft, m'lady," Mrs. Grynydd said, her accent thickening with her emotion. She extracted an enormous handkerchief from her pocket, and drying her eyes, managed the smile her master had requested. "I was Master Johnny's nurse, you see, and . . ."

"And now I am grown, but you have forgotten," Aldric finished, though he smiled in a way that almost made Mrs. Grynydd's cry again. "And Lady Aldric should meet the rest of our little group. Morton," Aldric called to the old butler, "Come and do the honors, will you?"

Morton made his slow, deliberate way to Mrs. Grynydd's side, and looking beyond him, Christina realized that in the gloom she had missed the three people who had trooped in after the housekeeper. None of them wore livery and all of them regarded her with the liveliest interest, Mrs. Davies, the cook, was of an age with Mrs. Grynydd; then there was Becky, the maid, and Mrs. Grynydd's granddaughter; and finally Tim Gadston, Becky's husband, whose duties were vaguely reported as having to do with the outside.

But for Aldric's valet, Gadston, a great-uncle to Tim, and following the next day with the baggage coach, that was all the staff, Christina realized as they each smiled a welcome at her and bobbed their heads politely. Five people to care for a house larger than any she had ever seen.

"But come now, Lady Aldric." It was Mrs. Grynydd who took charge as Morton faded back to his chair by the door. "You must be tired after yer journey. We've a sitting room upstairs in good order." She led the way to a beautifully carved wooden stairway on the far side of the room. "You'll be comfortable there while Becky prepares your room. Oh, what a grand time we shall have, puttin' the castle to rights! I've a notion we should start with the nursery." She smiled over her shoulder at Christina, who was suddenly glad for the gloom. "What bonnie babes you'll have, bein' as lovely as ye are and m'lord so handsome. Oh, what a day!"

Chapter 14

"Well, look here. You're even out of your bed, lamb, and I thought you might be sleepin' yet. Good morning to you."

Christina turned from the window and the gray drizzle beyond. "Is it a good morning, Nance? It looks singularly grim to me."

"Ah, well, 'tis only a mist that should lift soon. Come now, lamb, I've brought you a grand breakfast. The castle may lack for servants, but there's no lack o' good food. Mrs. Davies is a grand cook. Ye'll feel that much better, when you've tasted her currant bread."

"Will I?" Christina eyed the breakfast tray unenthusiastically. "Perhaps, but I think I will have the tea first."

"You must eat, lamb," Nance said firmly as she brought the breakfast tray, laden with currant bread, baked eggs, a rasher of bacon, a dish of strawberries and cream and pot of tea to a table near the window. "You'll take sick if you don't, and by the by, Mrs. Gryn said to tell you she will take you on a tour o' the house when you're ready."

Christina took a sip of her tea before she asked casually, "I wonder where my devoted husband might be that it is his housekeeper, not he, who will show me about his house?"

"His lordship and his steward are ridin' about the estate," Nancy reported as she bustled about deciding what Christina should wear on her first day at Pembridge. "He warned Mrs. Gryn that he's a precious great deal to do and will be away most of the day."

"So, I am abandoned to play the role in which he deliber-

ately cast me without warning—Lady Aldric At Last—
without any support, eh? It would serve him right if I
closed myself up in here and refused to come out."

Nancy could not tell if the threat was real or not, and
looked as concerned as she felt. "But Mrs. Gryn is so eager
to take you about, lamb!"

"Hmm," was all Christina said as she studied the gold-
trimmed edge of her cup. "And did you ask Mrs. Gryn
about a key for that door, Nance?" She gestured with the
teacup to a door near her bed. She had opened it by mistake
the night before and found herself contemplating Aldric's
room, his clothing draped haphazardly over a chair, and his
huge, canopied bed. It was a miracle he himself had not
been there to misunderstand and reject her with a look of
disgust.

"There is no key for the door, lamb." Christina was nib-
bling the currant bread, which actually was delicious, and
so did not see Nancy cross her fingers behind her back.

The maid had undergone a sea change in regard to
Aldric. She had felt almost as much hatred toward him as
Christina when her mistress had come ashen-faced to her
room that calamitous night, her wedding night, yet. But
then had come the frightening attack on Christina's life.
The marquess had not only come to her rescue but had
swept her off with him to safety. If he should be moved, in
time, to use that connecting door to transform his sham
marriage into a real one, Nancy believed that would be for
the best for Christina, and she was not one to stand in the
way of what was best for her mistress, however little her
mistress might share her opinion. "Now then will you be
wantin' to wear this sprigged rose muslin when you take
your tour with Mrs. Gryn?"

"I am not certain I will tour with Mrs Grynydd. She'll
only go on and on about the nursery and the heirs she mis-
takenly imagines I will provide his lordship."

Nancy took one look at Christina's bleak expression and
bit back the mindlessly jolly prodding she'd been about to
administer. Instead she met Christina's gaze head on. "Aye,

lamb, likely she will, but you'll think on it all even more if you stay here alone."

It was the truth. Christina finished her tea and made no protest when Nancy brought her the sprigged muslin.

Despite her age and a stiff hip joint, Mrs. Grynydd was an indefatigable tour guide. She took Christina from the great hall, with its ancient banners hanging high upon the walls, along seemingly innumerable corridors to peer into the dungeons, then on to the kitchens and back again, passing room after room, some empty, some with furniture turned ghostly by Holland covers, to, finally, the portrait gallery, where Christina could see Aldric had more than one ancestor to thank for his striking combination of black hair and eyes, light skin, and hard, chiseled good looks. There were fair, amiable-looking ancestors, too, but as Mrs. Grynydd described the exploits of several, Christina observed to herself that it was the black Beauchamps, as she named them to herself, who were most often the ruthless, ambitious Beauchamps.

Next, they laboriously climbed to the top of the tower for a breathtaking view of the valley that stretched out almost as far as Christina could see. When Mrs. Grynydd announced proudly that everything within sight belonged to his lordship, Christina murmured something half under breath about how prosperous the estate must be with so much land, but Mrs. Grynydd shook her head.

"It could be prosperous, but land must be tended, if it is to be prosperous, and Lord Aldric's father was no steward to his land or to his house. I beg pardon for speakin ill o' the dead, m'lady, but ye cannot know how hard it's been. Any other man but Master Johnny would've lost Pembridge, but that's the one thing the old master did right. He left us Master Johnny to take care of us in our time o' troubles. And speakin' of his lordship"—a broad smile broke through to rout the grim expression she had worn—"I'll warrant ye're eager to go to the nursery, m'lady. Ye'll see it's a grand place for wee ones." She plunged off down the narrow, stone stairwell of the tower before Christina could think to stay her. As they descended, the housekeeper went on, ignorant of the deepening strain on Christina's face, "Ah, I can hardly wait to dandle my lord's children on my knee! There'll be boys, o' course, but there'll be girls, too, and may they all have that hair o' yours, m'lady. I've never seen the like of it for beauty."

At the bottom of the stairwell, Christina acted, putting a hand on Mrs. Grynydd's stout arm and bringing her up short.

"Mrs. Gryn," she began carefully, "I do not know why Lord Aldric did not tell you himself, but as he did not, I must. You see, my lord and I are married in name only."

Poor Mrs. Grynydd could not swallow a sharp cry of dismay. "But, I do not understand . . . !"

"Nor do I understand, why he has said nothing," Christina picked up, after she damned Aldric beneath her breath. "Perhaps he intends to speak to you privately and has not had the time. However, the truth is that he brought me to Pembridge to protect me." It was not the whole truth, nor even the most important truth behind her marriage to Aldric, but if she must suffer through crushing the good housekeeper's fondest hopes, Christina did not think she must as well suffer through telling the humiliating, painful story that was the whole truth.

"How frightful that must have been for ye, m'lady!" Mrs. Grynydd exclaimed after Christina had told her of the attack in her bedroom. "I cannot imagine why anyone would want to harm a hair of yer lovely head! There's no understanding people sometimes, but you needn't worry yourself. His lordship will make it all come right. You'll see! And I think we'll not be tellin' anyone else of this, unless his lordship wishes it. To my mind, if ye signed the register as Lady Aldric, then ye must be Lady Aldric. Now, we'll just take a peek at the nursery, and there's the long gallery yet, then . . . "

"That all sounds very interesting, Mrs. Grynydd," Christina interrupted, quite as determined not to see the nurseries as Mrs. Grynydd seemed determined to show

them to her, "and I do want to see the rest of the house another time, but after being confined for two days in a carriage, I am longing to be outside a bit."

Mrs. Grynydd conceded immediately and graciously.
"Of course, m'lady! I should've thought o' that myself. I
turned sick the only time I rode in a carriage, you know. If
you want anyone to show you around outside, Tim will be
about the stables somewhere."

Christina said she did not require a guide, but Mrs.
Grynydd's mention of the stables put the idea of riding in
her mind. She found the pearl gray riding habit and
changed into it without ringing for Nancy, who was helping
Mrs. Davies in the kitchens. Her fingers unaccustomed to
struggling with buttons, Christina had some time to think
about what she had seen that morning.

Despite its tiny, mostly aged staff, Pembridge Castle was
not in dreadful disrepair. There were water stains on one or
two ceilings, perhaps, and the floorboards beneath the windows in the immense feudal dining room might need re-
placement, but it was not what one saw that told the story
of the previous ten years. It was what one did not see: the
light rectangles on the walls where pictures had once hung;
the empty mantels; the bare floors; the missing plate in the
dining room, and on and on. Aldric had had to part with a
great deal to keep his house intact. He had made the right
decision, of course; better to lose a rug than a castle. Still it
could only have been exceedingly difficult to watch his
family's treasures put upon the auction block one after another. And all because of her father.

Christina took herself outside where there was only the
unaccusing land and the sky. And Tim, the head groom,
ostler, and general handyman all in one. Redheaded, freck-
led, and built as solidly as a post, he greeted Christina shyly
but affably, too, until she told him she wished to ride. then
he shook his head and said, stammering a little, "B-but his
lordship said as how ye was to ride only with him, m-
m'lady. He'd not have ye gettin' lost an' all, I expect."

"His lordship worries overmuch," Christina returned.

And thinks he's a right to order my life as he pleases, she added sharply beneath her breath. Although why Aldric should please for her not to ride out alone, Christina couldn't fathom, and because there did not seem any good reason for the order, she assumed that he had given it arbitrarily, to establish his authority over her. To Tim she said, however, "I imagine he thought I would be weary, but I am not at all, and I do intend to ride. Now, Tim, either I can saddle a horse or you can. Which is it to be?"

Poor Tim. Christina had been giving orders all her life, while he had spent his life obeying. Her imperious gaze did not falter, and so, though he muttered beneath his breath about what his lordship would say, Tim saddled the only mate Beau had in the stables, a bay gelding of some years but good gait. Christina thanked him graciously and rode off, absurdly pleased to have gotten around Aldric's autocratic degree.

Aldric was a quarter of a mile away, upon a track that meandered up to Pembridge from the side, when he saw her emerge from the woods around the castle. She came out at a trot, but when she saw the meadow before her, she urged her gelding to a hard gallop toward the road that ran through the middle of the valley and on, eventually to Hampshire.

He had been visiting his tenants, giving them the good news that after years of demanding their patience about repairs and assistance, he could at last see they got what they needed. It had been rewarding work, but he was not in the entirely contented frame of mind he had anticipated.

Christina had nagged at him even before he had left the castle. He had gone into her room while she slept, though he could not have said why. By his own choice, she was not his wife in more than name, and yet he'd opened the door and looked in on her. Perhaps he'd wanted to assure himself no harm had come to her in the night. He had been so arrogantly certain nothing untoward could touch her at Pembridge, and yet he knew nothing of her enemy.

She had been fine, of course, sleeping peacefully, and he had felt a fool, but nonetheless, he had been powerless to leave immediately. With her hand cupped under her cheek and her hair confined in a fat braid, she had looked very young. But then she should. She was only seventeen. It was her sharp tongue, he thought, made her seem so much older.

With it still and her wide eyes shut, he had looked to the rest of her and admitted how delicate her face was. Her mouth was soft but small, her nose quite nicely straight, and her eyebrows the merest arcs. And then, even as his eye roamed to her hair, gleaming against the white of the pillow, he'd turned and left.

However his opinion of her looks might have changed, she was still Lely's daughter. Lely's! Great God, her father had done him so much harm, he'd have been within his rights to leave her unprotected in Hampshire. Yet when he got to the stables, the first order he had given was not that Beau be brought to him, but that she should not ride without him to escort her.

And at unguarded moments all the morning long, as he consulted with his tenants and his steward, she had intruded into his thoughts. He wondered if she had shut herself in her room. And if not, what had she found to do in a house where there were as good as no servants, the library was half stripped of books, and the furniture was draped in Holland covers, if there was furniture in the room at all?

Now, though, he saw he had worried for absolutely naught. As he ought to have known she would, Christina had been getting on quite as usual. She had willfully demanded her way and gotten it, because as an heiress to his fortune, she was accustomed to having things arranged as she desired.

He whipped Beau to a gallop, taking a path that cut through the woods and crossed hers. A fallen tree forced him to slow, which was to the good, for otherwise he might have ridden her down. When he came upon her, she had dismounted on the far side of the meadow, leaving Dan, her horse, to graze while she picked some wildflowers.

At the sound of a horse thundering up, Christina whirled and seeing who it was, lifted her chin defensively. Before the stallion had even come to a full stop, Aldric was off Beau and striding to her, his hands on his hips.

"What the devil do you think you are doing? I gave specific orders that you were not to ride unless I escorted you."

"I am disobeying like the child you evidently think me, my lord!"

Aldric's eyes narrowed. "You are a child if you act like one, and putting yourself in danger for the pleasure of defying me is not only childish but stupid and pigheaded besides."

"Pigheaded!" she cried, gray eyes flashing with indignation. "You are the one who is pigheaded, giving orders about what I may and may not do for no reason but that you enjoy exerting your authority."

"No reason! Devil it, you little fool! Someone is trying to kill you."

"In Hampshire!" Now she had *her* hands on *her* hips, and was leaning forward every bit as angrily as he. "You boasted yourself that no one could touch me at Pembridge. It was the reason you dragged me here. And what would you have had me do all day, anyway? Play the cold, less than enamored wife? Great God, but I understand now why you laughed to yourself at your suggestion. You knew how your loyal band of retainers would greet me, raving about having Lady Aldric At Last and babies in the nursery to boot!"

In fact, Aldric did feel slightly uncomfortable about the reception she had received. He had not realized quite how much Morton and Mrs. Gryn would take on over her. It had been another thing to chafe at him that morning, but he would be damned if he would admit it to her. She'd only demand she be sent back to harm's way.

"I could not be certain you would have any sympathy for Mrs. Gryn and Morton, Christina," he said instead and quite truthfully. "I was not laughing at you. There is nothing amusing in this situation."

"Least amusing of all is watching people build castles on land you know to be sand," she snapped, unappeased. "What in the name of heaven do you intend to tell them when I disappear, puncturing all their dreams?"

Without missing a beat, Aldric said, "That you ran off with your childhood love."

Her eyes flashed so that Aldric could almost see the sparks. "Very amusing, my lord, but I am deadly serious! I told Mrs. Gryn the truth."

"You told her about Lely?"

"No." Abruptly, Christina dropped her eyes from his and kicked at a rock with the toe of her riding boot. "I could not bear hearing another round of how lovely I am and what splendid children I will bear you, and so I told her that you brought me to Pembridge to protect me and that we are married in name only. It was the easy path, I know, but at least you may have the satisfaction of revealing the full truth: that I am the daughter of the dishonorable cheat who caused all her difficulties and that you married me to punish me for his sins. I . . . "

"Stop it!" Aldric ordered harshly. "You've gotten up a head of steam and are charging off God knows where except that it is in the wrong direction. I have no quarrel with what you told Mrs. Gryn. I thought it your right to decide what footing you would have with her, but that is only one misapprehension under which you are laboring, madam. The second has to do with why I married you. I am not so Gothic as you think, damn it! I did not marry you to punish you for Lely's sins. You will come riding with me and see why I did marry you."

"What a gracious invitation, my lord!"

He almost smiled. "Don't be sarcastic with me, my dear. It's a waste of time. I'm impervious to it. Come on. I'll play the lackey and help you up. That should appease you a little."

It did not appease Christina at all to have Aldric put his hands upon her waist and toss her into her saddle. She did not want him to touch her. Nor did she want him to arrange her riding skirt, but he did that, too.

They had gone a little way down the path, riding nearly side by side, when Christina realized Aldric was studying her consideringly. She had been distracted. His hands had felt so sure and steady when they had held her that she had not been able to take her mind off them. She flushed then, fearing what he might have read, but he took her by surprise. "Will you tell me how it is you came to be the only woman in the world who resents hearing her praises sung?"

Christina's eyes flared, but he seemed perfectly sincere, a friend asking about a matter he'd found curious for some time, no more. But the question was treacherous, somehow, and he was not her friend, she reminded herself sharply.

She elevated her chin dismissively. "I cannot think what you mean, my lord, and I do not care for the question."

It was as if he had not even heard her. "Do you think Mrs. Gryn a liar?"

"No! Oh!" Christina cried out in frustration. "You will get your way in everything! Very well then. Mrs. Gryn does not lie in the way the fortune hunters in London did when they told me my eyes reminded them of . . . I don't know, the mist or something equally absurd, anything to turn me up sweet. Mrs. Gryn believes what she says. It is her vision that is faulty. It is colored, because she dotes so on you."

"I see," Aldric said slowly. "And who is responsible for your opinion of your looks? Lady Lely?"

"My pier glass, my lord! And I have had quite enough of this discussion. I shall meet you at the end of this track."

Christina used her heels upon Dan and bounded forward, but more than Aldric, it was pity she fled, or the threat of it.

She knew how she looked. She had rarely seen her father, but she would never forget one memorable occasion when he had brought several of his cronies to Fairfield, and she had overheard him say to one that the pity was he not only had no son, but he really hadn't a daughter either. "She's a half boy with freakish height and nothing but arms and legs. Hair's a fright, too. Can't have gotten that from the Godfreys, by God, though she did get her seat from me. Ought to see her ride! Can take any fence or so the grooms tell me."

She had been only eight at the time, and he had not seen her after she had grown into a young woman, but Christina could not think she had changed so radically that her father's dismissive opinion did not still hold.

Chapter 15

Aldric spurred Beau but made no attempt to pull even with Christina until they came out of the woods onto a broad lane. Leading the way to the left then, he soon brought them to a neat farmhouse of four rooms. An old woman sat outside shelling peas into a large bowl cradled in her lap.

When she saw who had arrived, she sat her work aside and rose stiffly to her feet. Aldric waved her back to her chair, before he even pulled to a halt.

"Sit yourself down, Mrs. Evans. You needn't stand on ceremony with me."

The old woman grinned, showing more gum than teeth. "You may have played in my yard half the day when you were a boy, m'lord, but I shall be the one to say how I shall greet yer new lady. How do you do, Lady Aldric. Welcome it is you are to Pembridge."

When she began to make a curtsy, Christina automatically stayed Mrs. Evans with a gentle hand upon her thin arm, but the gesture was an instinctive one. Christina had not realized Aldric meant to present her to his tenants as his new lady. The lie she was forced to play made her stiff, and as soon as she had given Mrs. Evans a smile for the courtesy the old woman had done her, she stepped back to allow Aldric to get on with whatever his business was.

After he had asked the old woman about her health, he asked about her farm and how she, and the sons who farmed her land, had fared during the winter. Mrs. Evans had little good to report. Several cattle had died, and three of their most productive fields had been covered with water since early March.

"'Tis the weirs, m'lord. One was taken this winter, and two more last month by the rains. With naught to slow the stream, it rushes into the fields, and they are too wet to plant. 'Tis hard to lose those fields. They were our best. Robbie's thinking of takin' his wife and children to Birmingham. They say there's steady work there, and we cannot feed all the little ones with only two workable fields."

"Tell Robbie to stay," Aldric said almost sharply. "Working in the Birmingham mills is no life at all. And we'll soon have those three good fields of yours tillable. You say all three weirs along the stream have been swept away?"

"Aye," Mrs. Evans said, a wondering note in her voice. "But will you repair the weirs, m'lord? You've not been . . . "

"But I can now," Aldric interrupted her. "Indeed, not only shall I be able to have the weirs repaired, I shall have the drainage ditches cleared for the first time in years as well. I spoke earlier today with Jim Siles. He and his men will start the work tomorrow. If Robbie wishes to lend them a hand, he'll get to those fields the more quickly. I shall also be able to replace the cattle you've lost. Tell John to come to the castle tomorrow morning, and we'll discuss . . . "

But Mrs. Evans did not let Aldric finish. With a cry, she grasped his hand and pressed it fiercely with both of hers. "Oh, m'lord! 'Tis too good to be true! You've come about then? Really come about?"

Though Mrs. Evans had used almost the same words as Mrs. Grynydd, her joy was even more poignant, for she would be spared the loss of family. Christina's chest tightened uncomfortably, as she watched Aldric comfort the old farm woman in much the way he had his housekeeper. "Come now, Mrs. Evans. It is a time for smiles. All the fields will be planted this spring, and there will be as many cattle as Pembridge can support."

Christina said nothing when they mounted, and Aldric seemed no more inclined to conversation than she as they cantered on to the next farmhouse. Though built of stone like the first, it was only one room large, and rather than an old person to greet them when they rode up, four children came running from all directions. A moment later a young woman, perhaps in her twenties, perhaps even younger, came hurrying out of the house, a baby in her arms.

When she saw it was the marquess had come to visit her, she flushed with nervousness and hastily dropped into a curtsy.

"I am showing Lady Aldric around the valley, Janet," Aldric said, after he had helped Christina to dismount. "And we have come to see how you are getting on."

The young woman dropped another awkward curtsy in Christina's general direction, and murmured a breathless, "Pleased, m'lady"; then, in answer to Aldric's query, she stammered out the names of the four children clustered about her, eyes glued to their visitors.

"I am pleased to meet you," Christina said, smiling down into four pairs of identical, sky blue eyes. "I can see you were doing your chores, when we rode up," she went on, nodding to the pails and baskets three of them carried. "You must be a great help to your mother."

"I was gathering the eggs," piped the eldest, a thin girl who turned red when she heard herself speak. She was dressed neatly enough, but she wore no shoes.

The boy behind her was emboldened to step forward and hold up his nearly full pail of milk for Chirstina's inspection. "I was gettin' milk from old Betts," he announced proudly. "I'm the only one can work her teats."

"Jem!" his young mother squawked, mortified. " 'Tis not the way to speak in front o' a lady! Where're yer manners?"

The child looked utterly crestfallen, as well as mightily confused. Up until then, he'd always been praised for his ability with old Betts, and Christina smiled reassuringly at his mother. "Jem did not offend me, Mrs. Thomas. With his accomplishment, he is able to feed his family. He has reason to be proud. I wager you are good with most animals, Jem?" she asked, turning back to the boy.

Blushing to have Christina's interest fixed upon him, Jem could only bob his head up and down. It took the little girl by him to proclaim, "Jem can pick up the kittens already, though they was only born a day ago, and tabby scratches me if I try and touch 'em."

"Kittens?" Christina asked, smiling. "Now they are among my favorite creatures. Perhaps you could show them to me while your mother speaks with Lord Aldric."

She might have offered to give them each a diamond, the way they squealed with delight. The eldest girl slipped her hand into Christina's, which caused the younger, the one who had mentioned the kittens, to dart forward and do the same. The two boys ran ahead, leading the way to a lean-to where there was a box. Behind it lay a mother cat with five or six kittens burrowed into her. Murmuring quietly to the mother, Jem managed to pull one off of her and handed it proudly to Christina. The little thing's eyes were tightly shut still, and its fur felt as soft as down.

The children had her sit upon the box and handle each of the kittens in turn. On the spot, they made up names, with Christina acting as moderator when they squabbled. Absorbed in the kittens and the children, Christina did not realize Aldric had come, until the young Thomases fell silent, and she looked up to find that he was watching her.

"I hope the children have not worried you to death, my lady," Janet Thomas said, distracting Christina before she could discern if Aldric disapproved of her childish play and with mere tenant's children at that.

"Far from worrying me, Mrs. Thomas, they have entertained me delightfully." Christina smiled at the children and their anxious mother. "You may be very proud of them. They have very good manners, indeed. Here, Jem, you may return this little bit of a fur ball to its mother now. But, Mrs. Thomas," she went on, rising from the box and looking to the baby the other woman held, "before we leave, I should like to meet the newest addition to your family."

Mrs. Thomas beamed unreservedly, and held up the baby in her arms for Christina to see. "His name's Ted, my lady."

"Hello, Ted," Christina said softly. And when the baby gave her a toothless smile, she smiled back. "You're a charmer already, I see."

When Mrs. Thomas asked shyly if she would like to hold Ted, Christina did not look to see if Aldric would mind her taking the time. She took the baby and settled him into the crook of her arm, cooing to him until a smile burst out on his face again, and he waved his fists excitedly.

"He likes ye, m'lady!" Jem enthused, and all the other children chimed in, looking as proud of Christina as if she had won over a patroness of Almack's.

Mrs. Thomas smiled a soft, mother's smile. "I'm thinkin' you'll be glad to get your own baby soon, m'lady." Christina's expression did not change by so much as a flicker. "He is very dear, Mrs. Thomas," she said, handing the baby back to his mother, her smile perfectly in place. "As are all your children. I am pleased to have met them."

It helped that the children surged forward to walk her to her horse. Christina's smile became more natural, and responding to their chatter, she did not have time to dwell upon the thought that there was no possibility at all she would soon have a child of her own.

From behind her, she heard Aldric say, "Be certain to tell Dick he need not sell his bull now, Janet. I shall be able to buy the seed he needs."

"I'll not forget! He'll be happier to hear it than you can know, m'lord. 'Tis his last bull, and without a bull well, he'd not be a cattleman."

"Now he needn't choose between feeding his family and getting on in the world," Aldric said quite firmly. "Times will be very different at Pembridge now, I promise you. and don't forget to tell him Siles and his men will come soon to do the ditching that's needed."

Mrs. Thomas and the children were all smiles as Aldric and Christina rode away. At the end of the lane, Christina turned back to see the children stood watching them. When she waved, they jumped up and down waving back at her.

"They took to you," Aldric remarked.

Christina thought she heard a wondering note in his voice, as if he found it astonishing that children would like her. Her jaw set a little more firmly, she shrugged and replied dismissively, "I was something new in their world. Children are generally delighted by novelty."

"Perhaps, but you were good with them."

He had pressed the subject too far. She flung him a bitter look. "You sound surprised, my lord. Am I so hard that you thought children would be repulsed by me, or did you simply not give the matter thought at all, as you'd no need?"

Before the words were out of her mouth, Christina was furious with herself. She didn't wait for Aldric to answer the bitter, admittedly rhetorical question, and spurring Dan, rode ahead for a while, allowing the breeze to cool her cheeks.

Aldric gave her precious little time to regain her composure. Only a moment later he rode up to her and with an unreadable look in his eyes, directed her onto another smaller path that led to a clearing where a stream gurgled around a set of enormous boulders. Before Christina could slide off Dan herself, Aldric came and lifted her down, then strode off to the stream, all without a word. But it seemed he was not as abstracted as he appeared, for the moment Christina came near, he whirled about and pierced her with an intent look.

"I did not think of you in terms of motherhood. You are right." It little resembled a statement of wrong, seeming more a thunderbolt hurled from on high. Christina felt her cheeks heat. He had nerve, being angry with her, and she deliberately turned her back upon him, making for the boulders because they were the first thing she saw. Happily she found a perfect place to sit. It was only a little climb from the ground, but high enough she would hopefully be eye to eye with him, or, better yet, slightly above him.

When she had settled herself, Christina looked up, expecting Aldric to be watching her impatiently, but she found she had not made him wait at all. He was studying the stream, a stray stick in his hands. She didn't know how he knew she was settled, but he turned then, and meeting his eyes she became uncertain whether he had been angry as she had thought.

He looked almost uncertain, if someone with such a dark, penetrating gaze could ever be said to look uncertain. "Christina." The stick he held snapped in two. Aldric looked half surprised, then tossed it away and strode toward her. He had thrown off his uncertainty with the stick.

"I did hate you at first." The baldness of the statement made her blink, and his expression softened slightly. "At first, I said. We had suffered such wrenching loss here and to learn that everything that had happened need not have, that one man had cheated . . . I was consumed with rage and the need for revenge. I wrote to my sister at that time, and it was those early thoughts and plans, all formed before I had even laid eyes on you, that the Palmer pup reported. I did detest you then, merely because you were Lely's daughter, Palmer told the truth. I was infuriated that Lely had died and escaped me, and you were all that was left of him. I wanted you to suffer as my family had, was determined on it, even, but that was before I knew you. I hate Lely still, Christina, but I do not hate you any longer."

Christina could not hold his gaze. She didn't know whether to clap or cry. He thought he was being kind. And if he was not apologizing, he was explaining himself, which was remarkable in itself.

"I am glad I am not the object of hatred, my lord."

Her voice had been quite level. She did not risk saying more and was relieved when Aldric nodded as if satisfied.

"Which brings me to the point of our ride." He waited until she was forced to bring her eyes back to meet his most intent ones. "I did not marry you to punish you, Christina.

My people have endured great difficulties these last ten years. I could not allow that to continue."

"I did see their difficulties," Christina replied, her voice oddly soft. "It was impossible not to notice that the children were shoeless, or that Mrs. Evans's dress was made of sacking, while Janet Thomas's had been mended and re-mended. And none of that is to mention, of course, all that I heard you discuss with them, and I wish you to know, my lord, that I cannot regret more deeply than I do the hardships that my father caused you and them. I find it only fair to add as well that I respect very much the concern you have for your people. My father's tenants would not have recognized him, had he gone to visit them without his steward."

"These people's grandfathers worked the land for mine," Aldric said with a shrug that was so unconsciously arrogant, she almost smiled. "You understand then? I would have you believe I did not act against you personally."

"I think I do understand that," Christina allowed.

But her answer was too guarded to please Aldric. He made an impatient movement with his hand that caused Christina to stiffen.

"What is it you want of me?" she demanded before he could speak. "Do you wish me to say I have no ill feelings toward you for misleading me? If so, you must be disappointed, for I am afraid that I cannot."

On the instant tension crackled in the air between them. "What would you have had me do?" Aldric shot back, eyes narrowing. "Tell you the whole and politely request the return of the ill-gotten gains? Would you have tamely handed my fortune back to me?"

Aldric did not wait for an answer. Swearing savagely, he spun about and paced off to the stream.

Christina watched him, reminded how she had once likened him to a large, predatory cat. He moved that gracefully and looked that deadly.

The recollection did not serve as a distraction long enough. In the next moment she was biting her lip against a sharp, infuriating pain. He might well have succeeded with the tack he thought so absurd, but then, damn him, he did not know how effectively he had wooed her.

Christina scrambled down from the rock. Aldric swung around, his eyes restless and volatile as they lit upon her. Feeling anew all the bitterness of his sham, she met them head on.

"You simply do not understand, do you?" Christina flared at him. "You've your noble reasons for all that you did, and you are satisfied, but you could have married another heiress any time these past ten years and saved your people years of scraping. But you didn't. And why? Because you would not sacrifice your pride. You'd no such qualms about mine, though. My pride, you sacrificed willingly, and for that I cannot forgive you!"

She thanked God she was no longer trapped on the rock but standing a good many feet from Aldric. Whirling around, she stalked off to Dan, found a rock, mounted, and raced out of the clearing. About a quarter mile down the path, when she was well out of his sight, thank God, the tears began to come.

Aldric did not watch her go impassively. For a half second, he almost chased after her.

She was dead wrong to say marriage to any other heiress would have achieved the same results as marriage to her. Yes, the money might have been the same, but he'd never have been able to annul a marriage to any other girl and still retain her fortune, as he would be able to do in Christina's case. No other girl's guardian would have been so awestruck at dealing with a marquess that he or she would have failed to read the fine print in the marriage contract. He'd have been shackled to the girl forever; his life would never have been his own again.

No, the situations could not be likened at all. He had caused Christina distress, deep distress even. He admitted it, and admitted he regretted that he had, but she would not suffer for life, as she thought he should do. There would be an annulment, and then she would marry Will Palmer. The boy would take her, regardless of the fact that she had lived at Pembridge for weeks. He had belligerently told Aldric twice that he would, though his jaw had been swollen and he'd had to glare through one eye only. Palmer adored her. They would have half a dozen babies together and be happy as clams in Hampshire.

Abruptly, his jaw grimly set, Aldric swung up on Beau and kicked the stallion into motion, setting off in the opposite direction from that which Christina had taken. He had wasted enough time in his futile effort to explain himself to her. There were years of neglect to undo at Pembridge, and he hadn't the time to argue with her. Or the interest. He did not care what she thought. And even had he cared, he hadn't the breath required to make her understand him. She was set upon hating him, and she was as stubborn as one of the mules his tenants used to plow the fields.

Chapter 16

"**G**ood day, Lord Aldric."

"Mr. Carrington. I see you've come to town for market day," Aldric pleasantly returned the greeting of his vicar.

Mr. Carrington chuckled. "It would seem I have come to observe market day, rather. This confusion of wagons and cattle seems to be taking an eternity to untangle itself."

Aldric took in the cattle milling about and blocking the road along with several wagons that were attempting to turn around. He looked about to see what might be done, but Mr. Carrington leaned forward on his horse to glance down the principal street of Pembridge-on-Wye, the village some mile distant from the castle.

"I say, Lord Aldric," he remarked, "is that by any chance, Lady Aldric?"

Beau shied sideways, but aside from that Aldric did not betray his surprise as he followed the vicar's inquiring gaze. There she was, though, and closer to him than she had been in a fortnight. Since she had read him that lecture on whose pride he had sacrificed, she had avoided him like the plague. Occasionally he had caught glimpses of her in a shade garden he could see from his study, for it was the only place she seemed to frequent besides her room, and every night he heard her moving about in her room. Otherwise, he would not have known for a fact that she shared his home.

There were indications, however. Mrs. Grynydd had reported one day, apropos of nothing, that her ladyship was not eating enough to "keep a sparrow alive." At the admonishing look in her eye, he had rather sharply inquired what he was supposed to do about her ladyship's eating habits, and Mrs. Grynydd had replied so promptly that he could invite her ladyship to dine that it had been obvious she had intended to make the suggestion from the first.

He hadn't. Mrs. Grynydd did not know everything, and specifically could not know that Christina would not have accepted any invitation from him. She'd likely have considered it hell to dine in his exclusive company.

And of a certainty, she would not have allowed him to force food down her as he had had some fleeting vision of doing. Damn her. He thought more about her than he would have done had they met regularly.

Which was absurd. She was Lely's daughter, and if she was moody and off her feed, what could it matter? The day of their arrival, he had all but applauded her announcement that she would stay in her room for the duration of her stay at Pembridge, but he had been angry with her then for forcing him to play the ogre at Fairfield. No longer angry, he did not want to dwell upon her as much as he did. He had a world of work to do.

But she did appear somewhat thinner. He frowned. Was she making herself sick? She looked well enough in a muslin walking dress of an amber shade that complimented the bright hair he could see gleaming beneath the curved brim of her chip bonnet. And she held herself with the same lithe, graceful ease as usual. Surely she would be stooping or slumped if she was ill. Or would she? Christina? He could not imagine Christina slumping in any circumstances, though other girls of her height stooped whether they were ill or not. They feared being derided as Amazons, of course, just as he, in that memorable conversation with Moly, had derided Christina. Someone else had, he suspected, remarked on her height within her hearing, she was so prickly on the subject. Her response, typical of Christina, had been to fling back her shoulders and stand straight as an arrow.

The faintest of smiles curved Aldric's mouth as he watched her move along to inspect the ribbons on display at the next stall. She did have her pride.

And it was true he had not considered it, he added, the smile fading. She had been right about that, if not about everything she had said that day. It would not have mattered, of course, had he bethought himself of her pride. He could not have allowed her to take the fortune that was rightfully his to another husband. Still, he regretted the battering he'd given her. Regretted that she appeared thinner, too, for if he had been wrong to mock Moly for calling her figure elegant—it was, in fact, the essence of elegance—nonetheless, she had not much weight to lose.

" . . . must be very proud, indeed, my lord. Your wife is exceedingly lovely."

Damn. Had he said he did not want to be distracted by her? He had forgotten Carrington entirely.

An irritated muscle flexed in his jaw as Aldric turned to reply to the vicar, but even as he did, he found Mr. Carrington regarding Christina with such interest that he was returning his gaze to her before he knew what he did.

"Are not those the little Gadston girls approaching her?" Mr. Carrington asked. "Can she have brought them with her? She must like children very well indeed, if so."

"Yes, she does," Aldric said as he watched Tim and Becky Gadston's young girls trot up to pull on Christina's dress. He made no response to Carrington's veiled observation about the largesse of a marchioness who would concern herself with servants' children. He didn't hear it, really. He was distracted by her again, and thinking that the subject of children was another one to which he'd not given a thought. She would have them, of course, with Palmer, but not within the year, as she had likely been thinking.

She turned in response to the children, tipped her head slightly as she listened to them carry on about something, and then, as Aldric watched, she laughed.

He could not actually hear her laughter. He was too far away, but he could plainly see the smile that curved her lips and lit her gray eyes. He had not see her smile like that in what seemed a lifetime; had not even known he missed it.

"Ah, now the coil of wagons and cattle has untangled itself, we can go to your lady, Lord Aldric!" Mr. Carrington turned with something approaching a grin on his middle-aged face. "May I confess, my lord, that I am eager to determine whether her hair is as magnificent upon close inspection as it is at a distance? Lud, I do not believe I have seen such hair since my salad days! And she's a charming smile, too. You are indeed, a lucky man, my lord."

The improbable thought that his staid vicar was as smitten with Christina as a boy amused Aldric. The subsequent thought her smile might well fade before they ever reached her, sobered him. She should laugh. Damn it. She should eat, too, and enjoy herself. She was young and had her life before her.

Christina was one of the few people on the street who failed to see Aldric and the vicar dismount and walk toward her. Had the Gadston girls not cried out, half in awe and half in excitement, she'd have had no warning at all, but she guessed instantly why they were suddenly staring in such fascination behind her. Only Aldric had that affect upon people.

She knew she should not have come to market day! She had not wanted to come when Nancy had suggested it. She had protested that most of the people there would be his people, as Pembridge-on-Wye was situated on his estate, and that they would be craning their necks to see their new lady, which she wasn't. Nancy had not argued; she had prevailed in the most devious way. She'd gotten little Dory and Lizzie Gadston to plead with her to meet them there.

Christina would dearly have loved to have Nancy alone at that moment. Devil take her for always believing she knew what was best! Aldric was not only here but coming to her, and she had avoided him so successfully for so long.

She did not want to see him; did not want to be reminded how she had ripped up at him about not sacrificing his pride, though God knew, holding on to his pride had likely been the only thing that had kept him going.

She did not want to understand that! Blast him! He had sacrificed her pride; nay, he'd ripped it to shreds. He did not deserve any understanding, and she did not care how concerned for her he had seemed, wanting her to be assured he did not hate her any longer. He still did not want her!

Christina bit her lip, trying to still the sudden, fierce beating of her heart. She would be cool. He might be concerned for her in some ways; and she might even understand, a little, why he had done what he had, but it was imperative that she hold him at arm's length. He only approached her now because he had come upon her by chance and his people would expect their lord to greet his lady. She must remember that; remember that no matter how courteous or concerned he was, he did not want her.

Christina turned, prepared to say something, she had not decided what except that it would be exceedingly cool, but she had the wind taken out of her sails. There were two reasons for that loss of momentum. The second was the man walking hurriedly to keep up with Aldric's longer stride. He was a kindly-looking gentleman with thinning hair and a pair of gentle eyes that seemed positively to beam out at her from behind the thick spectacles he wore.

The first cause of Christina's sudden loss of angry purpose, however, was Aldric himself. She had tried not even to think of him all that fortnight, but perhaps she'd have done better to carry his picture before her eyes, she thought a little desperately. He looked so good. His black hair was most unfairly tousled from his ride, making him appear almost boyish, but that his shoulders filled out his light blue coat so exceedingly well and that he wore that coat and his buckskins and black, knee-high boots with a careless assurance no boy ever possessed.

"Ah, my lady!" The elder gentleman, the one she'd all but forgotten, was extending his hand, the smile curving his mouth as warm as that in his eyes. "What a pleasure this is."

"Christina." Christina's reaction to him had been so strong she could not quite meet Aldric's eyes. She flicked a glance over him, taking in only a blurred impression of blue coat and contrastingly black eyes, and as if from a distance she heard him say, "This is Mr. Carrington, our vicar."

She was already smiling at the vicar before Aldric had done. "I am pleased to meet you, sir."

"But surely not as pleased as I am to meet you, dear lady! I have been your secret admirer for what seems an age."

He beamed delightedly when Christina could respond with little more than a mystified, "Oh?"

"Yes, indeed, I have! You see Lord Aldric and I were obliged to wait while a herd of cattle proceeded to market at an understandably, but nontheless regettably, reluctant pace, and though I admired you prodigiously from the far end of the street, as I confessed to Lord Aldric, I was quite chafing at the bit to see whether your hair could possibly be as magnificent as I thought it to be. And I am delighted to report that it is! Why I fancy it might even burn, it is so bright."

It was her cheeks Christina felt burn. She could remember so well the day Aldric had said so much the same thing. Afterward he had asked her to marry him. All of it in order that he might get what he wanted and be free of her as soon as he could.

Christina murmured some sort of thanks, but the vicar never noticed her discomfort. He was taking a step back to study her jaconet muslin walking dress and curved-brim straw bonnet with its broad amber ribbons.

When he lifted his eyes in the next moment, they twinkled merrily. "I know it is unusual for a vicar to remark a lady's dress with such care, my lady, but I hope you will forgive me, for if I do not know every particular about it, and your bonnet and your parasol as well, my wife and daughter are likely to serve me stone soup for my dinner."

Christina could not help but smile at that, he was so absurd. "I believe you are a tease, Mr. Carrington."

"Well, I do admit I have been known to exaggerate, my dear lady. However," Mr. Carrington continued, a dryer note in his voice, "if you believe the women in my family will not wish to know every detail of your dress, then you have not lived in the country."

Having lived all her life in the country, Christina conceded Mr. Carrington his point with an amused chuckle, and then Aldric entered the conversation. "I take it from what you are saying, Carrington, that Mary is home from school?"

The vicar nodded. "Mary is home for the long holiday as is Kit. He is my son, Lady Aldric, and with the two of them home the vicarage seems rather full all of a sudden, though I will admit, very pleasantly so."

"Are they close in age, Mr. Carrington?" Christina asked out of politeness more than anything, for she did not expect to meet either young person.

"They are only two years apart," Mr. Carrington replied, "though you might not know it to look at them. Mary is small like her mother, and something of a rattle-pate like . . . well, there is no need to be too self-revealing, is there? Kit, by contrast, is taller than I am now, which has quite reduced my consequence in my own household."

Christina found herself laughing again, enjoying the vicar's humor, until, unbelievably, she heard Aldric say, "Why do you and Mrs. Carrington not bring Kit and Mary to dine at the castle this evening? I have not seen your children in such a while I might not recognize them."

"I should be delighted to accept your invitation, my lord!" Mr. Carrington exclaimed with the ready amiability that characterized him. "My family will be beside themselves to learn they are to visit the castle and meet the new Lady Aldric."

Mr. Carrington looked to Christina with such unfeigned pleasure that she could do naught but return him a gracious smile. But she did not want to smile at all. She did not want to play the hostess of Pembridge, and she did not want to entertain guests as Aldric's wife. Dear God, he had rejected her as his wife!

The searing thought put a glitter in her eye that boded ill for Aldric, but he gave her no opportunity to express her dismay, or outrage as she'd have called it. He was taking his leave even then.

"I must get on with my real purpose in coming to town," he said, addressing the vicar more than Christina. "Martin Seavers's wife is about to deliver him a baby, or so the midwife informed me when I went to visit their farm. If I don't find Seavers soon, however, the baby will have been christened before he gets home."

Aldric's eyes swept from the vicar to Christina, lingered a half second, and then he said merely, "My lady," and was gone.

The vicar chuckled and said something about the marquess being godfather to more children than any peer in the realm, but Christina scarcely heard him. She was watching Aldric's black head finally disappear in the crowd and thinking grimly to herself that she did not, would not, care what had been in his eyes. There could not have been a plea in them, anyway. He did not plead, not Aldric. He did not even ask if she wanted to play a role that was not hers. He simply decreed she would, for unfathomable reasons he had not thought to share with her.

Yet she would play his hostess that night, though she could easily have played ill. Mr. Carrington was simply too charming and dear to snub. Her argument was with Aldric, not him, and she even chose in the vicar's honor a dress of Nile green silk that emphasized her hair.

Having not been to dinner before, she had to ask Nancy in which room they would gather. It was the blue drawing room, one of the few with its furniture intact. She found the lord of the castle himself awaiting her there, dressed formally, the white of his cravat stark against the black of his evening clothes and hair, and she almost hated him for the catch he caused in her breathing. From the suddenly still look in his eyes, she guessed that he read her resentment, but she'd no opportunity to voice it: to tell him emphatically that she would never act his hostess again, for the Carringtons were announced and Christina had to uncurl her clenched fingers and smile a greeting, instead.

The vicar's family members were as lively and pleasant as he, and in other circumstances, Christina would have enjoyed herself thoroughly. But she was too acutely aware of the falseness of the role she played that night. It was something like a knife stab to her heart even to hear herself addressed as Lady Aldric, but of course there were several remarks about newlyweds and even specifically about her sham of a wedding. Near the end of the evening, when the ladies had left the men to their port, Mary Carrington, only fifteen and very much like Millie, particularly in her awe of Aldric, began to enthuse giddily on the subject of the marquess's courtship.

"Oh, la, Lady Aldric!" she exclaimed, clapping her hands. "I cannot imagine even being courted by such a man as Lord Aldric! Why, last year, when he merely asked me how my schooling went, I was struck completely dumb. I could not think of a word to say and turned lobster red, but you are so composed, Lady Aldric! I cannot imagine you ever being at a loss for words, and you are as striking as Father said. It is no wonder that of all the young ladies Lord Aldric must have seen over the years, he fell in love with you!"

Christina had not thought she would greet the arrival of the men with relief, but when they entered the drawing room at that moment, she let out a long shaky breath. She did not think she could have managed a reply for Miss Carrington, or at least not managed one that was not so bitter it would not have burned the young girl's ingenuous ears.

Given the excuse, Christina rose to ring for the tea tray. She had expected the conversation to turn another way, but Mr. Carrington inquired genially what the ladies had been discussing and as if from a distance, Christina heard Mrs. Carrington say, "We have been telling Lady Aldric generally how she has lived up to the very high expectations you gave us of her, my dear, and specifically, Mary has been rattling on about how strikingly she must have stood out from among all the other young ladies in town this Season past."

"She did, indeed." The low, lazy voice was Aldric's.

"She was a toast, in fact, and universally considered quite out of the common way, but my lady is so stubbornly modest, she likely did not realize it."

Acutely aware of the Carringtons, Christina managed to do the expected. She looked in Aldric's general direction and even ascertained that he was regarding her in a pleasant, kindly way. She smiled, again as expected, but the expression was so contrary to her mood, her lips felt as if they would crack.

Aldric was still wearing that wretched, almost paternal smile when the Carringtons finally departed and he turned to Christina to say, "Now then, that was not so bad as you expected, was it?"

Christina could not imagine what he had thought she expected. From the middle of the room where she stood, having risen to bid Aldric's guests good night, she looked to him and said in a voice that quivered slightly, "Not so bad? Well, I suppose you could say that, though for myself I thought it without a doubt, excruciating!" With a pleasure that seemed only to fan her anger, she saw that she had taken Aldric completely by surprise. And before he could, apparently, credit what he had heard, she added through clenched teeth, "And I will thank you in future not ever to arrange another little entertainment involving me again."

Now that Aldric had married her, there was no scarcity of candles at Pembridge Castle, and Christina could easily see Aldric's eyebrow arch sharply. "Allow me to remind you that this is my home, madam," he told her in a voice from which all trace of fatherly smiles had been quite erased. "In my home I shall do precisely what I please, when I please to do it. But I get ahead of myself, I fear. I should like to return to your original remark. Did you mean to say that you put on a performance worthy of Siddons this evening, and did not, in fact, enjoy the Carringtons?"

Black eyes locked on gray. "The Carringtons were all that is pleasant!" Christina ground out. "It was the sham role you forced upon me that I could not bear."

"Sham role?" Aldric inquired with a harsh, unamused

laugh. "I don't recall that I asked you to be reasonable, ma'am. All I asked was that you receive a few compliments from a vicar and his family, converse pleasantly with the same group, and so enjoy yourself. That is all."

He mocked her! "Enjoy myself!" Christina's voice rose as her anger soared out of her control. "How in the name of all that is holy do you expect me to enjoy myself in the home of a cheat? Yes, a cheat!" she insisted, defying the sudden blaze in his black eyes. "You damn my father for being one, but you are one, as much as he! You cheated me! You did! You misled me as cruelly as it is possible for a man to mislead a woman. You . . ."

"You," he broke in, the blaze gone from his eyes but replaced by such a flat, deadly coldness, Christina gave a cry of dismay. Aldric only leaned down the closer to her, making her heart bang against her chest. "Do you not find it as pleasant to hear home truths as to spout them, my dear ma'am?" he demanded icily. "A pity, for you will listen now. You are either stupid or a fool or both, if you think I misled you in the worst way a man can mislead a woman. Had I chosen to mislead you to that degree, I'd have told you I loved you, dearest Christina, and with so little I'd have had your skirts up around your thighs that night in Mrs. Sidley's cool, deserted gardens. You'd have been used goods, willingly used, I might add, and even dear, staunch Mr. Palmer would not have taken you. You may think on all of that in the splendid isolation of your room, if you care to." His black eyes held hers, and though they glittered now with contempt, Christina was powerless to look away. "I confess I care not what you do there, and of a certainty I shall not disturb the monotony you crave with any more little entertainments. After your so graciously worded request I would not think of inflicting a pleasant evening upon you again. Good night."

The door, when it closed behind him, cracked shut with such force Christina jumped. And having finally regained the power to move, she put shaking hands to her flaming cheeks and swore she would not cry.

Chapter 17

"Lamb! Did ye not enjoy yourself, then?"

There were times, infrequent but nonetheless real, when Christina wished that circumstances had not brought Nancy to regard herself as a relation more than a servant. She knew that despite her vow, she might cry at any moment.

"I enjoyed myself well enough."

She lowered her head, baring the clasp of her pearl necklace for Nancy, but the maid could still see her mistress's face in the pier glass. "What's this long face, then?" she queried stubbornly.

"Very well, then!" Christina cried, at the end of her tether. "If you must know, Aldric and I had a great row. Again. This time I cut up at him for inviting company. I hated playing his wife, Nance!"

"Ah, lamb . . ."

"Nance, please!" She resented Aldric for how close she was to tears almost more than anything. She hated crying, and she had done so much of it on his account. "I'll be fine, really. Please, just help me with my nightdress. I'm weary to death."

It was the shaky, unsteady weariness that comes after a bitter exchange. Exchange? Christina laughed without amusement. What a pallid word to describe that scene! She had been quivering with anger. She'd have said anything to strike out at him. And she had. Indeed, she'd struck a hit. His eyes had blazed with the impact.

She'd called him a cheat. And he was! Christina hit her

pillow and sitting up abruptly, hit it again. She was the one
with the right to anger, not he. Never mind the degree, he
had misled her! Nay, he'd as good as betrayed her. She had
the right to furious anger, to contempt, to curl her lip in a
disgusted sneer. Not he.

She hit the abused pillow again. It only folded where she
struck it, giving her as little comfort as her righteousness.

She had enjoyed herself that evening. After a week of
nights spent alone in her room, she'd have enjoyed Cloris.
Well, Christina gave an awkward, tremulous laugh, hugging the pillow to her now. Perhaps she'd not have wel-
comed Cloris, but she had liked the Carringtons and had
even at times during the evening all but forgotten her
painful circumstances.

Christina took a shuddering breath. She might have admitted that to Aldric. When he had said that about the
evening not being so bad, she could have given him his
due. Then, calmly and reasonably she could have requested
that he consult her before he had her play hostess again.
She would not have been obliged to say how hearing herself addressed as Lady Aldric hurt her unbearably. She
need not have humiliated herself. She could have said simply that she preferred solitude just then; that she did well
enough by herself; that he need not think he'd any responsibility to entertain her!

It was unbearable to have him show even a hint of caring
for her. Had he been cold and disdainful, how much easier
it would have been! He'd have left her to her fate at Fairfield, or if not, he'd have ordered her to stay in her room at
Pembridge and out of his sight. She'd have gone, too, and
been wildly glad he would not be her husband in truth.

Ah, but not Aldric. He must actually force his protection
upon her; must show her why her monies had been so important to him; must present her as Lady Aldric to his people; must invite guests to relieve the monotony of her days;
and then he must proclaim her a toast with a too kindly
light in his damnable eyes!

Oh, it was no wonder she had lashed out at him! Merciful heaven, he was like some cruel god dangling the most exquisite bait before her but being careful all the while to keep it just beyond her reach.

Christina heaved a sigh and lowered her head to the pillow she held upon her knees. It was as well she had behaved so wretchedly after the Carringtons had taken their good cheer off with them. Aldric was too attractive, and she too susceptible, but now she had given him a disgust of her, he would keep his distance as he had so coldly vowed to do.

But Aldric broke his vow as soon as the next day. Christina was in the shade garden, a small, private place bordered by large yews and shaded by a grand oak. She had spent most of her days there since the arrival of the workmen Aldric had hired to restore his castle. They made a great deal of noise, but far worse, they reminded Christina how fine Pembridge would look for the real wife Aldric would eventually select.

When she had first gone to the garden, she had sat on a bench beneath the oak and simply enjoyed the cool and quiet as she read. Then, almost idly, she had found herself pulling weeds here and there. She'd never turned her hand to such a thing before, but then she had never spent days with nothing much to do but think unwanted thoughts. When she had uncovered a shy, pretty plant that had miraculously survived the neglect of a decade, she'd become more earnest in her endeavors. Finally, she had applied to Tim for help.

She thought it was Tim who came to the garden that afternoon, as she worked on a bed of sweetly scented lilies of the valley. Hearing footsteps on the rock path, Christina turned to tell him where she wanted the ferns he had told her he had found for her.

But it was Aldric. The sight of him was so unexpected she froze, though she felt her cheeks color fiercely.

Christina ducked her head as if she had not seen him and squeezed her eyes shut just for an instant, trying to right herself. The only thing she could seem to think of was the one thing she had managed to avoid thinking of until then, and she felt a flaming embarrassment as she recalled how contemptuously he'd told her he could have taken her on the ground that night in Mrs. Sidley's gardens. The real rub was, of course, that he could have. Even had he not bothered to lie and say he loved her. No! Her eyes flew open. She must not agitate herself so.

She came to her feet only to find that, mercifully, if he had come to the garden on her account, the garden had distracted him.

She watched his eyes travel the winding paths, mark the freshly turned beds, then linger upon the tidied old ones. Still, inevitably, his eyes came around at last to her. There was emotion in them. Christina could not determine what emotion, precisely, though she thought she could eliminate anger. They weren't narrowed upon her or glittering with contempt.

He was standing almost ten feet from her, a bed of anemones between them, when he said quietly, "This garden was my mother's."

No one had told her. "Oh," she said, at a loss as to how to respond, for she imagined he must resent her presence there, though he did not really appear to. "I didn't know."

But he was looking around again, seeming, she decided finally, faintly bemused. That she could understand. He had not had a penny to spend on anything so frivolous as the gardens. The formal ones outside the yew hedge were a chaotic jumble of weeds, leaves, cracked statuary, and sagging benches.

"You've accomplished so much."

He was looking at her again. Christina's palms felt unpleasantly moist, and she was not sorry to have a reason to look away from him to the soiled gloves she wore. "I have enjoyed the work," she said, tugging lightly at the fingers of the right glove.

"Mother used to come every day, in the morning. I have always thought she enjoyed it so, because here, she had control, and she had not to contend with my father's waywardness." Christina thought he made the surprising remark more to himself than to her. He was not looking at her, she saw, when she glanced at him through her lashes, but neither was he dwelling bitterly upon the past. He had found the rabbit. She knew because his mouth lifted suddenly, and he went to it, which brought him to her, for the rabbit was propped against the bench near her.

"You found it," he said, the smile in his voice, too.

Christina did not think it necessary to reply, and was distracted anyway. She was wondering whether it would be too obvious if she quietly faded a few feet away. He had come too close. She could see, though it was late in the afternoon, that he had just come from his bath. There were traces of wetness in his black hair, and she caught the scent of the Hungary water he used.

She had actually turned to go as quietly as she could when Aldric caught her off guard, saying, "I gave it to Mother for her birthday one year."

The figure of the stone rabbit, with its feet stretched full length as if in flight and its long ears angled straight back from its head, had been well executed. Christina had smiled when she found it, but lifelike as it was, it still was a statue best characterized by the word "sweet."

Christina was a second late responding and even then she could find no more to say than, "Ah."

Aldric glanced from the rabbit to her. "I was ten," he explained, just the suggestion of a smile in his voice. "And I raised them."

He had raised rabbits?

Now his mouth quirked, slightly true, but nonetheless tellingly. He had read her thoughts, and Christina promptly dropped her eyes.

She watched as his black boots turned from the rabbit toward her. The silence stretched unnervingly. "Christina?" Her eyes remained glued to those shining boots. "Come now," he urged so softly it seemed his voice squeezed her heart. "You are no coward."

Oh, wasn't she, now? She looked up abruptly, her eyes betraying a flash of resentment.

He wasn't smiling, though, not even faintly as she'd expected. He looked as grave as a vicar at a funeral.

"I am sorry, Christina. I had no right or reason to speak to you as I did."

For a moment it did not seem there was any air to breathe. She was lost in his eyes and it was as if from a distance she heard herself say gruffly, "I've a sharp tongue."

"Aye." His gaze was steady on her. "You have, and I've given you reason and more to use it. But your sharp tongue has nothing to do with this. I was wrong."

She looked away from him swiftly as color climbed into her cheeks again. Wrong was not the correct word to use, for he had been right, as she had already admitted to herself. "I, ah, threw your kind impulse to divert me in your face," she said, her voice sounding mortifyingly unsteady.

"Christina?" He sounded so blastedly patient. He made her eyelids prickle, and she had to blink furiously before, at last, she dragged her eyes back around to him. And blast him, anyway! There was something about him, something more than black eyes and hard, masculine features, that affected her so deeply it seemed to Christina she had to catch her breath every time she looked at him. And just then his affect was all the worse, because he was regarding her so steadily.

"It is not excuses for myself that I want, Christina," he said, looking, or seeming to look, into her soul. "I have come to ask for your forgiveness."

"I was only trying to say there is nothing to forgive."

"There is a great deal to forgive." Aldric rebutted. "Would you have me on my knees?"

Perhaps it was the oh-so-slight, but still perceptible exasperation in his tone that righted Christina. She could respond a great deal more equably to it than to all that earnest, almost tender, contrition.

"That is an arresting thought, I allow," she replied, but her humor did not last, and almost to her surprise, Christina heard herself say quietly, "I am sorry, too."

Their eyes met and locked, and then Aldric said softly, "Well, I forgive you."

Her response hung in the balance a long moment, then in a rush of breath, almost as if she were afraid she would not get the words out, Christina said, "And I . . . I forgive you."

"I am glad." Aldric said it with a quietness that wrenched at her, but he did not force her to endure more of his seriousness than she could bear. He smiled in the next moment. Christina thought he looked almost mischievous, but could not credit the impression until he said, "I thought I might not only have to go to my knees to gain your forgiveness but perhaps even to go so far as to threaten you with a recitation on how breathtaking your hair is when the sun catches it."

"Oh no, Aldric!" It was too, too much, especially with that playful gleam in his eyes. "Please! Please, leave off on my looks."

She was begging, but she didn't care. The temptation to believe him, to bask in that look was so great, she couldn't bear it.

He studied her so thoughtfully, Christina wasn't certain that he would heed her, and she prepared to leave, but then he relented. "For now, I will heed your wishes, but perhaps I should warn you that you've freckles."

"What? I do not! That is one demerit I do not have."

She looked so indignant it was hard for Aldric to keep from smiling. Instead, he reached out and flicked her nose with his finger. She reacted as if he had slapped her, jumping back and nearly falling over the lilies of the valley behind her. "You do, actually," he said, the smile in his voice, if not on his lips, "because the sun is shining through the straw of your bonnet and there's a dusting of little tan and light squares across your nose. Don't worry though. In reality your skin is the same smooth roses and cream as always. Ah, ah, no groaning, now. It is the truth, and I've a mind to make amends for all the hurt I've done you by bringing you to understand that you are a lovely young woman before you leave Pembridge."

Christina had not known she had any hope left in her until

then, when he so casually, even pleasantly, mentioned her eventual departure. Once, long ago, Mrs. Palmer had hired a conjurer to perform tricks at one of Will's birthday parties. One of the tricks had involved the man whisking a cloth from a glass and exposing it to the audience. Christina felt like that glass, suddenly bared and unable to hide itself. Aldric had only to look to see the wretched, sickening pain that could only mean she had, despite everything, clung to hope.

She swatted at an imaginary gnat and allowed her fingernails to curve into her palms. The sting gave her a focus, and her voice emerged admirably dry, if a little low, as she queried, "You admire Sisyphus then, my lord?"

Aldric laughed. She had not heard him laugh so in a long while and bit her lip. "No, my dear, I do not admire Sisyphus and do not intend to fail." He touched her, nudging her chin lightly with his finger, and bringing her eyes flying back to his. Christina knew her expression was more closed than ever, but she could not help it.

Aldric wryly shook his dark head, one corner of his mouth curving up in the faintest of lopsided smiles. "You've that look about you that says you are determined not to listen to a word I say. But I put you on notice, Christina. I have heard you dismiss yourself for the last time. Kit Carrington couldn't take his pup's eyes off of you last night, and he wasn't hanging out after your fortune, either, as you thought was the case with all your suitors in London."

"Only the poor ones," she quipped, not having to work at wryness. But she could not remain in his grasp any longer.

He let her go without protest. "I'll not make you endure more compliments today. I intend to go slowly with you."

"As if I were an unbroken horse?" she retorted.

"Precisely." His black eyes gleamed with his amusement, and she wished she could say it was amusement at her expense. She'd have been less undone, had it been. She tried to look away, to ignore how achingly attractive he was, but he was already saying, "Actually, I do believe I have the right to slip in at this point that your gray eyes are magnificent when they are flashing."

"Oh!" She whirled to stalk away, truly angry that he should continue to try and charm her when he did not want her, but Aldric caught her arm. Even so light and impersonal a touch as that he used upon her sent something almost shocking racing through her, and she stopped at once to lift her arm away from him.

"Nay, now, don't bridle again," he said, half laughing even then. "I promise to stop teasing you for now at least, as I've news you would wish to hear. I've had a letter from Moly. Shall we sit?" He indicated the bench, and Christina had little choice but to go to it, though she was careful to sit as far from him as possible. Aldric did not seem to notice. All seriousness now, he reported that Thompkins had settled in as a groom at the Grange.

"He has consulted with young Will on one point and though the boy had an answer, it seems Thompkins wishes to be certain that as far as you can recall, it is accurate to say that no one in particular put you in the path of any of these accidents."

"No." Christina shook her head. "It was the first question I asked myself, but I could think of no one. Everyone at Fairfield knew I rode every morning and that I often rode in the direction of a stream that meanders through the estate. Likewise, anyone could have learned which saddle was mine, or looked out the window at Morland House and seen me sitting on that bench in the gardens. The accident with the cart is the only one I am truly at a loss to explain. Cloris knew the route we would use, as she had asked me to stop by her dressmaker's to pick up a dress she had to have for that night, but even so, she could not have known the carriage would be stopped before a cross street that not only slanted toward the main street but had a heavy cart parked on it, just waiting to be let loose."

It did seem an impossible series of events to arrange. Still, Aldric marked that Cloris's name had arisen once again, and he determined to advise Thompkins how frequently Christina's stepsister seemed to lurk on the edge of events.

Chapter 18

"I am sorry, Dory, but I am not done yet." Smiling regretfully, Christina gestured to a clump of periwinkle standing in a bucket. "If I do not plant this today, it will die, and your father will be most unhappy, for it was he who so generously made me the gift of it."

"Can you come later, my lady?" Dory inquired hopefully.

Christina was not able to resist the entreaty in the girl's eyes. "Yes, if I finish before I must go and dress for dinner. I shall come to see what you and Lizzie are up to at the falls. Do be careful, though," she thought to call out as the two little girls, one six and the other only four, began to trot away.

"We will!" they both chimed back, waving.

Christina did not think she would have time to meet them at the pool. She had a great deal of Tim's periwinkle to plant and then there was the need to dress for dinner.

She dug her next hole a little more vigorously than was, perhaps, strictly necessary. She knew she ought not to be getting in the habit of Aldric's company. Well, perhaps she was not quite in the habit of it yet. She had only joined him twice now in the evening, but she acknowledged she had set a precedent that would not soon be broken. Look at how she had not gone off blithely with Dory and Lizzie to enjoy a walk to the waterfall. She had restrained herself in order to have time to dress, to make herself presentable for him.

And yet . . . she bit her lip. He had invited her to join him for dinner with such circumspection, she could not see how she could have declined, unless she wished to be the most churlish ogre ever born, and sadly, she admitted she lacked the strength to be so off-putting.

He had invited her as they returned to the house together the day he had come to her . . . no, to his mother's shade garden. They had just decided it might be helpful to Mr. Thompkins if she were to write her own account of all that had occurred, when Aldric had said ever so lightly, "You must feel under no obligation because I invite you, Christina, but I find my own company night after night rather tedious and would be very pleased if you should join me for dinner. Decide precisely as you please, and you needn't do so now. I must leave you here, anyway. There's my steward, Mr. Baldwin, coming up the drive now, and I must speak to him."

With an amiable wave he'd taken himself off to meet a small, darkish man approaching the house on a horse that was also small and dark. Christina had had a smile for the similarity of the steward and his beast, but the smile had faded soon. He had made it almost impossible for her to retreat back into her angry isolation, and so she had known she would accept his invitation, though she recognized the dangers, particularly as he had set himself to be charming.

Still, she had assured herself she did possess a shield of sorts. She would not soon forget how casually, almost pleasantly, he had mentioned that she would eventually leave Pembridge. He did not hate her. She accepted that, and accepted as well that he enjoyed her company enough that he preferred it to unrelieved solitude. But when the time came, he would wave her off without regret.

She did not intend to allow him to charm her so that she forgot. As a precaution she had gone down to the first dinner armed with an array of neutral topics of conversation, and as a result there had been only one fraught moment. In the course of a discussion of the castle, Aldric told her he had once been locked in the dungeons for hours.

As Christina had only been able to bring herself to peer from the step nearest the door into the dank darkness of

Pembridge's dungeons, she'd looked up to stare at him. "Merciful heaven! How old were you?"

"Ten or so," he'd said, studying her, but she hadn't noticed, caught up as she was in imagining how he must have reacted as a child to the place she'd found foul and fearsome as an adult.

"Did you have a light?"

"An excellent point." He had smiled at her, though once more she had scarcely noticed his expression. "Yes, I did, but only for a while. My lantern eventually burned out."

"How long were you there?"

"Not long enough to merit the look on your face, Christina."

She had recovered in the next moment, telling him about how very grim she had found the dungeons and then rattling on about dark places and children, saying almost anything, really, to hide the fact that she had felt the degree of dismay that she had, because he, no other, had been the child in the dark place.

That had been the only sticky moment, though. He had complimented her, true, saying in this instance something about her elegant profile, but she had been prepared for flattery and had returned him an easy thanks before asking him about his plans to improve the strain of cattle on the estate. He'd grinned, damn him, guessing her strategy, but she had found her own reason to grin, at least inwardly, when he could not resist the subject and had plunged into an explanation of the plans she had heard him mention briefly to Mr. Carrington the night before.

"My lady! Lady Ti!"

The shrill scream brought Christina's head up. She scarcely recognized the voice as Dory's, there was such panic in it, but Christina had given no one else leave to address her as Lady Ti, because Lady Aldric had sounded so cumbersome on the child's young lips.

Instantly rising to her feet, Christina began to run in the direction of the path that wound up the hill to the falls, and met Dory running headlong at her. The child was gasping for breath, winded from her run, and so distraught she could not speak. Her eyes filled with tears, and Christina took both her hands in a gentle grasp.

"Is Lizzie in difficulty, Dory?"

The deliberate calmness of her voice had the effect of slowing Dory's wild breathing. The little girl nodded frantically, swallowed hard, then blurted, "She fell in the pool! I threw a big stick to her, but I cannot swim, and I came for you!"

"You did splendidly, Dory, but listen to me. You must do more. Run to the stables to your father and tell him what has happened. We will need a horse to bring Lizzie back quickly and some blankets to get her warm. Hurry now, while I go on ahead."

Christina gave the child a push toward the stables, then began to run more furiously than she had ever run before in her life. A stitch cramped her side after a while, but she ignored it, praying as she ran that little Lizzie had the stick her sister had pushed to her; that the water plunging down from the tops of the foothills was not so cold as seemed likely; and with a spurt of speed, that she could arrive in time.

Hearing the roar of the falls gave Christina the strength to sprint the final distance, and she arrived just in time to see Lizzie's little head disappear under the water. The child had floated near the waterfall and when the spray hit her, it had knocked the stick from her grasp. Without thought, Christina kicked off her half boots and flung herself into the water. She could not swim well, but one of her governesses had believed that a young lady ought to be able to save herself, if the need arose, and had taken Christina to one of the lakes that dotted Fairfield to teach her the rudiments of getting about in water.

The water in Hampshire had been warm, though, and Christina had been dressed in a bathing costume that had not included a wide skirt and underclothes. Merely to keep her clothes from dragging her down, Christina had to kick with all her might. "Lizzie!" she called, dread seizing her when the child did not resurface immediately. The water was as icy cold as she had feared. Already she could feel it sapping at her strength, but still she moved her arms in half circles as she'd been taught and struggled to kick against her clinging skirts.

"Lizzie!" she screamed shrilly, and miraculously, though the child could not possibly have heard her, Lizzie came up thrashing wildly only a few feet away. Christina screamed for her again, and just keeping her own head above water, managed to propel herself forward.

Lizzie saw her and lunged. Unprepared for the fierceness of the child's reaction, Christina went under the water. She caught Lizzie by the waist and managed with a mighty kick to lift the child away enough to get her own head out of the water, but even as she sucked in a huge breath of air, Lizzie lunged again and clapped on to her neck with a death grip.

"No! You are sinking me," Christina shouted, but the little girl was too terrified to understand and actually tightened her hold on Christina. They both went under again. Lizzie's panic turned into such a frenzy of kicking and clutching at Christina's neck that even when she did bob to the surface for a second, Christina could not get a good breath.

She gulped water, and though she was aware of a splash behind her, she scarcely marked it as she and Lizzie went down again, this time so far, she felt a wild thrill of fear, knowing they could not possibly surface before she must breathe again. Her lungs on fire, she kicked and flailed in panic, getting nowhere it seemed until suddenly a hand caught her by the hair and wrenching it unmercifully, yanked her upward. Miraculously, at the same moment, before she understood what was happening, Lizzie was pulled off of her, and then she surfaced, spluttering and gasping for breath.

"Easy, now! Easy, Christina," a voice shouted above the waterfall's noise. "Lie back," it instructed, but she was beyond relaxing, and the next thing she knew, as she continued to mill the water with her arms, she was grabbed diagonally across the chest, and brought up hard against another chest. "Stop!" an authoritative voice shouted directly into her ear.

How she knew it was Aldric, Christina could not have said, but she did, and she attempted to turn and grab him, exactly as Lizzie had grabbed her. He held her clamped too tightly against him, though, and yelling again for her to lie still, began pulling them both in the direction of the bank. She only vaguely realized they were moving purposefully, but Aldric's hold upon her was so unrelenting that finally some of her panic began to recede.

Without fear overriding every sensation, she realized her legs and arms were numb with cold and that she lacked the energy to move anymore.

She could not even seem to summon the effort to get herself out of the water. Aldric had to heave her inelegantly onto the bank where she flopped like a fish. Gasping for breath, she foggily heard him exclaim, "Damn! She's blue. Throw a blanket here, Tim. What of Lizzie? How is she?"

Concern for the child penetrated Christina's daze. Spitting up some of the water she had swallowed, she struggled to lean up a little and follow the direction of Aldric's gaze to Tim, who was bending over his child. "She's retching, m'lord," he reported without looking up. "I'm thinkin' that's to the good, though! She must have drunk half the pool."

"We must get them to a fire as quickly as we can," Aldric said as Christina sank back to the ground, exhausted. She was shuddering, but she didn't realize it, though she did hear Aldric say, "I'll help you take Lizzie up before you, Tim, so that you may get her home to your hearth. Nay, no argument, man! Lady Aldric is not so weak as the child."

Dimly Christina realized Aldric had left her. She heard the sounds of more retching, then vaguely moans, and finally she heard Tim ride off with Lizzie, but she did not realize Aldric had returned to her side until she felt his hand at her throat. Then she heard as much as felt him rip her dress down the front. She gave a startled cry that sounded more like a moan, but he only pulled the harder on her clothing. When she tried to resist, albeit ineffectually, he slapped her hands away.

"Stop, damn it!" he ordered harshly. "You'll die of cold in these sodden clothes. It's why I sent Tim away. Here, I've a blanket."

She was shivering uncontrollably, her teeth chattering so they rattled in her head when Aldric began to rub her with a blanket so scratchy it could only have been a horse blanket. She marked the discomfort, but it was as nothing compared to the blessed warmth that surged into every part of her he touched.

On and on the rubbing went, until she was warm at last, and Aldric wrapped the blanket tightly under her arms. She shivered one more time, as if for good measure, but she was sufficiently recovered to think to thank Aldric. When she lifted her eyes to his, though, she lost the words. For upon the sign that she had somewhat recovered, Aldric's brow suddenly lowered and he began to blast her with such an angry tirade, Christina could only blink.

"What in the name of heaven possessed you to do such an idiotic thing?" he raged, scowling thunderously. "Dear God, you can barely swim! The child would have drowned you in another moment, and you would have both been lost! You did not even have the presence of mind to strip yourself of all those clothes. Heaven help you, but you might as well have worn a necklace of rocks! Who taught you to swim? No one who knew how, I'll warrant. You couldn't manage the child. She was squeezing the life from you. . . . "

On and on he went. Christina might have taken offense, but as he lambasted her, he scooped her up into his lap and held her against him, allowing the warmth of his body to seep into her. She wasn't cold now, except for her toes, but she was unbelievably sleepy.

When her eyelids fell, though, Aldric shook her. "Are you listening?" he demanded.

She had not been listening to him for a while, but she

thought it wise to nod in the affirmative. However, she was powerless to keep her eyelids from drifting shut.

"You are not," he contradicted, but gruffness had replaced the anger in his voice. "You are going to sleep, and you cannot do that yet. I cannot mount Beau with you dead asleep in my arms. You must stand until I am on him, then I will be able to pull you up to me."

Stand? Had he asked her to fly, Christina could not have been any less inclined to do what Aldric said she must, but he had not asked for her opinion. Without further ado, he stood up and let her feet slide down to the ground. The breeze felt pleasant on her bare legs. And that brought her eyes wide open.

She was naked beneath the blanket. Christina swayed a little and with a muttered oath, Aldric lifted her again and stalked to a great rock that stood sentinel by the pool. He propped her against it for all the world as if she were a piece of wood. She hardly noticed. He had stripped her of her clothes! She had been too befuddled with the shock of nearly drowning and the cold to take in what all that ripping had meant. Even her chemise . . . she looked down swiftly. No, it was gone. She had been completely bared to his view.

She couldn't face him and looked longingly at the ground, willing it to come to swallow her.

"Stay on your feet, damn it!" Aldric shouted. "Do not move an inch, and do not, above all, sink to the ground. I'll never reach you."

Well, she thought, more grumpily than relievedly, he didn't seem to have been unduly affected by the sight of her in all her naked splendor. Huddled in the increasingly itchy blanket, she watched Aldric catch Beau and lead him to a rock. It was then she realized Aldric had not taken the time to saddle his stallion before he rode to her rescue. She felt a flash of gratification, but it lasted only until she thought how impossible it would be for the two of them to ride the restive stallion without the benefit of a saddle.

Any comment on the matter seemed beyond her, however. And so when Aldric rode up and held out his hand to her, she took it. "Put your foot on mine," he directed, "and I'll swing you up before me. You may have to let go the blanket for a little, but I'll wrap it around you again before you are too cold."

But not before she blushed to the roots of her hair. She had to lift both arms to pull herself into place on Beau, and the blanket not only fell open but would have fallen all the way to the ground, except that Aldric caught it in time.

If her scarlet hue had escaped him, Christina knew her cry of dismay could not have, but Aldric appeared to take no notice at all of either Christina's embarrassment or the cause of it. Frowning with concentration, he held Beau still with his thighs and wrapped the blanket around her again, then took off his coat and draped it about her shoulders for good measure.

Putting his arms around her, he clucked at Beau, urging the stallion to a walk. Uncertain of her balance, Christina grabbed the front of his shirt with a tight fist, while she used the other hand to hold her blanket in place.

Given the difficulty of staying upon an unsaddled horse while riding sideways and holding a blanket closed around her, Christina could not for a little concern herself with how she was dressed or not dressed, as the case was. But eventually she caught the horse's rhythm and did not have to concentrate quite so determinedly merely to keep her seat. Then she had an absurd image of herself as Lady Godiva, though she was really only naked from the knees down, and too exhausted to stifle the cry, she wailed mournfully, "But my legs are bare!"

Aldric did not respond with any sympathy at all. "So they are," he agreed with heartless dryness. "Very bare. The trees have gone quite pink with shock. I don't doubt but that they'll cut you dead the next time you come this way."

It was the right thing to have said, of course. Christina gave a watery chuckle and burrowed her head close against his chest. He felt so warm and strong, she had an urge to burrow her whole body against his. She didn't, but only because she thought Beau would unseat her if she did.

Then she remembered again about her dangling, bare legs. "But what of the servants?" she groaned into his chest.

"The servants? What will they think of your bare legs?"

She nodded, her cheek rubbing up and down against the soft lawn of his shirt.

"Well," he said, and she thought she heard him chuckle. "If they are lucky enough to see your legs, my dear, I imagine that in addition to the pints of ale that will be lifted in honor of the idiotic bravery you displayed on behalf of a child of one of their own, there were will be a good many more pints raised to the luck that brought them a glimpse of what they cannot but agree are beyond doubt the most delectable pair of legs in the kingdom."

Exhausted and more than a little dazed by the too near brush she'd had with tragedy, Christina still managed to tip her head back and smile rather crookedly when she met Aldric's black eyes. "You are undoubtedly only teasing me again about my looks. But do you know what? I am coming to the belief that you are a great deal kinder than you would have anyone know. Yes. Much, much kinder, my lord."

With that, Christina lost the battle to keep her head upright. It sank sideways to lie upon his chest, and her eyes fell shut.

In her half-aware, half-dozing state, she could not be certain that Aldric did lean down to brush a kiss across the top of her sodden head. She thought he did, but he might only have been flicking a twig from her hair. However, if he did not kiss her, she really did think she heard him murmur just afterward, "I wasn't being the least kind about your legs, little peagoose. If anything, I understated their long, delectably shaped appeal. It is another in a long line of points to Moly. Damn him, if it isn't. And now I've saved your life, I think it would not be inappropriate for you to address me as Johnny. My friends do, you know."

But Christina didn't reply. She was asleep by then, lulled by Beau's slow rocking gait and by the deliciously warm feel of Aldric's arms around her.

Chapter 19

"Ach, lamb! Look at you just sittin' there, your tea tray scarcely touched. I thought you said you were all new again."

Christina took in Nancy's militant stance, legs apart and arms akimbo, and managed a smile. "I am recovered, Nance. I swear it. I am only sitting quietly because Dr. Morrison advised me to go slowly this third day as well."

"An' that's why you're not even readin' the book in your lap? Because you must rest? Readin' doesn't seem a tirin' activity to me. I think you're sittin' quiet as a mouse because you're missin' him, though I don't doubt you'll tell me nay."

Christina's mouth curved ever so slightly. "Then I suppose there is no point in my saying you are wrong if your mind is already made up."

"He'll be back, lamb. There's no need for you to fret."

"I don't think you may fault me for fretting if I am sitting still as a mouse, Nance," Christina pointed out, her gaze drifting to the window. "And I know perfectly well that Aldric will return to his castle. He has only gone to Norfolk, after all, not China, and to do nothing more exotic than buy cattle. I cannot imagine that he means to drive his prize bulls to London before he brings them here."

Nancy chuckled, pleased by the humor that seemed to mean her mistress's mood was not so low as it appeared, and turned her attention to straightening the room, though she was not so busy she could not chat as she worked.

Word had come that Lizzie was sitting up that morning,

Dr. Morrison having proclaimed her almost entirely recovered from her ordeal. "Becky and her Tim are blessin' you every hour, lamb. Why, if you hadn't kept her head above that water, she'd have drowned, poor wee little thing."

After the good news about Lizzie, Christina only listened to Nancy with half an ear. As her eyes drifted again to the window, her thoughts returned where they had been all morning. She did miss him. Nancy had been, as she would have said, as right as rain.

Christina bit her lip. It might have been funny if it hadn't been so serious. She had spent most of her fortnight at Pembridge avoiding him, yet the house felt empty now that he had gone. She had reason to resent him, even hate him, yet her spirits had been heavy as lead since his departure. Six days, the probable length of his journey, seemed an eternity to her, and yet when he did return, he would not be returning to her. Oh, she would be in residence at Pembridge, unless Mr. Thompkins made some startling discovery, but when Aldric turned his steps toward home, he'd think of the castle, of his tenants, of the work he had yet to do. If he thought of her, his steps would likely slow.

Not that he had failed to be solicitous about her condition when he got her to his castle, half drowned. He had looked in on her several times and on the evening of the second day, when she had gained strength, had joined her for dinner in her room. And when he had come to tell her he had had a letter from a friend in Norfolk who had several prize bulls for sale, he had asked her if she felt well enough to be left alone, implying he'd have delayed his trip on her account.

She had assured him that she was quite well enough for him to go. With Nancy and Mrs. Grynydd hovering over her, she did not need Aldric to make certain she rested, took the tonic Dr. Morrison had left for her, and ate properly.

What she wanted of Aldric, he wouldn't wish to give. Had he not come to her rescue at the pool and fretted over her and held her so securely in his arms afterward, she might have gone on believing that she could fight her attraction to him, that all she had to do was remember that he did not want her. But he had held her. She knew how comfortingly secure his arms were, how solid his chest beneath her cheek, and with a fierceness that rattled her, she longed for him to hold her to him again.

When he had come to bid her adieu early that morning, she had hardly been able to look at him for fear that he would read her desire in her eyes. She had pretended to be half asleep and had as a result been considerably startled when he had leaned down to brush his lips across her brow. "No heroics, while I'm away, Gray Eyes," he'd whispered lightly. "I expect to find you hale and dry when I return."

And then he had gone, and she had cried weak, silly tears because that little taste of his sweetness made her long for more.

"Are you goin' out to yer garden today?"

Christina looked up, half startled to realize she had quite forgotten Nancy. It was on the tip of her tongue to tell the maid that the garden was not hers, but she bit the words back. She could not make Nancy bear the brunt of her disconsolate mood.

She went out to the garden, too, though she was still too weak from her ordeal to work. Tim came and all but fell upon his knees before her for the third time in as many days. As Becky had done much the same on her way to the garden, Christina almost irritably told Tim to leave off. She had nearly drowned Lizzie not saved her, she said, and they were all making a great deal of nothing, and now it was time to think of other things. He smiled a little, and she laughed and said he was, after all, very welcome, for Lizzie was a darling child and anything she had been able to do was its own reward. Then becoming rather brisker, she asked if Tim had time to consult with her on some plans?

Christina had not forgotten the half bemused, half wondering way Aldric had looked around the mostly restored shade garden. Though she could not hope to accomplish a similar change in the formal gardens in only six days, she thought it would be possible, if Tim could spare her the laborers, to have those gardens cleared and ready for new plantings.

Later, she acknowledged with a hollow laugh how far she had come. She was no longer sequestered in her room, holding herself apart from the restoration of the castle and even resenting it. She was actively engaged in a part of those restorations, and she knew too well why. In part, she was quite naturally seeking some way to thank Aldric for saving her life a second time. But in even larger measure, she knew, she sought to give him pleasure because he had held her in his arms, brushed his lips across her hair, perhaps, and told her her legs were the stuff of legend.

And she did not even know whether he had meant all that about her legs! Christina bit her lip sternly but could not suppress the telling quirk at the corners of her mouth. He had said it twice, and the second time surely had thought she was too exhausted to hear him. Oh, she was a fool to hope for so little reason! She was, and yet she turned all her energies that day and the next into restoring Aldric's formal gardens.

On the third day of Aldric's absence, Christina was interrupted in her endeavors just before luncheon. It was Mrs. Grynydd coming to tell that she had a caller. "She gives her name as Lady Elise Danley," the housekeeper said, then paused before she added, "'Twas for m'lord, she asked, but when Morton told her his lordship was not home, she asked for his wife. Do you wish to receive her, m'lady?"

Christina did not need the uncertain note in Mrs. Grynydd's voice to warn her against receiving Lady Elise Danley, whomever she might be. The mere fact that the woman had asked for Aldric set off warning bells enough in Christina's head, but she heeded neither her own nor Mrs. Grynydd's instincts.

Like a child who discovers a sore and cannot ignore it, she went inside, only taking the time to be certain the blue muslin she wore hung properly and that her hair had not come loose from its pins. She wished she had done a great deal more the moment she entered the receiving room to which Morton had shown her visitor. Lady Elise Danley was dressed in a striking burgundy taffeta that perfectly set off the dark gloss of her hair and the rich brown of her eyes and subtly contrived to emphasize her full, thrusting bosom.

The only advantage Christina could see that she had was her height, for Lady Danley was of a diminutive size, but she was not certain she could contrive to look down her nose at a woman who was as beautiful and desirable as the petite, lushly endowed, exceedingly feminine woman before her.

"Good morning, Lady Danley. How may I help you?"

It was a perfectly polite opening and should not have provoked the dismissive laugh Lady Danley gave. "Help me, child?" the woman trilled, raking Christina with a disdainful look. "I can't imagine you could do anything to help me. I only stopped by to see for myself who it was Johnny took to wife. He made no mention of his plan, you see, when we were together in April. Ah yes, I see you understand he came to me during the time he was ostensibly wooing you. He is such a voracious man, and we suit each other so very well! But now that I have seen for myself why he thought his wedding plans too unimportant ... . "

Christina found her tongue, finally. "As I take it the two of you communicate no longer, Lady Danley," she interrupted with a mocking coolness that caused the other woman's eyes to fly wide, "I shall convey to Lord Aldric that you came to visit. He is a man of great honor, as I doubt you are capable of understanding, Lady Danley. What his reaction will be, I can only imagine, but I do know he would be dismayed were I to entertain his former mistress." Christina turned her back upon her unwanted guest, dismissing her summarily and moved with a deliberately measured, regal pace to the door. Over her shoulder she added distantly, "I will send Morton to show you the way to the door. Good day."

She did not look back again, but even so she had had the

distinct satisfaction of seeing Lady Danley's face flame unbecomingly, first, when she had been informed she could have no understanding of honor, and second, when she had been termed a former mistress. But though Christina had left her unwanted visitor red-faced, her satisfaction lasted only until she had closed the door to the receiving room behind her.

She took with her too clear a mental image of Lady Elise Danley and had too accurate a recollection of every word the woman had said to remain triumphant. Lady Danley had called him "Johnny." As if Christina had dreamed it, she thought she remembered Aldric murmuring that *she* should address him so. It had been on their ride back from the pool. He had said something about saving her life, and that his friends called him Johnny. She'd not quite dared to do it, though, even to herself. But Lady Danley did, with ease.

Damn! And damn again. It stung so much, that evidence of their friendship, but it did not sting half so much as that knowing "he is voracious"; even more than the knowledge that the reason Aldric had mysteriously deserted her for those several days when he had, indeed, been wooing her, had been to go to his mistress. His luscious mistress with whom he was voracious.

Christina curled her hands into fists, fighting the urge to throw one of the few vases that had escaped the auction block at the wall. She did not even understand all the word implied.

She had only been kissed twice in her life, both times by Aldric, and the first time, the more dizzying time, he'd just returned from trysting with his mistress. Perhaps Lady Danley had not completely satisfied his voracious appetites.

Christina did throw her kid slipper at the wall of her room. It bounced nicely, and she did it again. But still she was angry. Not with Aldric, oddly. She could not learn anything worse about his feelings for her than she already had. She was angry at herself.

Lady Danley ought not to have affected her so deeply.

She ought not to care that Aldric had a mistress who was as seductively beautiful as any woman Christina had ever beheld. She ought not to want to race back downstairs and scratch the woman's slumberous eyes out.

But she did care! She fervently wished she had spoken the truth when she had dismissed the vile woman as Aldric's former mistress. She had allowed herself to hope again, even despite that very recent remark of Aldric's that indicated he fully expected her to leave his house and his life.

She must leave. It simply was not possible for her to keep Aldric at any sort of distance when she lived in his home, and though she deplored her weakness, Christina realized she must accept it and get on with what was best for her. She needed to forget Aldric, not to fall further in love with him every day. She must leave Pembridge as soon as possible.

She did not order the carriage brought around on the instant only because she was not certain either where she could go or how to obtain the funds to get there once she had decided on the place.

The next day, four days after Aldric's departure, Christina entirely unexpectedly received the answer to her questions, or perhaps it had been prayers she had sent up. When she returned from a walk, she saw a carriage pulled up before the house, and recognizing it, she gaped momentarily before she began to run as fast as she could.

Christina would have run right into Will's arms, she was so glad to have him come to deliver her just at the moment she most needed deliverance, but glancing beyond him, when she burst into the same receiving room in which she had spoken with Lady Danley, she saw, to her astonishment, that Will had not come alone. The first person whose eyes Christina met were Cloris's, and she stared blankly for a moment, unable to imagine why Cloris would journey to see her. Nor did her elder stepsister's shuttered expression give her any hint, but that it confirmed Cloris had not put herself to the trouble out of a sudden burst of love.

But Christina was given no more than half a second to ponder the mystery of Cloris's presence, for a squeal from near Will turned her attention, and before she knew it, Millie was hurtling forward.

Christina reeled off balance under the girl's friendly assault, though when her eyes met Will's, she sobered somewhat beneath the searching look he gave her.

"What a surprise this is," she said, hugging Millie about the shoulders. "A very pleasant one."

"We ought to have forewarned you, I know, Ti," Will began. "But, well, we know how you like surprises, and so we thought . . . "

". . . to give you a surprise," Millie giggled. "When Will said he wished to see how you were getting on in your new home, Cloris wished to come, too, and I would not be left behind, of course, and Mrs. Lester kindly agreed to accompany us, for Mama is suffering an attack of the grippe that is not serious, so Dr. Barnaby says, but is most uncomfortable."

Christina had not even noticed Mrs. Lester, a widow of few means who lived near Fairfield. She bid the elder woman welcome to Pembridge, and then before she could lose her courage, she went on to say in the most neutral tone she could summon that she wished to return with them to Hampshire.

"You are leaving your husband!" Cloris cried, her lips pursing with disapproval. "But that is unheard of! Think of the scandal."

"If Christina wishes to leave Pembridge, then she shall," Will said, giving Cloris a look that made her color. Christina wanted to applaud. She had never seen him be so firm with Cloris, as he had usually left that unpleasantness for her. Looking to Christina he added with quiet emphasis, "We have come to be of whatever assistance we can be to you."

"And we have missed you so very much, Ti!" Millie joined in at once. "Will mopes about everywhere and so do I."

"I do not mope about everywhere," Will protested, straightening as he eyed Millie with some vigor, "You are exaggerating as usual."

"You never smile," Millie retorted, undaunted. "You look like this." She adopted such an absurdly lugubrious expression that Christina had the most untimely urge to grin.

Will, however, was not at all amused. "You need to be taken over someone's knee, Miss Millicent," he advised the young girl in a tone that indicated he thought he might well be the person to do it. "You are too old to behave so forwardly."

But the little minx only tossed her head. "Tom Parston did not seem to think I was so young when he tried to kiss me," she observed with the falsest innocence imaginable.

Will's brow lowered threateningly. "Tom Parston tried to kiss you! Devil it! You must have encouraged him."

"I did not!"

Christina considered stepping in to separate the combatants, but Mrs. Grynydd came with the tea tray, and the conversation took a more general turn when Mrs. Lester asked about the castle. Christina agreed to lead a tour, though she warned that there was a great deal of work being done. At that she had the distinct displeasure of hearing Cloris remark in an audible undertone, "Of course there is, now he has your money."

At another time, Christina would have responded with some cutting retort of her own, perhaps something about how sharp-tongued a spinster can be, but she did not say anything that day. She hadn't the spirit for it. Cloris was right.

And anyway, all she could think about was leaving Pembridge now that she had a party with whom she could make her escape. She knew she must get away before Aldric returned, or lose her chance, for he would never let her go until Thompkins had made Hampshire safe for her. Aldric might not care to behave voraciously with her, but he did possess such a strong, if misguided sense of responsibility that he would fight to keep her where she could be naught but miserably unhappy.

To her frustration, however, Christina found it difficult to get Will alone to make plans. Cloris, particularly, seemed to stick like a leech to him, while Millie would not be parted from her.

It was not until the next morning that Christina did finally have an opportunity to speak privately to Will. He came into the breakfast room just as she was finishing.

He remarked in surprise when he saw her, saying he had not expected she would arise for another hour at least. His manner was a little awkward, as if he did not know quite how to behave with her, and given their last meeting, Christina only found it surprising that he had come to see about her at all.

She, too, felt strained, but she determined that she would act with him as she always had, and so hopefully return them to their formerly comfortable footing. "I cannot tell you how grateful I am to you for coming, Will. I really do wish to leave Pembridge as I said yesterday. What I did not say is that I wish to leave as soon as possible. Today, even, if possible."

"Has he been cruel to you, Ti?" Will demanded, his jaw tensing as he frowned darkly.

"No, no not at all!" Christina shook her head quickly. "Aldric has been . . . quite courteous, though distracted, of course, for he has been extremely busy attending to his estate and his people."

"His people?" Will asked dryly. "You sound as if he is a king."

Christina only shrugged. "It is different here than in Hampshire. The Beauchamps have held sway over this land so long, they are far more important to the people than whoever is currently sitting on the throne in far-off London. They look to their lord for everything, and Aldric feels the weight of that responsibility keenly."

Will studied Christina a moment before he observed quietly, "It would seem you have forgiven him, at least in large part. I had thought, when you said you wished to leave, that you must still hate him."

Hate him? It seemed to Christina almost as if a different woman had flung that harsh statement at Aldric. Before Will's watchful look, she flushed a little, but she met his eyes, nonetheless. "No, I do not hate him still. I said that when I was raw with hurt. As to whether I have forgiven him, I can hardly say, though I can say I do understand better why he did what he did."

"And yet you wish to leave him?"

Of all the things Christina did not want to do, she did not want to give Will room to misunderstand. "Yes, I want to leave Aldric. I want an annulment and nothing more to do with him, but, Will, I do not want to marry anyone else."

Will seemed to find the coffee Becky had poured for him of exceptional interest, for he stirred it several minutes before he finally said softly, "I see." And then, "You love him still, I think."

"I . . ." Christina looked off abruptly to the window, though she saw nothing of the day. She saw Aldric, bending over her, brushing a kiss across her forehead as he called her Gray Eyes. "Yes," she all but whispered, letting go a breath. "Yes, I am afraid I may. But he does not love me." She looked back at Will then. "And I cannot live with him, knowing he does not. I must leave, but if you do not wish to take me with you, Will, I would understand. I will make other . . ."

"Nonsense, Christina," Will interrupted, laying his hand upon hers. "I hope that I shall always be your friend, and that you will always come to me if you are in difficulty. Of course, you may come with us. We cannot leave today, however. The horses must rest at least until tomorrow."

"Oh, Will, how can I thank you? You are too good."

"Nonsense, again, Christina!" He flushed a little and let his gaze drop from hers. "In truth, I've an admission of my own. I suppose I was so set on the idea that we would marry that I never looked around at anyone else, but since . . . well, I have, at least a little, and I find, well, I canno be certain, I would not make the mistake of assuming again, but, ah . . ."

Christina's strained expression eased as Will's color deepened and he floundered so helplessly. "I think you are trying to say you have found someone else who interests you, Will," she prompted him softly.

"I feel a fool," Will admitted, looking as foolish as he said he felt, with a sheepish grin spreading across his face. "She is so young and even silly, yet I find myself thinking about her a great deal."

"And she has always adored you."

"She has?" He looked at Christina with a pleased surprise that turned into astonishment as he absorbed the full implications of what she had said. "But then, you must know whom I mean?"

"It was obvious yesterday when you nearly exploded at the revelation that Tom Parston had kissed her."

"I will wring Tom's neck," Will vowed in a growling tone that made Christina want to smile.

"I don't think you need worry over Tom," she said gently. "And I am very happy for you, Will."

They both had suspiciously bright eyes as they looked at one another a long moment, then Will straightened and said in a very brisk, manly tone, "Well, now that's settled, and at least you'll not shrink from coming to stay with Mother and Father. You must, you know, when we reach Hampshire. Thompkins has not discovered who it is has tried to harm you."

They did not have the time to discuss Thompkins further, however, for Christina heard steps at the door and removed her hand from Will's just as Cloris stepped into the room. The girl eyed them closely, but made no comment at finding them together as she took her seat and gave Becky her order for breakfast. But when Will informed her that they would be leaving the very next day with Christina in tow, she could not remain silent.

"This is most ill-advised!" Cloris exclaimed, her small eyes narrowing. "Your place is with your husband, and do not think that Mother will welcome you back with open arms! She will not."

"I do not labor under that illusion, Cloris. I intend to stay at the Grange."

Something flashed in Cloris's spiteful eyes then. It came and went so quickly Christina could not read it with certainty, but she did determine that she would keep an exceedingly wary eye upon her stepsister.

Chapter 20

Even before it began, Christina encountered difficulty on her journey to Hampshire. Anxiety about Aldric's return nipping at her heels, she had hoped to depart early on the morning after Will's arrival, but Cloris awoke complaining of a headache, and though she dosed herself with an elixir, she returned to her bed and would not get out again. She said she was not much improved the next day, but Christina was too frantic by then to cosset her stepsister further. Still, Cloris dragged, and they did not get away from Pembridge until after luncheon, a day and five hours late.

Two hours later, perhaps even less, it began to rain. Christina had little reason to worry overmuch, for the rain was a gentle one, but as they continued, the rainfall became increasingly heavy, until they were driving in a downpour through which they could scarcely see. Christina fretted that they would become mired in the mud, but before that happened, the coach wheels slid sideways on a slick section of road. The odd movement created an unnatural pressure upon the rear axle, and it broke with a loud crack that was as startling as the bump with which the rear of the carriage bounced into the mud.

At the jolt, Cloris let out a screech, Mrs. Lester came awake with a wail, and Millie looked with startled eyes to Will, who leaned forward to pat her hand and assure her they were not in serious difficulty. Christina put her head out of the window, heedless of the rain, to assure herself that Will's coachman was not hurt.

He was not, but he was wet through and grim when he came to report that there was no hope of repairing the carriage there. He did have one piece of good news, however. He remembered from their journey through the same area only three days before that there was a village ahead. With Will's approval he unharnessed one of the carriage horses, and the groom, whom Cloris had brought along as her contribution to the journey, set off at once in the driving rain to see if he might locate a vehicle there in which the party could be safely conveyed to shelter.

The groom was successful, if slow, for it took some two hours before they were finally shown into the private room of the village's small inn. The rain had stopped entirely by then, but Christina was able to derive little satisfaction from the belated cooperation of the elements. The coachman's pessimistic guess that they would not be able in so small a village to obtain another axle for a carriage the size of Will's proved accurate. This time it was the coachman who went on to the next village, where he hoped to find what he needed at the larger posting inn there. If he failed, Will instructed him to return with a hired carriage, but nonetheless, Christina could not but fret. Even with luck, they would not be on the road before noon the next day, and she was still no more than a three-hour ride from Pembridge.

Her taut nerves were not to be soothed, either. Cloris's every word was a complaint, much of it shrill, and all of it directed at Christina. "If you had not been in such a scandalous hurry to leave your home and husband, none of this would have happened! You are as selfish as ever! Why, you needed to give us only half a look to see we were all fatigued to death. Even Will. Were you not weary of travel, Will? You said you were fatigued half to death before we arrived at Christina'a."

Will said something placating, but Christina took little comfort. Though she had had good reason to wish to leave Pembridge, she did feel half selfish for demanding that the travel-weary group return to the road so soon and now felt responsible for their current discomfort. When Cloris started again, this time on the likely wretched meal they would have, Christina rose abruptly, apologized for any discomfort she might have caused, and announced she was going for a walk.

Will offered to accompany her, as did Millie, but they did not insist when Christina said firmly she would prefer to take her walk alone. As she left, they were getting up a game of cards with Mrs. Lester.

Christina spent a few moments in the room she would share with Millie, fetching a light cloak against the damp of the evening and a bonnet. Nancy was there and not pleased to hear she meant to walk alone, but Christina insisted she would be perfectly safe in a village of no more than thirty people, whereas Cloris, she said, was in danger of dying by strangulation if Christina remained shut up in a small space with her even a moment longer.

Nancy chuckled in reply and whether it was that good-natured sound or the beauty of the evening after the rain, Christina soon forgot her vexatious stepsister.

She did not forget Aldric, however. She wondered what he would think when he returned and found her gone. Perhaps she was fretting for naught. Perhaps he would not care, would say if she wanted so much to be gone, then good riddance. Would he send for Lady Danley?

Christina kicked out at a rock, causing it to sail into the air and land with a splash in a creek near the inn. Due to the rain, the creek was high, and Christina watched it swirl and froth from the perspective of a footbridge that led to the fields the villagers worked. She had crossed the footbridge, and taken a path that led along the creek when she heard footsteps behind her. Perhaps she was tense on Aldric's account, but she felt an odd prickling along the nape of her neck and whirled sharply. To her relief she saw it was the groom, Martin, from Fairfield, and she smiled.

"Martin! You startled me. I did not hear you come."

"You were not intended to, my lady."

Christina stared, taking in his words only slowly, they were so unexpected. The sly smile on his face registered more quickly, however, and she took a step preparing to turn and flee, but her caution came too late. He was upon her in a single, swift bound, grabbing her arm and twisting it cruelly behind her as he stuffed a dirty rag into her mouth.

Christina did not remain stunned long. She twisted and fought him, landing a painful blow to his shin, but Martin worked handling horses. He had a wiry strength and in a matter of seconds had dragged Christina behind some willows and tied her hands, though she fought him all the while.

When he flung her over his shoulder, Christina began to buck with her entire body, but the groom held her so tightly she flailed at the air, and he had only a little difficulty trotting along the riverbank to a horse he had tethered at the edge of the fields. He flung her down hard in front of the saddle and swung up himself before Christina could catch the breath he had half knocked from her.

When he spurred the horse to a trot, heading it toward some woods, Christina panicked and began kicking as wildly as she could. She succeeded in startling the horse and making it shy, but she also earned Martin's anger. He cuffed her so hard on the side of the head, her ear rang. "Keep that up, and I'll snap your neck," he growled viciously.

Christina knew with a leap of real fear that it was no idle threat. He had already tried to strangle her.

When she went still, Martin gave a harsh, triumphant laugh. "I see you understand me, m'lady, fine. That's good. Very good. Yer stepsister would have you dead this time for certain, but she gave me leave to use you first in a hut I saw in the woods as I was riding to the village earlier. If you are a very good girl, I'll use you kindly, but if not . . ."

He laughed evilly as he ran a callused hand over the rounded curve of Christina's bottom. She squirmed, trying to evade the intimacy, but he only gave the ugly laugh again and slapped her hard before he turned his horse onto a path that led into the dark of the forest.

* * *

By a stroke of luck, Aldric never reached his destination that day, though he had arisen early enough to arrive at Pembridge by noon. At first light, far earlier than was his wont, he had come fully awake. For a little he had tried to blame his wakefulness upon the difficulty of resting well in an inn bed, but that explanation did nothing to explain the energetic lightness in his step as he went down for breakfast, nor did it address his first thought upon awakening.

Even then, he did tell himself that he thought of Christina only because she was at Pembridge, and he was eager to get there to make ready for the arrival of the prime bulls he had bought in Norfolk. But it was not of cattle that he thought, as he kicked Beau into a canter only a little while later. He thought of red-gold hair, and gray eyes, and the way she had snuggled into him when she had been wet and cold and silkily naked beneath her woolen blanket.

And of those, long, long, curved legs. Suddenly Aldric's smile flashed, and he laughed aloud. He was done resisting her. It was absurd. He had nearly worked himself to death every day, trying to put her out of his mind, only to fall into his bed exhausted and lie wide awake listening to every sound she made in her adjoining room. No longer, by God! She would join him in his bed as a wife should.

She was Lely's daughter. It was true. She was, but she was not Lely, any more than he was his father. If he considered her blemished by her father's sins, then surely he would have to hold himself accountable for his father's. Lely had cheated that day, and his soul would be forever damned for that, but, galloping down the road to Pembridge, Aldric finally admitted the point that had always gnawed away at him. His father had made a criminally stupid wager. No man, no matter how certain of victory, should wager more than he can afford to lose, and his father had wagered every penny he had that was not entailed.

Yes, he could admit it, he realized, feeling somehow both sad and lighter all at once. He could admit it. His father had been a weak man, gay and charming, perhaps, but unwilling or unable to fight the feverish excitement that led him to wager dangerously. He had been an easy mark for Lely, and had to be held accountable at least in part for his own downfall.

But his father's errors and Lely's sins lay in the past. His life lay in the present. With Christina. Great God, but he had never felt such a cold, gut-wrenching fear as when he had galloped up to that pool and seen Lizzie Gadston all but holding Christina under the ice-cold water. He had been shaken by that fear even when he got her back to Pembridge. He'd not been able to let her go. Though Nancy had come running to her mistress, he had carried Christina upstairs and put her to bed himself.

He remembered that Nancy had grinned knowingly but that he had scowled back at her, still trying to deny what was plain as day. She would smirk all the more now, would the faithful Nancy, and he would see she got a raise in her pay.

"Nay! M'lord! M'lord! The child!"

Aldric came alert instantly, pulling up on Beau and looking around to see who had screamed and about what. Without realizing it, he had reached Beauchamp land, and he saw he knew the woman pelting through her gate to the road.

"Sal!" she was screaming. "Sal! Get back here!"

There was a child crouched in the ditch just beside him. Aldric had not seen her. He swung down from Beau to assure Kate Simmons her daughter was unharmed.

"Did she run in front of me?" he demanded, wondering if Christina could distract him that much, but Mrs. Simmons, puffing and out of breath, shook her head rapidly.

"Nay, m'lord! I couldn't find her, and when I saw her in the ditch, I was that afraid she would jump out beneath your horse. Ah, m'lord, I am that sorry for stoppin' ye so! Still, it may not be the worst thing. You'll want to know that though you were ridin' hard as the wind, you missed your lady by an hour."

"Missed my lady?" Aldric repeated.

"Aye." Mrs. Simmons nodded, eyes widening at the suddenly piercing look his lordship bent upon her. "She passed this way in a carriage. Mr. Simmons heard in the village it was a friend of hers, a Mr. Palmer, came to take her for a visit, and her stepsisters with him."

To Mrs. Simmons's astonishment, the marquess grabbed her arm and in a suddenly harsh voice asked, "Stepsisters, Mrs. Simmons? Two stepsisters?"

"Aye, m'lord. Two," Mrs. Simmons repeated almost fearfully. "Goin' to Hampshire they was, Mr. Simmons said."

"Sweet Christ."

Why she had put herself in danger, why she had gone with Will, Aldric would not allow himself to consider. A sense of the greatest dread filled him and sent him leaping up on Beau and galloping back down the road so urgently that Mrs. Simmons stared after him with her hand over her mouth.

Cloris. She was a woman, but a woman could hire her ugly deeds done, and he had recollected a small thing while he had been in Norfolk. On that long-ago night when he had been taking Christina's measure for the first time, Cloris had approached Christina and Will. He had not spared the stepsister even a glance, but Moly had, and for no reason at all he recalled that Moly had likened the look she gave Christina to a stiletto's blade. It might mean nothing, probably did mean nothing, but she was the only person he knew for a certainty had regarded Christina with hate.

Aldric told himself he worried for naught, that his suspicions were fantasies, that even if Cloris were the villain, she would not have the opportunity to hurt Christina when they traveled in a carriage with at least two others. Nonetheless, he galloped after Christina without heed either for the fact that he had been riding all day, or for the rain that began to fall shortly after he left Mrs. Simmons on the road.

Galloping hard, not slowing for the storm that had stopped Christina altogether, Aldric came first upon the carriage, sitting tail-end down in the mud. A man who had been paid to watch it told him where its occupants were, and Aldric pulled up in the inn yard only a little after Christina had gone on her walk.

His clothes wet and filthy with mud, his expression fierce, Aldric threw the innkeeper into a gaping panic when he strode into the inn furiously demanding to know where Mr. Palmer's party was, but soon enough, Aldric was throwing open the door of the private parlor, causing the occupants within to gasp with surprise.

He swept the room with a piercing glance. Will, young Millie, and an unknown woman were playing cards before the window, while Cloris sat apart with some embroidery in her lap. But he did not find Christina.

"Aldric!" Will surged to his feet. Had Aldric been in a reasonable frame of mind, he might have noted that there was, along with surprise, a note of something like satisfaction in Will's tone, but Aldric was not in a reasonable frame of mind at all. Fear made his voice harsh. "Where is she?" he demanded.

"She has only gone for a walk," Will said with a patience that might have surprised Aldric at another time. "She will return . . ."

"You!" Aldric dismissed Will and rounded upon Cloris. Something savage coursed through him when she went pale beneath his gaze. Never taking his eye from her, he stalked forward to lean threateningly over her, making her cower in her chair. "If one hair of her head is harmed, I will see you hanged, Miss Bexom," he promised in a dangerously soft voice. "Do you understand? I will see a rope put around your neck and pulled taut so that your neck is snapped in two."

A chorus of dismayed exclamations went up from the others in the room. Aldric paid no heed, and Cloris seemed not to hear them at all as she gazed like a trapped animal into the piercing, black eyes that promised such cruel retri-

bution. Speech failed her, and she shook her head frantically.

"Don't bother to deny that you are the villain of the
piece," Aldric cautioned silkily. "I've a man in Hampshire
looking into the matter, Miss Bexom. He knows all about
the man you paid to kill her. He is a Bow Street runner and
will testify against you. It is a capital offense you've com-
mitted, and I will make certain that you will be sentenced to
be hanged by the neck. . . ."

"No! No!" Cloris blurted, frightened to the point of panic
by Aldric's lies. "He was only to frighten her into leaving
Hampshire."

"Cloris!"

Will loomed into her view, distracting her from Aldric.
Seeing the expression on the young man's open face,
Cloris went as red as she had been pale only the moment
before. "Christina had everything! Everything!" she cried
piteously, stretching out her hand to Will. "She had all the
money and looks and position, and even you! I only
wanted to frighten her into marrying and leaving Ha—"

Will started to make some interruption, but Aldric cared
nothing for Cloris's reasons. Brutally, he grabbed her arms
and jerked her to her feet. She screamed, but he shook her
violently. "Stop that!" he thundered. "Tell me what unpleasant fright you planned for her today. Where is she?"

"No, no! I planned nothing . . . ."

Almost by sleight of hand, it seemed, Aldric produced a
knife from his boot. The blade gleamed deadly in the low
light of the room, and Cloris gasped. "Now then, Miss
Bexom." Aldric held the knife before her eyes. "Where is
she? Or would you rather I marked your face to look as evil
as your soul?"

The words began to tumble from her as she stared trans-
fixed at the knife. "No, oh no. No, please. Martin followed
her on her walk. He . . . he has become obsessed by her like
every other man she encounters! He saw a hut in the woods
when he rode to the village earlier. He has taken her there
to. . . ."

But Aldric knew why a man would take Christina to a deserted hut. He flung Cloris from him so hard, she fell to the floor. She gave a pained cry, but Aldric turned to Will to command fiercely, "Watch her! If Christina is hurt, she'll pay."

Aldric paused only long enough to demand of the innkeeper if the man knew of a hut in the woods along the road that ran north of the village. "There will be reward in it, if you do," he added, loosening the man's tongue so that he received precise directions about the shortest path to the place.

Chapter 21

"Get in there, m'lady fine." Martin sent Christina sprawling through the door of the hut. "I've been wantin' you a while, I have. Thought it was a waste, killin' you, but I do what I'm paid for."

Christina could feel his eyes on her, but she lay still, gathering her energies. Though the jolting she had taken riding head down on the horse had dizzied her, fear had helped to clear her mind. Her heart was pounding like a kettle drum, and she was not so dazed as Martin believed.

"Hey now, y'er still as a corpse." Martin squatted down by her, the odor of his unwashed body nearly gagging her. She counted her breaths to calm herself, and when suddenly he pushed her over, she flopped as if she were insensible. He gave a dissatisfied grunt and leaned closer. She was not prepared when he slapped her. Her eyes shot open, but even as he gave his horrid laugh, Christina used her hands, tied behind her, as a lever, and lifting her legs struck out at him with all her might.

Taken by surprise, Martin went reeling backward. Christina scrambled to her feet and lurched for the door. She was nearly there when he caught her and flung her back into the room, leaping on her with a guttural cry. She fought wildly, rolling and bucking and kicking so that Martin cuffed her again. He hurt her, but he also knocked her gag loose, and she raked his arm with her teeth. The blow he gave her then made her head ring, but wild as she was, Christina came at him again, butting her head into his chest.

He went up on his knees. "Blast, I'll tame yer spirit, I

will!" he vowed, a feral light in his eyes as he raised his hand to hit her again. Christina let out an ear-piercing scream and bucked again so his blow only grazed her. Swearing, he made a fist to knock her senseless, but as she let out another scream the door of the hut flew open.

Martin gaped, and Christina, unable to see the door, attended to herself, taking advantage of his momentary distraction to pull her knees to her chest and roll clear of him.

"Get out of here, Christina. Get into the woods until I come for you." Crouching on the floor on her knees, Christina stared through her disheveled hair, unable to comprehend how Aldric could be there. He did not spare a glance from Martin, but when she did not move he commanded sharply, "Now!"

She went, taking care to stay out of the way of the two men. Martin had risen to a half crouch. As she backed out the door Christina saw the knife gleaming in Aldric's hand and then she heard him say softly, "Now, Martin."

From outside, Christina heard the men's feet shuffling on the floor as they circled one another; she heard Martin taunt Aldric and the deadly silence that was Aldric's reply. She heard a grunt, then Martin laughed, then there was more shuffling, and all the while she listened, she ran about the clearing looking for something sharp on which to cut the rope binding her wrists. A hard thud sounded from the cabin, when finally she saw what she needed. An ax had been left beneath a tree to rust. Still, it served its purpose. When the rope split, she grabbed up the ax with a cry and raced back to the hut.

Realizing suddenly that she heard nothing, Christina slowed, eyes intent upon the door. A dark shape materialized, and she stopped, waiting, holding the ax steady in her hands. If it was Martin, she meant to kill him.

But it was not Martin who came through the door, and with a sob of gladness, Christina threw down the rusty ax and ran to Aldric. He staggered as she threw herself at him with such force.

"Aldric!" she cried.

Simultaneously he growled, "Do you never do as you are told, woman?"

"I meant to help! Oh, Aldric, how did you find me?" She was holding him to her, her arms about his waist, as if the heat of his body could erase the experience of the last hour. He did not return her embrace. She realized that he was standing stiffly, and suddenly let go of him. "Are you hurt?" she demanded, fear kindling in her again.

But Aldric shook his head. "No. Martin is dead, though."

"Good," Christina said fiercely. "I am glad, and I do not care if that is wrong. He was an evil man. Oh, Aldric, I am so grateful to you!"

Her voice shook, and she wanted to go back into his arms, but Aldric's expression did not invite her to touch him again. There was a white line around his lips and his nostrils were flared as if he were furious, but he spared her no more than a raking glance, perhaps to assure himself she was unharmed, perhaps merely to confirm how little he cared for her, before he lifted his head to look to the road. "Someone is coming."

Christina had not heard the horses, but she gave little thought to who came. She stared hard at Aldric, trying to determine if he was really angry, and why he might be, after he had ridden to her rescue yet again. She realized then, how disheveled he was. The shoulder seam on his coat was ripped, his cravat was torn and limp, and everywhere, but particularly on his boots and buckskins, was mud. Looking closely, she even found a streak of mud on his face. He had ridden hard after her, through the rain even. She bit her lip and tried to control the surge of hope that threatened to fling her back into his stiff arms.

There were three riders, Will in the lead and two men from the village behind him. "My God, Christina, are you hurt?" Will shouted even before he pulled up his horse.

"No! Aldric came in . . ."

"Who is with the girl?" Aldric cut in angrily.

Will flushed at his peremptory tone, but answered readily enough. "I left a man watching her. She will not get away, but what of Martin?"

"I killed him," Aldric said flatly. He looked to the two country fellows behind Will. They tugged on their caps, acknowledging his rank, and Aldric inclined his head. "I would be grateful if you men would bring the man's body back to the village. His horse is there."

"Aye, m'lord," they said, dismounting as they spoke and proceeding into the hut.

"Has anyone contacted the magistrate?" Aldric demanded of Will as he crossed to Beau and mounted the stallion. Christina noted that there had been a distinct difference in his tone when he addressed the two farmers. With them, he had been lordly graciousness itself. With Will and her, he was brusque to the point of rudeness.

She could not allow herself to hope. It was madness. He was done with her now. That was why he was so remote. Still, she drifted toward Will, as if she expected to ride with him back to the village. Aldric cut her off, bringing Beau in front of her and holding out his hand imperiously. He did not seat her before him in his lap, though. Due to the saddle, he said it would be easier for her to ride behind him. Feeling daring, Christina wrapped her arms around his waist. She held her breath a second, but he did not object.

His back was strong but narrow and lean at the waist. Christina pulled her mind from the heady feel of him to ask again, "How did you come to find me so providentially, my lord?"

There was a hesitation, as if Aldric had to bite back his first words, and Will riding beside them, said, "Yes, Aldric! I was never so surprised in my life as when you came charging into the inn."

Aldric gave the young man a swift look. From her position, Christina could not see his expression, but Will straightened slightly in his saddle. Then Aldric said, speaking as if he measured each word, "When I learned that you had left Pembridge, Christina, in the company not only of

Mr. Palmer, but your elder stepsister as well, I was concerned."

"You knew it was Cloris, then?" Christina asked.

"Not with any certainty. I'd have had her locked away, had I had any proof."

"But what brought you to suspect her?" Will insisted. "I thought Robert the more likely suspect."

"He is a cold fish," Aldric allowed. "However there were one or two things that pointed to Cloris. For one, it was she who determined the route Christina would take the day the cart bowled into her carriage."

"But how did she know where my carriage would be stopped? The coachman had been at Fairfield for years. He could not have been party to her scheme."

"He was not." Aldric agreed. "She was clever enough not to take more than one servant into her confidence. No, I suspect it was the driver of the dray they paid. Martin had only to keep watch for you, signal the man to pull out, and then saunter up the hill to the cart, he would have left on the hill earlier."

"But why?" Christina demanded.

She felt Aldric shrug. "I think she had gone by that time from wanting to frighten you into marrying away from Hampshire, to wanting to be done with you altogether."

"But why? Why does she hate me so?"

Christina was not aware how raw her voice sounded, only that Aldric touched her hand briefly. "She is mad," he said simply. "Mad with envy."

Christina's head drooped, her forehead coming to rest on Aldric's back. "Of course, the blasted money."

"She envied you more than the wealth you had, Ti." Will looked uncomfortably to Christina. "She resented our affections, too. I can scarcely credit it, but she said as much."

To listen to Will, Christina had turned her head without lifting it, so that her cheek lay against Aldric now. When he made no protest, she remained as she was, holding him about the waist and half resting against him.

To Will she said with a rueful smile in her eyes, "And I thought her interest in you was merely a ruse to annoy me."

"But you knew she'd an interest in me?"

"She made no secret of it, Will, but I confess I did not realize either how strong her feelings were."

"She envied everything about you." Christina half turned, for it was Aldric who had spoken. She caught the clean, male scent of him and wanted to bury her nose in his back and breathe so deeply she could erase the reek of Martin's sweat from her memory. But Aldric was continuing. "She said she envied your position as well, by which I suppose she meant that your father was a baron and your mother an earl's granddaughter. She also said she envied your looks."

"My looks?" Christina queried into his back.

"Aye. Unlike you, she is not blind."

He was angry. There did not seem to be any question of it, he spoke so mockingly but still he had made her a compliment, if a roundabout one. Christina entertained a fleeting fancy to press her lips to Aldric's back. He would never feel the kiss through his coat, and she would never have another chance to touch him so tenderly. Now that he had discovered, and eliminated, the source of the danger to her, he could wave her off to Hampshire with an easy mind.

"What is to be done with Cloris?" Will asked, addressing Aldric.

Christina forgot about the kiss, waiting for his answer. She could not imagine ever breathing easily, if Cloris was free, but she did not relish a public trial, either.

Aldric replied grimly to Will, "She ought to be put on public trial and hanged."

Hanging by the neck . . . Christina shuddered, and she felt as much as heard Aldric swear beneath his breath. "She deserves it," he curtly informed that shudder of revulsion, but when she made no reply Aldric added, in a somewhat more moderate tone, "There are places where she could be kept. They are grim, I imagine, but perhaps preferable to hanging."

Christina simply buried her head against Aldric's back. She could not make an answer. Had Martin harmed her or Aldric, then she could have decided between sentencing Cloris to death or a lifetime of confinement in a place even Aldric termed grim, but as it was, she could not summon the hate needed.

The two men said nothing either, and the issue hung heavily in the air until they emerged from the woods a stone's throw from the village. A young boy from the inn was on the watch for them, and sprang up to yell back over his shoulder in the direction of the inn, before he came running as fast as he could toward them.

"The lady! She . . . !"

Christina thought he was remarking upon her return, and was surprised when she peered over Aldric's shoulder to see that the boy was not looking at her, but at Aldric and as if he had important, but unpleasant news.

"What is it, lad?" Aldric prompted when the boy stopped, panting, before the horse. "T'other lady, m'lord! Jumped, she did, from the window. Morris was outside her door, keepin' watch like, and heard her scream, but he weren't in time to catch her."

Christina gave a cry of distress. Aldric was not so nice. "Well, she has saved us a deal of trouble, at least," he pronounced somberly.

"Aye," agreed Will, surprising Christina. "It is for the best."

"What of the magistrate, lad? Mr. Palmer sent for him. Has he come yet?"

"Aye, m'lord. Squire Lawrence awaits you at the White Horse."

In fact, Squire Lawrence hastened out of the inn to greet them. He knew of Aldric, and overcome by the honor of speaking directly with his lordship, hastened to assure them that he would carry out his duties at their convenience.

Aldric peremptorily arranged it that Christina should be spared the ordeal of answering questions. He and Mr. Palmer knew all that had occurred, he said, and Christina, only too glad to be spared, went up to Millie, who promptly burst into tears at the sight of her.

Millie had not thought Christina could possibly return unharmed, though she did allow, "If anyone could get to you in time, I knew that Lord Aldric would. You should have seen him, Ti. He was so very fierce!" Millie went on to describe to Christina how Aldric had raged into the inn and exactly how he had threatened Cloris to force her to tell the truth. "I think he would have cut her face, too. He was that wild with concern for you."

He did seem to have been concerned for her, but Christina knew that it might as well have been Aldric's pride that had driven him to act as he had, and so she turned the conversation to Cloris. Millie said simply, echoing Aldric, "She was mad, Ti. She envied everything you had, including Will. I think it was his unmistakable revulsion that drove her to take her life. But let us not tell Mama, Ti!" Millie looked pleadingly at Christina. "Let us spare her, tell her only that Martin attacked you and caused Cloris's death."

Immediately Christina put out her hand. "Of course, we shall spare her, my love. I would not want her to know about Cloris. Nothing would be gained."

Christina was extremely glad when Nancy came to supervise a bath and a change of clothes. She scrubbed herself hard, wanting to wash off the smell and touch of Martin. But when it came time to eat the light meal a maid brought to their room, Mrs. Lester, who had taken to her bed until she was called for food, managed to eat a good deal more than she, for Christina grew increasingly nervous as she waited for Aldric to summons her in order . . . she tried not to put it into words and so saw a clear image of Lady Danley.

Aldric's messenger was an apple-cheeked maid, a young thing, who blushed when she told Christina his lordship wished to see her below in the private parlor.

Aldric had bathed, too, and his clothes had been brushed clean and hastily mended so that he looked new, or almost, for he had not bothered with his torn cravat. But if his clothes were restored, his mood had not been. When Christina entered, he was leaning against the mantelpiece, with his arms crossed over his chest and his expression hard as flint.

She did not think the muscle she saw flex in his jaw a good sign but took the lead anyway. "All I seem to have done of late is thank you for coming to my aid, but I wish you to know, my lord, that you've my deepest gratitude for what you did today. I would have been extraordinarily lucky to escape from that hut with my life."

"Indeed, you would have," he agreed, an angry light flaring to life in his black eyes and incidentally proving Christina had read that flexing of his jaw aright. "You behaved like a fool, and I will have an accounting of why you rushed to put yourself in such danger. My God!" he went on, giving her no time to answer. "Are you so mad for Palmer that you would risk your life to be with him?"

"No!" The denial burst from Christina before she could even consider how she should best respond, but having exclaimed the truth, she added more reasonably, "I told you long ago Will is like a brother to me."

"I should say he has behaved like a deuced odd brother, ma'am."

Christina did not care for his sarcasm, or for that formal "ma'am" either. "I did not say Will regarded me as a sister, though I do not believe he really was in love with me. He had simply gotten it into his mind ages ago that we would marry and never fully reconsidered the matter. Now that he has, he has actually found someone far better suited to be his wife."

"What?" Aldric came away from the mantel at that and caught Christina by the shoulders, giving her a shake. "Then what on earth possessed you to leave Pembridge?"

"Why are you so angry, my lord?" she countered, studying him with hope, despite herself.

"What? Why am I so angry? Damn it, woman, you put my life in danger! I will know why!"

It was not the answer Christina had sought. She bowed her head. "I thought it would be for the best," she murmured.

"To get yourself murdered would be for the best?" he demanded incredulously. "You are lying, damn it! I want the truth!"

Aldric shook Christina again, this time with considerably more vigor. She flung up her head, furious suddenly. Who was he to make such demands, anyway? "Well, you may demand all you want, but you've no power over me any longer, my lord! Nor any right to manhandle me this way! Let go of me this instant. I will not discuss this subject anymore!"

Aldric's eyes blazed in response, and he pulled her up so that their faces were only inches apart. "Madam, I am your husband. I have the right to take you over my knee and beat the answers I want out of you."

"I won't tell you!"

"You will!" He shook her so the braid Nancy had pinned atop her head popped loose from its pins and fell heavily across his wrist. Aldric stilled instantly, but his eyes did not soften. "Why, madam? Did you leave merely to defy me, or is there someone you meant to run to?"

"What if there is?" Christina demanded defiantly. "What does it matter to you? You intend to annul our marriage as quickly as you can get to the proper authorities."

"Who is it?" he demanded, his black eyes blazing so wildly that Christina finally flinched.

"No one!" she all but screamed. "There is no one for me to run to. You are quite on the wrong tack. But I do not want to discuss this further, Aldric. It has been a horrid, wretched day. I am sorry, sorrier than you can imagine, that I brought you so near harm. I would never have forgiven myself had anything happened to you. Never. Oh, please. Leave off. It cannot matter. You don't want me." She could feel tears welling in her eyes and furious again, struck out at his chest with her fist. "Let me go and be done with it! Go to your mistress!"

The room fell quiet. Aldric felt how fine-boned Christina was in his hands, and he could see she had to bite her lip to battle tears. Yet, she was the same girl who had held off Martin for the precious time it had taken him to get to her; and she was the fury who had hefted an ax in her hands and prepared to come to his aid in that hut.

The silence in the room stretched as he studied the top of her coppery head and marked that her braid did not burn his wrist but felt instead like silk.

"Christina," he said finally, "I do not have a mistress."

She took a breath but still the words fell out. "You do. She came to Pembridge."

"Ah."

It was a very knowing sound. Christina threw up her chin, forgetting how difficult it would be to look cool and superior with tears in her eyes. "Damn you," she said bitterly when one spilled out of her eye and splashed onto her cheek. "You've reduced me to tears. That should be enough! Let me go."

"Christina, I don't have a mistress," Aldric repeated. She made a growl of protest and tried to break free, but he held her still, though his grip on her arms did shift and he no longer held her punishingly. "Just after we arrived at Pembridge, I wrote to Elise to tell her our affair had run its course. I suppose she came to argue the point. I am so sorry I was not there to spare you the scene she must have put on. She can be ugly. Was she?"

"She was beautiful, actually," Christina said in a rather small voice. "But she did tell me where you were this spring, when you left town for those days."

Aldric's eyes never left Christina. "I am not surprised. She'd have said anything to strike out at you. I wager she did not say that we had made the assignation before I ever met you, and that I went to her two days late and left a day early. You will remember my return, of course. I found Robert Bexom accosting you and wanted to kill him."

Their eyes held. Christina could not quite breathe with Aldric looking at her as he was. "Fine agent of vengeance I am," he said softly. "Christina, I have fallen hopelessly in love with you."

"Oh!"

He smiled then just a little at her cry of wonder. "I find I cannot let go of my copper-haired, elegant, and so very long-legged marchioness."

"Oh, Aldric!"

"Johnny."

She blinked. "Johnny. Do you mean it?"

"About the long legs?"

"Oh, you beast!" But she didn't strike out at him. A little shakily she asked, "What of my father?"

He winced with chagrin. "I've come to what is likely common knowledge. You are not your parent. Can you forgive me, Christina? Can you, really? You said you hated me."

"I did hate you then, but because I . . . I loved you. Hopelessly. Oh, Al . . .   Johnny!"

He slid his hands from her shoulders to her neck and caressing the hollows there with his thumbs, said huskily, "And I you, for the longest time. I have just been the blindest fool."

"But I am . . ."

"Shush," he stilled her with a light kiss on the mouth. "I'll hear none of that ever again. You are the most elegant slip of a thing I have ever seen. Fine is what you are, Christina. Exceedingly fine."

And then he kissed her long and hard and they were both breathing heavily when he lifted his head to whisper softly, "Do you understand?"

And she nodded. "Oh yes, Johnny, I do."